MOLLY SAND MUST DIE

LAURA SNIDER

SEVERN  RIVER

PUBLISHING

Severn River Publishing
www.SevernRiverBooks.com

This is a work of fiction. Names, characters, businesses, places, events and incidents are either the products of the author's imagination or used in a fictitious manner. Any resemblance to actual persons, living or dead, or actual events is purely coincidental.

ISBN: 978-1-64875-598-9 (Paperback)

ALSO BY LAURA SNIDER

Ashley Montgomery Legal Thrillers

Unsympathetic Victims

Undetermined Death

Unforgivable Acts

Unsolicited Contact

Unexpected Defense

Unconditional Revenge

Standalone Thriller

Molly Sand Must Die

Smith and Bauer Legal Thrillers

Justice Bites

To find out more about Laura Snider and her books, visit

severnriverbooks.com

To Ashley, Amanda, and Kristen.
I am so fortunate to have a set of ride-or-die, bury the body friends like you.

PROLOGUE
OLD PETE

Present
June 15, 2018

Death was a part of life. To live was to die. Everything died. Plants, animals, people. Old Pete would be among the dead one day. He accepted that. He'd come to terms with it years ago. He was but a cog in the wheel of the world. This sort of thought process wasn't new to him. It was one of the reasons he'd earned the nickname Old Pete long before society would label him as "old." He was an old soul.

These days his body had caught up with his soul. He was old in soul and old in body. Oldness in body, he'd learned, brought a whole set of bothersome troubles along with it, though. Back pains, tooth pains, arthritis. Worst of all was the insomnia. Gone were the days when he'd lay down next to the Mrs. and fall into a deep, gentle slumber lasting through the night until the rays of the early morning sun reached in to touch his closed eyelids. Now, he slept fitfully, lying awake for hours at a time, staring at the popcorn ceiling above.

The night of June fourteenth into the fifteenth had been different. He'd finally broken down and taken one of those pills the doctor had suggested. It was an over the counter "sleep aid," that was what the doctor had called it. An "aid" for his "little sleep problem." A problem that hadn't felt little at all. The box described it as "gentle," whatever that meant. He took that "gentle" pill and it had knocked him out. *Gentle my foot.* If that was gentle, strong would lead to the permanent kind of sleep.

His sleep was dreamless, deep, and dark, unsettling in its unnaturalness. The morning crept up on him, tearing him out of his dense sleep at four-thirty sharp. He sat up, startled to come to so suddenly, so violently. Had he heard something? Was someone in the farmhouse, lurking about in the night? He strained to hear, his heartbeat thumping in his chest, but he heard nothing aside from the light snores of the Mrs. and the rooster crowing at the sky, begging the sun to rise.

It was nothing, you old fool. It's all in your head.

One "gentle" little pill couldn't subvert years of habit. He had risen at the same time every day for the last sixty years, and he'd continue doing it until the day he kicked the bucket. He was a farmer with livestock. Farming was more than a job; it was who he was. Caring for his little piece of the world was in his blood, in his bones, as much a part of him as his lungs and heart. There were no vacations, no time off. It was the way he liked it, the only life he dreamed for himself. The animals needed food, day in and day out. They counted on him. He hadn't let them down yet.

Stretching, he stood and pulled on an old t-shirt, nearly threadbare but soft from years of washing by the Mrs. His spindly legs slipped into a pair of overalls that seemed as though they'd grown over the years. His body was shrinking. Another benefit of aging. He was shriveling, like a grape left out in the sun, wrinkling and puckering as the weeks, months, years, decades, slipped past.

Pulling on a pair of socks and work boots, his hands moving slower now than ever, he took one last glance at his beloved wife's slumbering form before stepping out into the hallway. The old wooden floorboards groaned under his weight as he tiptoed his way toward the staircase, careful to avoid the creakiest spots. He placed his hand on the staircase railing, gripping its familiar shape. He'd grown up in this house, holding this same banister as a small child, growing into it as an adult.

He grabbed a lantern on his way out the front door, flipping it on as he stepped out into the endless country darkness. He moved in a graceful autopilot, like a dancer repeating a routine for the thousandth time. Thinking was not required. His muscles knew how to move, where to lead him.

The screen door snapped shut, and he was greeted by the stillness of the farm. The air was crisp this time of year. It was mid-June, his favorite time of year, when the weather was warm enough to keep the creak out of his bones, but not yet muggy and stifling. The barn smelled of fresh hay and must. He grabbed a pair of work gloves from a shelf and filled two large buckets with slop, enough for the pigs' breakfast.

A sharp stab of joy struck him as he continued through his morning routine. His movements were methodical, built from years of repetition. He whistled as he made his way out of the barn and toward the pig pen. He had four pigs, each named after a Beatle. John, Paul, Ringo, and George. It was not a large operation by Iowa standards, but he liked the animals. They were whip smart and held a touch of danger, domesticated animals that quickly turned wild if left to fend for themselves.

Old Pete kept his small band of pigs for nostalgic reasons. His father had raised pigs and so had his grandfather, great-grandfather, and great-great-grandfather. As far as the land platting went back, a member of Old Pete's family had worked this very piece of land, had a small drift of pigs, and plenty of bacon in the ice box.

Pete was not about to break that kind of tradition, although his son probably would. Old Pete's boy didn't love the land like all his fathers before him, but Pete was proud of him anyhow. The boy had grown up and gone to medical school. A doctor. The emergency kind. Who could find shame in that? But still, it was sad that a century-old tradition would die out with Old Pete.

Quit that negative thinking, Pete told himself. *You're not dying today.*

He shook his head and continued walking down the path toward the pigs. He could hear them snorting and rooting around, even in the dark. It sounded like they were already eating something. A critter had gotten into the pen again, most likely, and it had not ended well for that critter. Pigs were not passivists. They were aggressive, and they'd eat anything. Anything.

That was when he noticed the disturbances in his well-worn path from the barn to the pigs. Dirt kicked around, disruptions in the grass, indents in the ground, drag marks. His eyes tracked the marks, watching as he continued to make his way toward the pig pen.

It's nothing. A critter caught by a barn cat. A barn cat caught by a large critter. It was no reason to worry, nothing out of the ordinary. These things happened in the country.

Then he saw the shoe. It was lying right there beside his path. It shimmered as it caught in the light of his lantern. *What in the Sam hell is that doing here?* he wondered as he stopped beside it and lowered his lantern to get a better look.

It was a high-heeled fancy to-do. Black with a red sole. It did not belong on a farm. His wife would never wear something like that. Not even in her younger days. She was a boot-wearing gal. Always had been. That was one of the things he loved about her. No frills. Just her.

Old Pete stared at it for a moment, wondering what to do, then he shook his head and continued walking. The pigs needed breakfast. The shoe could wait. The rooting and chomping noises grew louder as he made his way down the path. The pigs were definitely eating something. He hoped it was a wild animal, a squirrel or raccoon.

When he reached the fence, he raised his lantern and nearly dropped it when the soft tendrils of light cut through the darkness and touched upon the pigs' meal. They'd nearly eaten it all, but there were hunks of hair, long hair, possibly from a woman, and blood everywhere. Buckets of it. It flowed out of the pen like a river of death.

It's not a person. It's something else. A sick joke.

Old Pete's mind desperately grappled for answers that had only one solution. A purse hung on the fence, dangling there like it was on display at a store. He stood, dumbfounded, gaping at the scene, but only for a moment. A small sliver of time that allowed his mind to process the situation and kick into gear. Adrenaline forged through his old body, forcing him into action, moving faster than he had in years.

He dumped the slop into the pig's trough and moved to the other side of the pen, where the swine gnawed on what was left of their ghastly appetizer. Then he took the empty slop pails and began banging them against the fencing. *Bang. Bang. Bang. Bang.*

"*Paul, Ringo! You get away from there, now,*" he shouted as he struck the fencing as hard as he could with the steel pail, his arms tingling with the reverberations of the sound.

"Go on and get your breakfast." Paul, George, and John moved toward the slop bucket. Ringo, who had always been the wiliest of the bunch ignored Old Pete.

"I said go on, *git!*" Old Pete slammed the pail against the fence, right next to Ringo.

After another bite, Ringo looked up at him, a piece of pink fabric–a shirt perhaps–dangling from his mouth. Old Pete struck the fence one more time, then Ringo snorted and joined the others.

Old Pete reached into his front pocket and removed his phone with shaking hands. It was a swanky, colored contraption with all those things the kids called "apps," none of which he understood. Phones were for calling. That was all he needed his to do. Yet, his daughter thought he "deserved" more.

She'd bought him this new fancy phone for Christmas. He didn't like it, but she'd been so excited to give it to him that he had no choice but to accept it. He always did have a weak spot for his little girl. Not for the first time, he was now left cursing that weak spot. The phone had no buttons. It took several moments for his fumbling fingers to press the spots on the screen labeled 9-1-1.

"9-1-1 what's your emergency?" A dispatcher answered.

Old Pete recognized the voice. It was little Susan. Not so little anymore. "Susie, I need some help."

"Pete?" Susan's voice was suddenly intense. "What is it? Do you need an ambulance?"

Old Pete's gaze shifted to the pools of blood. "No. I need a coroner."

Susan gasped. "Oh, my God. What happened?"

"It's not me or the Mrs."

She sighed audibly. "Then what?"

"There's what's left of a body, I think, here in the pig pen. I came to feed them, and they were already chowing down on something. It's a woman, maybe. There's a purse hanging here on the fence. But they've eaten all of her. I got them cornered for now. I watch those forensic shows. Gotta protect the evidence. Or what's left of it. I know that. But someone ought to get on out here lickity-split."

"They're on their way, Pete. You hang in there."

Pete ended the call and went back to his task at hand, guarding what was left of the person. All he could see was hair, but there could be more scattered around in the mud, as unlikely as that may be.

It wasn't common knowledge, but pigs ate clothing, bones, meat, nails. It didn't matter if the material was organic or not, they'd eat it. Old Pete once knew a guy who had a heart attack in a pig pen and all that the authorities found of him were his false teeth. The swine ate everything else. Old Pete hoped there was more than just hair and blood left of this person. Something the family could bury. He also hoped that the person had been dead before the pigs started eating.

As Old Pete stood there and waited, he couldn't help thinking about his long-understood adage. Death was a part of life. He had accepted that long ago. But it wasn't supposed to be like this. Alone, with livestock munching on your flesh and bones.

1

TYRONE

Present

June 15, 2018

Homicide was not common in rural Iowa. To Tyrone's amazement, the locals rarely locked their doors at night. They left their keys in their cars and their guns in the glove box. It was all foreign to Tyrone, a Chicago native. Leaving anything unlocked in the city was like giving it away. A bike without a chain might as well have a sign saying *free to anyone.*

But still, Tyrone had taken the job in Fort Calhoun, Iowa, a small-ish town of approximately 20,000 people. It wasn't small for Iowa, but it was small to him. He'd spent the first ten years of his career as an officer working for the Chicago Police Department, all of which were spent on patrol. He enjoyed the work, but it was a means to an end. He wanted to be a detective. He wanted, no needed, to investigate.

Unfortunately, so did every other cop in Chicago. That was why he'd accepted the position as a detective with Fort Calhoun five months ago. He'd checked the crime rates, and even though it was small, Fort Calhoun had a higher-than-average crime rate. When he took the job, he'd planned to solve one or two major crimes, get some experience under his belt, prove himself, then return to the city where he belonged. After five months of petty thefts, drug-related home invasions and drunk drivers, he was starting to question his decision to leave the city.

Then he got the call. He was already dressed for the day in a pair of jeans and a collared shirt. He'd just popped a piece of bread in the toaster and cracked three eggs to scramble when his phone started buzzing against his apartment's laminate countertop. It was supposed to look like granite, but it just looked like crap to Tyrone.

"Gully here," Tyrone said, picking up after the second ring.

"Detective Gully," a now familiar voice said. "It's the Chief. I'm out at Old Pete's farm."

"Old Pete?" Tyrone said. The familiarity between law enforcement and locals was strange to Tyrone. In Chicago, he had rarely dealt with the same person twice.

"Looks like we have a murder on our hands," the Chief continued. "We've got blood everywhere and signs of a struggle. Can you get out here?"

The local Chief of Police was an older man, old enough for retirement but too stubborn to leave. He spoke slowly, without urgency, which irritated Tyrone. Their job literally was emergencies. There should be an emergent sense in everything they did, even communication.

"I'll be there in a few." Tyrone got the coordinates and left his uncooked breakfast on the counter, grabbing an energy bar on the way out. He was at the scene in less than fifteen minutes, and he wasn't the only one.

Flashing lights surrounded the old farmhouse. Patrol vehicles with the logo of different agencies stamped across the side. *Fort Calhoun Police Department. Iowa State Patrol. Calhoun County Sheriff's Department.* Tyrone parked beside the vehicles and got out to search for the Chief. He didn't have to look far. All he had to do was follow the trail of voices in the unnerving country silence. It led to a large group of officers milling around behind a big red barn.

"Tyrone," the Chief said when he approached. "Thanks for coming."

Another officer stood next to the Chief. Officer Jake McKee. A local patrolman. He'd been with the department for close to five years and he'd wanted Tyrone's detective position. He'd been a shoo-in until an officer with ten years of experience in Chicago applied for the position. Jake hadn't taken the disappointment well.

Jake looked up at Tyrone and sneered.

"What's going on?" Tyrone asked.

The Chief's gaze drifted to a nearby pig pen. An old farmer stood there, talking to a sheriff's deputy in a brown uniform with a star on his chest. Tyrone's gaze shifted around the scene, taking in the massive amount of blood. There were pools of it everywhere.

"We've got a murder," the Chief said.

"And you suspect the pigs?" Tyrone said. This had to be a twisted joke. A form of hazing. They'd called him out to investigate pigs for a homicide. He knew small towns could be backward, but this was next level.

"I told you he wouldn't take it seriously," Jake said, his cold gaze boring into Tyrone. "Give me the case."

The Chief ignored Jake and continued talking to Tyrone. "The victim has been a missing person since February."

Tyrone raised an eyebrow. "How do you know that?"

"We found her identification. It was in her purse." He held up a clear evidence bag containing a driver's license. "It's Molly Sand."

Jake whistled and took a step back. "I changed my mind. I don't want this one."

"Why not?" Tyrone asked. The guy had just been begging for the assignment. The quick shift had Tyrone wrong footed, unsure.

"Frank Sand is a bruiser," Jake said. "The kind of guy with the power and influence to ruin careers."

Tyrone blinked several times, his nerves settling. "Okay." He'd dealt with plenty of heavy hitters in Chicago. People with connections to former presidents and major league baseball players. He was not unaccustomed to the rich and powerful, and he could handle it.

"The guy who used to have your position. Haven't you ever wondered what happened to him?" Jake said.

Tyrone hadn't, but he certainly did now.

A cruel, joyless smile spread across Jake's lips, and he leaned forward, eager to assault Tyrone with the story. "He stopped Frank Sand on an operating a vehicle while intoxicated traffic stop. Frank was driving all over the road. Swerving like a chicken with its head cut off. He blew a .2 on the PBT. It seemed like a slam dunk case until Frank's attorney got involved. She made such a stink, somehow turning everything on us. *We planted evidence. We are corrupt. Blah. Blah. Blah.* And the locals bought it. Now the former detective is a janitor at Fort Calhoun High School."

Tyrone would have to tread lightly. He did not have any interest in janitorial work.

"Don't worry about that," the Chief said, clapping Tyrone on the shoulder. "I'm sure you'll solve it in no time." Then he walked away.

"Because if you don't..." Jake made a slitting motion across his throat before following the Chief.

Are they setting me up for failure?

They very well could be. But the only way to combat that was to succeed, and that's what Tyrone intended to do. This case was his now, and he would make the best of it. It was time to act.

First, he called for a forensics team to come from the crime laboratory in Ankeny, Iowa. It was the only criminal forensics laboratory in Iowa. It would take them a while to get there, but they were experts, and someone needed to get out here to start collecting blood samples.

His second call was to arrange for the slaughter of the pigs and the dissection of their stomach contents. Their stomach acids likely destroyed any DNA or forensic evidence, but he needed to cover all his bases.

Finally, he made a call to Frank Sand himself. Murder investigations always started with the husband. He would not treat Frank Sand any differently. Maybe that would lead to the death of Tyrone's career, but he was not compromising this investigation by affording Frank Sand special treatment. He'd seen plenty of officers make that mistake in Chicago. The rich and powerful were just as capable of murder as anyone else. Maybe even more capable.

2

MOLLY

Four Months Earlier
February 1, 2018

It was three in the morning when Frank came home, stumbling into the bedroom with a weak smile and watery eyes. Was he having an affair? Again? *Why not?* Molly couldn't do anything to stop him. She was trapped, and they both knew it.

"Late night," Molly said, staring down at her fingers, intertwined and resting in her lap.

She was perched at the end of the bed, her body wrapped in a thigh-length silk robe. She'd been waiting for him, searching social media for any sign of what Frank was up to that night. A picture posted at a bar. A tag from someone younger and blonder than Molly. *Anything.* But she'd seen nothing. That left her awake, worrying, wondering if he was up to his old tricks. If he was at some hotel, rented for a few hours of fun.

"Yeah." Frank worked odd hours at the various bars, restaurants, and gyms that he owned and operated around Fort Calhoun, but he rarely stayed out later than two. "I'm beat."

Molly nodded. She was tired, too, but she kept that to herself. She hadn't been sleeping well, and his late nights weren't helping. Still, her sleep was her problem, not his. Frank would not want to hear about it; he wouldn't listen if she tried to tell him.

"Well," Frank clapped his hands together. "I'm going to take a shower and catch a little shut-eye." He tossed his cell phone on his bedside table, stripped naked and got in the shower.

Molly didn't move.

Ping. Frank's phone chirped and vibrated with a message.

Molly's gaze darted toward it, then skittered away.

Ping. Ping. Ping.

The phone moved with the vibrations. It was nearing the edge of the nightstand where it could easily fall off.

Ping.

It could fall and crack the screen. The floor in the bedroom was hard-wood. A large rug stretched across most of the room, but the nightstands were not on it.

Should I get it? Frank did not like her touching his things, but he also didn't like it when they broke.

Who is texting now anyway? It was three-thirty in the morning. Frank didn't take business calls before noon unless it was an emergency, and nobody texted when it was *that* urgent.

Ping. It teetered on the edge.

Molly crawled across the bed and grabbed it, flipping it over so she could see the screen. "Oh, my God," she said, nearly dropping it. There was a picture of a naked woman, no girl, she couldn't be more than twenty, with the index finger of one hand in her mouth and the other hand in her crotch area. The text read, COME ON BACK, BABY. I'M READY FOR YOU AGAIN. Next to it were the cat and eggplant emojis.

Ping. The phone buzzed in her hands and a new message populated the screen. There were no faces in this picture. It was a close-up shot with the phone between the girl's legs. GET IN HERE. Three eggplant emojis followed.

Frank was cheating. *With who?* Molly's gaze darted to the closed bath-room door. The shower was still running, but he'd be out soon. Her fingers flew across the screen, typing in his passcode. *1 2 3 4 5 6.* Frank hadn't told her, but she knew him well enough after ten years of marriage. He wanted easy, not safe.

Ping. Another message. The girl's fingers were inserted inside herself in this image with the words, I bet your wife doesn't do this.

A flash of something passed through Molly, but she couldn't quite describe the feeling. Was it anger? Frustration? Embarrassment? This girl knew Frank was married, and it hadn't deterred her. She was using it as sexual banter.

The water stopped. The shower door swished open. Molly was running out of time. She clicked on the message and a name popped up. *Rebecca.* She scrolled back through the images, clicking on the first picture. It was the only one that showed the girl's face. It was half obscured by Rebecca's long, light brown hair, but Molly still thought she recognized her. She worked out at Frank's gym, *Frankly Hot and Heavy*.

Molly tried to scroll back to earlier messages, but there weren't any. Frank had deleted them.

"Why do you have my phone?" Frank's booming voice startled her.

"I, uhhh..." Thoughts and emotions scratched their way through Molly's mind, dragging and digging in different directions. She couldn't grab hold of anything, couldn't form words.

"Why do you have my phone?" Frank was naked aside from the towel around his waist, his beer belly hanging over it.

"You were getting texts. It almost fell off the nightstand." Molly swallowed hard, then turned it around, showing him the screen. "Who is Rebecca?"

His expression changed, the anger melting away, replaced by horror. "She's nobody."

Molly held the phone out to him, suddenly desperate to get rid of it. Her hand shook. He accepted it and placed it back on the nightstand.

"It doesn't look like nothing. Were you with her tonight?"

"She's nobody. It's nothing." He came to her side, dropping onto the bed beside her. The whole thing shook, and the mattress dipped, causing Molly's small frame to slide toward him. "I'll end it," he finally said.

Molly said nothing. There was nothing to say. Either he would or he wouldn't. His track record for the latter wasn't promising.

He shifted his body toward her. "You believe me, don't you?"

Molly shrugged, leaning away from him. She didn't want to touch him.

"You have to believe me. I love you, Molly." He tugged at the belt of her robe. "You love me, don't you?"

"Yes," she said.

Truthfully, she didn't know how she felt about him anymore. He didn't love her. What they had was a game of cat and mouse. He was the cat, she the mouse. If she stayed in her cage, trapped, behaving as he pleased, he wouldn't attack. But he was always prowling, always waiting.

"You can't get a divorce, you know that," his tone had turned cold, flat. "You need me." He slid the collar of her robe down her shoulder, exposing the teddy beneath it.

Molly did need him. That was one of her many problems. They had two children and she had no job, no family, no education, no degree. She'd been wanting to go back to school for years now, to learn to be a nurse or a teacher, but Frank wouldn't hear it.

"You love me. I love you. Let's make love," he kissed her bare shoulder.

There was that word again. *Love*. Frank only used it while asking for forgiveness. And he only wanted forgiveness to ease the tension in the air. Not for her, but because it made him uncomfortable.

"Is it 'love' with me and 'sex' with Rebecca?" Molly asked.

"I already told you," Frank said, "She's nothing. Nobody. Now do as I say," he ripped at the side of her robe.

She grabbed at it, trying to keep it on, but he pulled harder, tearing the fabric.

"If you won't make love," he shoved her, placing both hands on her shoulders, "Then I'm going to fuck you."

Molly shook her head. "No, Frank. I will, I'll make love."

"Too late."

He climbed on top of her, straddling her. She struggled beneath his weight, her body desperate to fight back, her mind telling her to *be calm, he only likes it more when you fight*. But her body would not follow her mind's instruction.

"You are mine," he said, issuing a dark, guttural laugh.

She could feel him growing hard against her stomach. He placed a hand to her neck and penetrated her with a hard jerk, tearing his way inside her unprepared body. Searing pain shot through her. She cried out, but it only excited him, making his jabs more violent, more intense.

A tear slid down her cheek, and she forced her body to relax. He would finish faster. It would hurt less if she could relax. She made her mind go somewhere else, to disconnect. He controlled her finances, her body, but she still controlled her mind. Her thoughts were still her own.

3

TYRONE

Present
June 15, 2018

He liked to watch suspects when they were alone in interview rooms. It was when they were their most honest. They knew they were on camera, they were in a police station. Yet they dropped their guard, forgetting that they were supposed to be grieving or scared or whatever false emotion they wanted Tyrone to believe.

Frank Sand was no different. Tyrone watched him now, sitting in the small room, making himself as comfortable as possible in one of the four blue, plastic chairs. The man was slouching with his arm slung over the shoulder of the chair, scrolling through social media. He looked like he didn't have a care in the world. Maybe he didn't.

"Look at that guy," Jackie said. "He makes me sick."

Jackie was a patrol officer. The Chief had assigned her to assist Tyrone in the investigation into Molly's death. Jackie was young, in her early twenties, but she was a hard worker. Like all new officers, she made mistakes, she lacked knowledge, but she made up for it with determination. There was a huge learning curve with the job, one nobody quite expected. Officers needed to know the law inside and out, like attorneys, but they only had a fraction of the education.

"Let's not jump to conclusions," Tyrone said. He'd been thinking the same thing, but he'd been an officer longer, and he'd learned the danger of zeroing in on a suspect too fast. Cases were usually as they seemed, but not always.

"Even if he had nothing to do with her murder, he's still acting like an arrogant prick."

"That's true. Don't expect that to change during the interview either."

One of the first things he'd learned when he moved to Fort Calhoun was that some people were untouchable. They were well-connected, high-income men. The kind of men who exploited the good-old-boy system. Frank Sand was one of them. He owned most of the businesses in the area. He had restaurants, bars, and a popular gym called *Frankly Hot and Heavy*.

Unfortunately for Frank, Tyrone was not a good-old-boy, and neither was Jackie. They were outsiders, a female cop, and a black out-of-towner, and that emboldened them. There were no favors to repay, no pats on the back.

"Well, I better get this show on the road," Tyrone said, taking one last look at the camera before turning his back. "You watch from here."

"Sure thing," Jackie said, her shoulders rounding as she issued a heavy sigh.

Jackie wanted to be in the interview room. She'd hoped he'd let her be there this once. But she didn't question the decision. She might later, but only to understand the logic behind his choice to approach Frank with one officer instead of two. The answer was simple, Tyrone didn't want Frank to get his guard up. He wanted him to feel as untouchable as he'd always been in the past. Two officers would indicate they were looking at him closely.

Tyrone made his way to the interview room. He paused outside, his fingers lingering on the doorknob. He took a deep breath, centering himself, steeling his emotions, before turning and entering. The door creaked.

Frank shifted in his seat, sitting up straighter. He abandoned his social media, mid-scroll, and placed his phone face down on the table. Frank Sand was a big man, tall and wide, but only in the belly, his arms and legs were thin. He was in his mid-fifties, clean shaven with a head of mousy brown hair that had grown thin on top. He was a prime example that owning a gym was not the same as working out at one.

"Took you long enough," Frank said.

"The wheels of justice take time."

"That sounds like some voodoo witch-doctor bullshit. Did you make that up yourself?"

Tyrone stared at him for a long moment, wondering if he'd meant the reference to a witch doctor to be derogatory. Would he have said the same thing to any of the townie cops? The way Frank was looking at him, green eyes narrowed, Tyrone would bet the answer to that question was a resounding *no*.

"Do you know why you are here?" Tyrone asked. He pulled the plastic chair across from Frank away from the table. Its legs made a *whomp, whomp, whomp,* sound that bounced off the walls of the small room, amplifying the noise. Then he sat down, never taking his eyes off Frank.

"I'd guess it has something to do with my wife."

Tyrone had a file clutched in his hand, a thin one with only a few documents. He set it on the table in front of him. It didn't contain anything confidential or unknown to Frank Sand. Tyrone had only brought it to use as a prop. He flipped it open.

There, on the front page was an image of Frank's wife, Molly Sand. A stunningly beautiful woman, but in a plastic, unnatural, sort of way. She had the kind of beauty that stole your breath and forced you to look, but it was cold and clinical, built in a doctor's office, not a womb. She was young, not even thirty yet with a small, straight nose, extraordinarily full lips, and chestnut colored hair, highlighted in blond, that fell in soft waves down her back.

"I want to remind you that you've already been Mirandized," Tyrone said.

"Yeah, no shit. I can hear. What I don't have is time." He glanced at his watch, a Rolex likely worth more than Tyrone's car. "It's six o'clock in the morning. I should be sleeping. I've got businesses to attend to. You may punch a clock, but my work never ends. I have an empire to run." He flashed a toothy grin, baring his teeth like a challenge.

"I didn't *bring* you here. I asked you to come. Your decision to acquiesce to my request was your own."

"Whatever. Can you get to the point?"

"You don't seem very concerned about your wife."

"She's been missing since February. You jackrabbits haven't found hide nor hair of her since then. I don't expect it's any different now."

Tyrone blinked hard at the term *jackrabbits*, forcing his mind to remain on the facts of the case. He would attempt to unpack the meaning behind that term later, when he was in the comfort and safety of his apartment.

"Tell me," Tyrone said, tapping the eraser side of a number two pencil against Molly's picture, "how did she disappear?"

Frank sighed, heavily. A passive aggressive display of irritation. "I've told you a million times."

"That's where you're wrong. You've never told *me* anything. In fact, this is the first time we're meeting."

"Well, I've told someone. It was that bull sized girl cop." Frank leaned back, looking up at the ceiling, thinking, "Jackie something or other."

"Officer Marsh," Tyrone said, forcing his eyes to remain on Frank instead of tracking toward the camera. "Officer Jackie Marsh."

"That's her." He chuckled. "Built like a linebacker, that one. She'll never get married looking like that."

"Not sure marriage is high on her agenda."

"Probably for the best. No point wanting things you can't have. What's that saying? Shit in one hand and wish in the other, see which fills up first."

"Perhaps. That's not a phrase I've ever used."

"Yeah, well, you're not from around here. I can tell. You're one of those city boys from up north. Detroit or Minneapolis or something."

Tyrone gritted his teeth. He had left the realm of boyhood many, many years ago, and he was not about to tell this jerk anything about himself, including the city he called home.

"I understand you've spoken with Officer Marsh about Molly's disappearance, but I have not heard the details. So," Tyrone tapped Molly's picture again, "indulge me."

Frank's eyes drifted to Molly's photograph, then darted away. "There isn't anything to tell. I left for work, and when I came home, she was gone. That's it."

"No note?"

"No."

"Or letter?"

"Aren't notes and letters the same thing?"

"Perhaps."

"Listen," Frank said, slapping his palms down on the table, "this has been a real joy, but I really must be going."

Tyrone had hoped to get more information before revealing any of his cards, but his prime suspect was ready to walk out the door. He had to do *something* to keep him present and talking. Tyrone didn't have anywhere near enough evidence to arrest or detain Frank. If he wanted to leave, he could.

"Before you go, there is one thing you ought to know."

"What's that?"

Tyrone leaned forward and lowered his voice. "We found your wife."

"Molly?"

"Yes. Are you still ready to go?"

Frank's posture stiffened and his eyes widened. "I need to make some phone calls."

Frank didn't ask where they found Molly or if she was okay. That was significant, but it was no smoking gun. He needed something solid. He needed Frank to admit that he knew a fact that he shouldn't know. If that happened, Tyrone would grasp onto it like a lifeline and pull until he forced a full confession out of Frank.

"Make all the calls you want." Tyrone stood and headed toward the door. "I'll be back in a little while."

He left Molly's husband, always the prime suspect in a murder investigation, alone in the interview room, and headed for the camera room. There, he would watch Frank frantically making call after call. With some luck, Frank would say something dumb, tell the person on the other end a significant fact, perhaps something about pigs. Suspects often did forget that they were on camera.

4

MOLLY

Frank fell asleep immediately after he finished, and Molly lay awake watching the clock tick forward, hoping for sleep that never came. Her mind wouldn't shut off. By five o'clock, she gave up and rolled out of bed. Frank was snoring loud enough to shake the walls. Molly had read somewhere that snoring was a sign of sleep apnea and if left untreated, a person could die in their sleep.

If I could only be so lucky. But that was too convenient, too easy. There was no easy way out for Molly. Frank had made that clear from the day they got married.

You belong to me, he'd said on their wedding day.

Back then, she'd thought it was romantic. He belonged to her, she belonged to him. It didn't take her long to realize the belonging was not reciprocal and there was nothing romantic about ownership. How naïve she'd been back then. She'd thought money could fix everything.

It was easy to believe when she grew up sleeping on a damp floor, her stomach so empty it had stopped grumbling and felt like it was concaving. Molly's childhood was spent waking up to find her mother passed out with a rubber tube wrapped around her arm, and an empty syringe lying feet from her outstretched hand. The family had moved around often, attempts to avoid the government discovering what was happening in the home. But eventually, Molly's mother passed out in the wrong place at the wrong time and found her way into a jail cell.

Molly had been nearly a teenager by then. She'd been placed in a foster home and, naively, she thought her life would get better, but it didn't. It just became different. She still moved often, traded from one foster home to the next. Her awkward body had filled in with curves in all the "right" places, and she found herself hiding from foster dads who tried to get a little too cozy, apologizing to foster moms who blamed Molly for their husband's actions.

Stop it. Stop remembering, Molly told herself. This was what she did after she discovered Frank's affairs, after he took advantage of her. He'd move on like nothing happened, and she blamed herself, rehashing her past. It was her fault, like it was back then. If only she could do more, be more, be better, none of the bad things would happen.

No. No. No.

Molly made her way into the bathroom, closing the door. The cold of the marble floor bit into her feet, but she welcomed its sharpness. Pain was real. She made her way to the medicine cabinet, shaking a few green and white pills into her palm, swallowing them dry. She needed to get out of her funk. If not for herself, then for her kids. The pills would help.

As she closed the medicine cabinet, her gaze fell onto her bathroom sink. The countertop was his and her style, white marble set against a deep blue vanity. A vase of white flowers, chosen by Frank's designer, twisted their way toward the ceiling. Molly kept her various lotions and perfumes lined up on a two-tiered glass organizer sitting next to her sink. Each item had a place, especially her expensive perfumes, including her Chanel No. 5, which was missing.

Oh, no.

Had she lost it? It would irritate Frank. He hated when she lost things. Her gaze shifted to the medicine cabinet. Maybe she'd been taking too many of the green and white pills lately. The label said *take as needed*, and she needed them more than ever these days. Or was Frank messing with her? He would ask her about it. He could have stolen it to shift blame away from himself, his affair and his behaviors, to accuse her of something.

Well, two can play at that game.

She began searching through Frank's drawers. It only took her a moment to find his bottle of Giorgio Armani *Aqua Di Gio Eau de Toilette* cologne. She grabbed it and took it into the walk-in closet, placing it beside his summer shoes, tucked away in the back of the closet. He'd find it, eventually, but it wouldn't be for a few months. It was his turn to *lose* something. Maybe he'd stop calling her an "airhead."

She pulled a robe over her shoulders and slipped her feet into slippers. The soft material was luxurious against her skin. Both items were expensive, but Molly didn't do the shopping, so she did not know their actual cost. She tried looking it up online, but the brand was the type that didn't list their prices or display their pieces online. It was that exclusive.

She stepped out of the bathroom and into the hallway, leaving her husband snoring like a hog. She padded down the hallway and stopped at the next two rooms, slowly opening the doors and peeking in on her two children, Matthew and then Genevieve. Her two rambunctious sweethearts were deep in sleep, both nestled under their down comforters.

Their rooms were decorated in traditional boy/girl colors, again a design choice by Frank and his designer. Genevieve's walls were a soft pink with rainbow and unicorn decor. Matthew had dark blue paint with images of Marvel superheroes and framed words like *Pow!* lining the walls. Their father was trying to force gender roles on them, but they'd found a way to counter it. Matthew's head rested on Genevieve's rainbow pillow. Genevieve's chubby little arms were wrapped around a plush spider man.

Molly smiled at her smart, brave children. They both had rainbows and superpowers within them. She hoped her influence could outweigh their father's, and they'd grow up to be unique people, not carbon copies of every girl and boy of the past. She closed their doors softly and made her way across the hallway and down the winding front formal staircase and into the kitchen.

Molly popped a pod in the Keurig and waited for her coffee to brew. She drank it black even though she preferred cream and sugar. She was twenty-eight, almost thirty. Her metabolism wasn't what it used to be. She needed to cut calories wherever she could. Frank purchased her clothes, and he refused to buy anything larger than a size two.

She would like to do her own shopping, choose some less form fitting, less beige clothing, but she didn't have money of her own. She had no credit cards, no debit cards, not even a checkbook. Frank controlled the accounts. That was one of the reasons why she wanted to go back to school. It was also why Frank had never allowed it.

She drank her coffee and spent the morning watching trash television, trying to keep her mind off Frank's text messages. When had the affair started? Was it months, weeks, or days after the end of the last affair? She had no way of knowing.

"*Prostitution whore!*" A woman's voice screeched from the television, catching Molly's attention. The woman stood and flipped the dinner table, dishes and glassware crashing to the ground as she continued spewing epithets at another woman.

I wish I could be like that. If Molly had an ounce of that woman's fire, she'd—

"Mommy?" A small voice came from the stairs.

Molly turned to see Genevieve and Matthew coming around the corner, their eyes bleary with sleep. Her heart fluttered, filled to bursting at the sight of her two little angels. Who was she kidding? She could have all the strength in the world and Frank would still win. She wouldn't do anything to harm her kids. Not physically, emotionally, or financially. Leaving Frank wouldn't impact the first two, but the last, she didn't know how they'd survive. They needed his money.

"Can we watch a show?" Matthew asked.

Molly patted the couch on both sides of her. Matthew crawled onto her left side and Genevieve to her right. They pressed their little bodies into hers, wiggling until they fit like a set of puzzle pieces. Molly switched the channel to PBS kids, a show about dinosaurs and trains. This was Molly's favorite time of the day. When life was going so wrong, these two children were the one thing she'd gotten right.

Molly leaned over and kissed the top of Matthew's head and pulled both kids closer. She wanted to remember everything about them at this age. Their scent, the feel of their skin against hers. They would not stay like this forever. They would grow up, move out, and then it would only be her, Frank, and his mistresses.

His mistresses.

This was the fifth time. Would he ever stop? She thought back to her conversation with him the night before. He had said he'd end it with Rebecca, but he hadn't even bothered promising that he wouldn't do it again. Because he would. There was no keeping him from getting what he wanted; and he wanted lots of women.

Molly heard the door to the basement apartment open and close. She turned around, but the children didn't move. It was seven o'clock. Nolan always got up at that time. He was the children's au pair, and Molly's only friend in the world.

"Good morning, gorgeous..." Nolan's voice was chipper at first, but it darkened when he saw her expression. He crossed his arms and jutted out a hip. "Alright. What happened?"

Molly looked at her two children. "Why don't you two go into the kitchen and grab some breakfast. There are some doughnuts on the counter."

"Okay!" The kids said in unison. They hopped up and rushed out of the room.

Molly watched them dash off, wishing she could borrow even a small amount of their childhood joy.

"Okay. Spill," Nolan said, dropping onto the couch next to her.

"He's cheating."

"Again!" Nolan's eyes widened. "That bastard. Some people deserve to be eunuchs. Your husband is one of them. Same chick or different one?"

Eunuch was right. If he'd only known what Frank had done after she'd confronted him about the affair. But she didn't tell him, wouldn't. Somehow, that was too embarrassing to admit. Too hard to form into words.

"Different girl."

"Who? Do we know her?"

"Rebecca. That's all I know. I think she works out at the gym."

Nolan chewed on his lip. "The usual age?"

"Yeah." All of Frank's past dalliances–at least those Molly had discovered–were all between the ages of eighteen and twenty.

"It could be Rebecca Rice," Nolan said.

"I don't know. I just know her name is Rebecca and I recognize her face." Molly didn't go many places other than the gym and Nolan knew it. That was why he was her eyes and ears outside the home.

"It's probably Rebecca Rice. Don't you worry, honey." He gathered her small hand into his larger hands, patting it. "We'll figure it out. Your pal Nolan's got this. I'll get the tea, and I'll spill it, honey. I'll knock it over right where everyone can see. Just for you."

"Thank you."

"But seriously, what are you going to do about him? You know I love you, but you can't keep letting this happen."

Molly cocked her head to the side, thinking. The confrontation with Frank had ended the same as always, but she felt different about it this time. Maybe the fifth affair was the charm, the fifth time he forced her to submit to him. She didn't want to continue as though nothing had happened; she couldn't. She needed a plan.

"Maybe you could use it as leverage. We all know he won't change."

"What do you mean?"

"Use it to force him to let you go back to school," Nolan said.

"Maybe," Molly said.

"You ought to get something out of it—" Nolan looked like he wanted to say more, but they were interrupted by the sound of Frank's heavy footsteps coming down the stairs.

"Oh good," Frank said, coming around the corner. He yawned and didn't cover his mouth. "Just what I wanted to see first thing in the morning. A fairy."

As always, Frank was back to his usual self, no longer guilt-ridden or cowed. He was not worried about Molly's forgiveness. It was expected. This was their dance. He screwed up, he apologized, she accepted it.

Not anymore. She couldn't bear to spend the rest of her life this way. A constant circle of betrayal laced with hints of violence.

Nolan snorted.

"Why are you here?" Frank said.

"You know why I'm here." Nolan's eyes flashed with fury. "Neanderthal," he said the last word only loud enough for Molly to hear. He hated Frank, but he didn't want to lose her and the children.

"You shouldn't. Matthew doesn't need a sissy teaching him how to act." Frank's gaze flicked to Molly. "This has gone on long enough. It was fine when Matthew was a baby, but he's getting older. He doesn't need to see a man doing a woman's job."

Molly's heart stuttered. She couldn't lose Nolan. She couldn't.

Nolan placed a protective arm across Molly's shoulders. "Bring another woman in this house and you'll have war, honey. All. Out. War. And you, sir, you are not equipped for that. With me, you have peace."

Frank shook his head and walked toward the door muttering, "The things I do for peace." He was fully dressed in jeans and a collared shirt, his regular work-day outfit. He opened the door and closed it behind him without saying goodbye to Molly or his children.

"I hate that man," Nolan said.

Molly sighed. She wanted to feel the same way, but she needed Frank. With a childhood like hers, need was close enough to love. To ask for more was greedy.

"Where is he going today?" Nolan asked.

"I don't know," Molly said. "One of his businesses. He never tells me which one."

Frank always knew where Molly was–that was the purpose of the tracker on her iPhone—but he didn't return the favor. They had a *don't ask, don't tell* policy in their marriage. He didn't have to ask her where she was because he always knew, and he wouldn't tell her his location even if she asked. It sounded one-sided because it was.

That was their relationship in a nutshell. One-sided. It was time she did something to change that. Genevieve and Matthew were getting older. They watched how their father treated their mother. Going on like this, pretending, it would only ruin their futures, their lives. It was time for a change. But how would she do it? How could she escape with those that she loved, her children, and the things that she needed, financial security?

5

ANGEL

Past

February 1

Every day was dramatic. That was the blessing and the curse of practicing family law. It was a people profession, and people were unpredictable. Especially when they were going through a divorce or a child custody battle. It was the lowest and most desperate point in many of their lives, and Angel Malone was there to witness it. Her clients were reality television in the flesh. They behaved badly, were ill-tempered, needy, and demanding.

"Why do I do this to myself?" Angel muttered as she stared down at the long list of interrogatories sent by opposing counsel.

It was a rhetorical question, of course. She knew exactly why she practiced family law. Money. She handled a few criminal cases here and there, but surprisingly, people were willing to dig deeper into their pockets to exact revenge on an ex than they would to protect their own freedom.

Angel was at her desk in her office, a small law firm bearing her last name *Malone* and her partner's last name, *Parker*, Parker and Malone, PLLC. She'd dedicated her professional life to this firm, starting back when it was Parker Law. It took years to convince George Parker that he needed her, that a partnership was superior to a sole practitioner, but she'd done it. And now her name was right there on the placard next to his.

Angel ran a hand through her long, brown hair, pulling it over one shoulder. She was going to have to call her client and go over the questions. Interrogatories were part of discovery, an exchange of questions requiring sworn answers, and she was not looking forward to the conversation. It would be fine if opposing counsel hadn't been quite so invasive. One of the questions was, *Have you ever engaged in anal intercourse?* It was meant to embarrass Angel's client. There was no legal reason for it.

"Angel," a voice came through the speaker on her phone, startling her. It was the office manager and legal assistant, Chloe.

"Yes." There was no inflection at the end, no upward tilt to the word, forming it into a question.

"Is now a bad time?"

"No," Angel said with a sigh. "It's been a long morning."

Angel had so many clients and everyone seemed to think their case, their situation, was the most important. One would think that her clients would keep the questions to a minimum considering her $275 hourly rate, but they didn't seem to care about the cost when they called and texted and emailed to ask the same things over and over and over again.

That was until they got their first bill. Then they still wanted to talk to her all the time, but they added little digs like *you're probably going to charge me a fortune for this question but...* As though they hadn't signed the fee agreement and completely understood that her time was money, and they would have to pay for it.

"I get it." Chloe was not one to hold a grudge. "Frank Sand is here for his appointment."

Angel glanced at the time. Ten o'clock already. There was never enough time in the day. "Go ahead and send him in," she said, setting the interrogatories aside and grabbing a fresh legal pad and pen.

A moment later, there was a soft knock on the door.

"Come in," Angel said, rising to her feet.

She threaded her fingers together, lightly resting them in front of her hips. She'd worn a navy-blue skirt suit with a white cashmere sweater. It was an outfit that was both professional and feminine. She preferred pant suits, but she would not wear one when meeting with a traditionalist like Frank. He expected women to look a certain way, and she was not immune from that expectation, even as his attorney. Maybe especially as his attorney.

The door swung open, and Chloe stepped inside, holding it open for Angel's client. Frank stepped past Chloe, turning so he was face to face with her, his chest brushing against hers. It was not necessary. Frank was a big man, but he wasn't *that* big. He could have easily stepped past her without touching her at all. He was trying to cop a feel. Chloe was young, blonde, and curvy. She caught the gazes of many men, including Angel's husband.

Chloe's eyes widened when Frank pressed into her and she took a step back, imperceptible to Frank but obvious to Angel. She did not reciprocate the admiration of men. She tried to deter the unwanted touching, to stand back. She dressed frumpily in loose-fitting clothing and didn't wear makeup. Yet, it still happened.

"Thank you, Chloe," Angel said. "That'll be all."

Chloe gave Angel a grateful look and scurried out, closing the door behind her.

"What? No coffee today?" Frank said.

"Not today. Have a seat." Angel nodded to the two chairs positioned across from her desk. They were Italian leather, brown, modern Chesterfield style.

"I feel like I've been called to the principal's office," Frank said, dropping into the chair closest to the door. "Please, Mrs. Malone, don't put me in detention. Or do," he said, leaning forward and winking. "Put on a form-fitting shirt, a pair of glasses, and some high heels." Frank whistled. "I'd be up for detention any day."

Angel gave him a tight smile. "What brings you in today?"

The best way to deal with his bad behavior was to change the subject. There was no point in correcting him. He wasn't going to change.

"Oh, Angel, my Angel."

She stiffened but forced the smile to remain on her lips. Frank was a longtime client. Steady income for the firm. If divorce were a degree, he'd have his doctorate by now. He was on his fifth marriage. A bad husband, but an ideal client. At least on paper. He always paid his bills on time and had plenty of cash to burn.

"You're wound so tight," Frank said. "Do you want me to come over there and give you a shoulder rub?"

"That won't be necessary. What brings you in?"

"Right." He straightened his back and fiddled with a fictitious tie. "Down to business." He was one of the richest men in Iowa, but he didn't dress like it. He was a jeans sort of guy.

"Time is money," Angel said.

"I'm good for it."

"You are."

"But you're right. Let's not waste our precious minutes. I need help with this." He slid a stack of documents across the desk, turning it so it was right-side-up for Angel.

Angel looked down. The caption read, *Petition for Modification.* Her gaze settled on the names contained in the caption. *Frank Sand, Petitioner, and concerning Vivian Sand, Respondent.* Vivian was Frank's first wife, and the document was filed in their original divorce case number.

"What's this all about?"

Frank chuckled. "I thought you were the one that's supposed to be telling me the answer to that question."

Angel continued to scan the document. *Modification of custody, placing full custody of the minor child, F.S., with the Respondent, Vivian Sand.* Vivian and Frank's divorce was finalized years ago. At the time, Frankie Jr. had only been three years old. The agreement had been shared care with each party having equal time, week on, week off exchanges.

Frank still paid child support, but that was only because at the time of the divorce his income was astronomically higher than Vivian's. But Vivian was no couch potato. She'd been a stay-at-home mom while married to Frank, but upon divorce, she quickly obtained her realtor's license and then her broker's license. She had the perfect mixture of charm, cunning, and ambition that had her taking the local market by storm. These days, nothing in the area sold without Vivian's fingers touching it.

"Frankie Jr. has to be almost eighteen, right?" Angel asked.

"He'll be eighteen this summer."

Angel debated asking him the exact date but decided against it. He wouldn't know. Children's birthdays were things that secretaries tracked and notified Frank as the date drew near. Angel could easily dig the child's birthdate out of an old file. It wouldn't be hard, and she was billing him by the hour. Finding that date would score another fifty bucks at least.

"That doesn't make a lot of sense, modifying custody just before the kid is eighteen."

Frank shrugged. "She probably needs money."

"Vivian has plenty of money, doesn't she?"

"She always needs—or wants—more. She's got a champagne lifestyle on a beer budget."

Angel gave him a hard look.

"It's all that plastic surgery and junk she puts in her face. It's ten thousand a month, at least."

Angel shook her head. "I'll never understand it."

"You don't now. You're only, what, thirty? Wait until you get to our age. You'll do the same thing."

Angel was thirty-five, but she wasn't going to correct him. He was close enough and guessed in the right direction, moving her closer to young rather than older. Frank was fifty and Vivian was approximately the same age. She was Frank's only age-appropriate wife, and that was only because he was barely twenty when they got married. His current wife, Molly, was only twenty-eight.

"I doubt that." Angel made good money, but not *that* kind of money. Especially since her husband, Mike, claimed he was a "stay-at-home dad" when their two kids went to daycare every day.

Frank shrugged.

"Alright, well, we'll need to file a formal answer to this petition. As you know, my retainer is five-thousand-dollars."

Frank leaned forward and reached into his back pocket, producing a fat bank envelope. "Five thousand on the nose." He tossed it onto the desk. It landed with a *thunk*.

Angel's gaze followed it, but she didn't reach out to grab it. They'd done this dance for what felt like thousands of times. One of Frank's four exes was always dragging him back to court for one thing or another. Children were usually the most contentious part of divorce matters. Luckily for him, he only had three children, two with his current wife, Molly, and one with Vivian.

Child support was expensive. Far more expensive than anyone ever expected. People pretended custody disputes were about the kids, but that argument fell flat when they started out saying they'd agree to shared care, but changed their minds, demanding full custody once Angel plugged the financial numbers into the child support calculator, and it still had them paying.

Angel turned to her laptop and clicked on a document saved to the desktop. It was a fee agreement form with *Parker and Malone, PLLC*, written along the top next to the law firm's business logo. She typed Frank's name in the box labeled *represented party*, and wrote, "Modification matter with Vivian Sand, Calhoun County Case Number CDDM0019276," under *scope of representation*. Then she pressed print.

A moment later, the printer spat the document out. She stood up, grabbed it, and returned to her desk, knowing full well that Frank had been staring at her backside the entire time. She could feel his gaze following her closely, like a stalker's hot breath against her bare neck.

"This is the fee agreement and scope of representation." She turned the document so that it was facing him. "Look it over and sign on the signature line."

Frank did not read it, he simply signed and pushed it toward her. "I have one other thing I want to discuss with you."

"Oh?" Angel lifted an eyebrow.

"I want to discuss a potential divorce with my current wife, Molly."

Angel would be lying if she said she was surprised. She often thought of Frank and that *Friends* episode when they started calling Ross *the divorcer*. Frank truly was a divorcer, but not in the same funny, hopeless romantic way as Ross Geller.

"Alright," Angel said, flipping to a fresh page on her notepad, "but this one is going to cost you."

6

TYRONE

Nobody wanted the brand *liar*. The word "lie" sounded malicious, but there was a difference between a lie and an untruth. Especially in investigations. Lies were intentional, but untruths were more complicated. People saw what they wanted to see. Or they'd close their eyes moments before impact, and their brain filled the empty space with something that was close to true, but not quite right.

Frank Sand was a liar. In the moments since Tyrone had left the interview room, Frank had transformed into a wholly different person. Watching Frank through the video screen now was like seeing the truth. The man brimming with arrogance was gone, replaced by someone high-strung, frantic, and desperate. Frank was a snake that had shed his first skin.

He still held his phone, but he wasn't scrolling it while lazily draped over a chair. He was pacing back and forth along the length of the room, making calls on repeat. It was like he was stuck in a time loop, repeating the same actions. He dialed, held the phone to his ear for several seconds, then brought it down before starting all over again.

"Who do you think he's calling?" Jackie asked. She didn't look away from the screen as she spoke. Tyrone didn't either, but he could see her in his peripheral vision.

"It's hard to tell. An attorney would be my guess."

"*Fuck*," Frank said after what was probably the hundredth time dialing. "Pick up. Pick up. *Pick up.*" He stared at the small object in his hands with enough hate to cause a chill to run up Tyrone's spine.

It was shortly after six o'clock in the morning. Most people were still sleeping. Frank's chances of reaching anyone were slim to none. That was part of the reason Tyrone had chosen to pick him up for questioning right away. Tyrone held every advantage. Frank probably hadn't even been to sleep yet. He'd had a long day at work, he was tired, and it was unlikely an attorney would burst into the interview room, bringing the questioning to a screeching halt.

"Come on, come on," Frank said, bringing the phone to his ear again. He hadn't stopped pacing for a good five minutes. But then, suddenly, he stopped mid-stride. "Finally," he said into the phone. "I've called you a hundred times." He paused. "I figured that, but this is important." There was another pause. Then he looked right at the camera. He stared at it for a long moment as though considering, then turned his back to it, bringing his hand up, cupping the mouthpiece.

"I guess he has something to say that he doesn't want us to hear," Jackie said.

"Apparently," Tyrone said with a sigh. "I better get back in there."

There was no point in watching from the recording room if Frank wasn't going to speak freely.

"While I'm gone, will you call over and check on forensics. See if they've got anything solid on that blood." They had preliminary results on a few samples, most of it belonged to Molly, but he needed confirmation. He needed every swab tested. No stone left unturned. "I'd like to know if it all came from one person, or if we can place someone else at the scene." With luck, the killer cut themselves during the struggle. And it did appear that Molly had put up quite the struggle with all the disturbances in the grass.

"Sure thing."

Tyrone left the small room with Jackie and reentered the interview room with Frank. He entered as silently as possible, turning the doorknob slowly, gradually opening the door. Frank's back was to the camera, which meant his back was to the door as well.

"Listen," Frank hissed, his voice low. "I'm telling you that it didn't work. It didn't *fucking* work."

Tyrone's foot caught on the door as he crossed the threshold, making a small sound. It was barely audible, but Frank still jumped and whirled around.

"What are you doing?" Frank said. The words hissed out of him high pitched and desperate.

Tyrone closed the door behind him with a soft *click*. "Coming back. Is that a problem?"

"You're trying to sneak up on me." Frank pressed a button on the phone, then lowered it to his side.

"I'm just coming to talk to you. That's all." There was a beat of silence, then Tyrone nodded at the phone. "Who was that?"

"Don't worry about it." Frank pocketed his phone for the first time since he'd arrived.

"Someone you don't want me to know about?"

"Is privacy a crime?"

"No." Tyrone gestured to the table. "Do you want to have a seat?"

Frank reluctantly pulled the chair away from the table and sat. Tyrone did the same. They stared at one another, the silence stretching long between them.

"It was my au pair. If you must know," Frank finally said.

"What's an au pair?" Tyrone didn't believe him. Frank was a liar, after all.

Frank scoffed. "Of course, *you* wouldn't know."

Tyrone didn't know what he meant by that, placing such an emphasis on the word *you*. Was it because he was in law enforcement, a low paying position compared to Frank's millions, because he was black, or some other reason? Ultimately, it didn't matter. It was personal and an insult. Whether it was due to his income or his skin color, he'd probably never know.

"She's a live-in nanny," Frank said.

"What's your au pair's name?"

"Rebecca."

"No last name?"

"Rice."

"How do you go about finding something like that, an au pair? Do they advertise in the newspaper?"

"Nobody advertises their services in the newspaper anymore except prostitutes and scammers."

"I guess I ought to read the newspaper more," Tyrone said, raising an eyebrow.

"Yeah, you should. Then you idiots might be able to solve a crime."

Frank was trying to get a rise out of him, but Tyrone didn't take the bait. Criminals did this kind of thing all the time. It was a way to distract from themselves, their actions. There was a time in Tyrone's career when he would have fallen for it, allowed his temper to take control of his mind, but not anymore.

"How long is this going to take?" Frank said.

"As long as it takes."

Frank dropped back into his chair. He wasn't fidgeting anymore. He had transformed back to his former, arrogant self. Something about that phone call had calmed him.

"I can't help but notice something," Tyrone said.

"What's that?"

"You haven't asked me anything about Molly."

Frank grunted.

"I told you that we found her, but no other details."

In truth, there weren't a lot of details to tell. There was blood everywhere. Molly's purse with her identification and her shoes were all discovered at the scene along with shreds of clothing inside the pig pen. The pigs had taken care of the rest. They'd found only one other thing—a phone cord—which could be the murder weapon.

"I don't care," Frank said, crossing his arms. "She abandoned her family."

There was no emotion in Frank's voice, and his reactions were calm, making it impossible to untangle the truth from the lie—if he really didn't

care because he thought Molly had abandoned him, or if he was fabri-
cating a story to explain his disinterest.

"Do you know where we found her?"

"I'm guessing you plan to tell me one way or another."

There, he was wrong. Tyrone didn't intend to tell him anything just yet.
"When did Molly disappear?"

"There's a police report. You should read it."

"I might just do that."

Tyrone hadn't been part of the missing persons investigation. That had
been Jackie's job. He'd been new to the force when Molly disappeared, but
still seasoned. An adult missing person was a good early assignment for a
newbie cop. Nobody took it seriously. Adults had a right to disappear. Even
mothers of small children. Maybe especially mothers of small children.

"I shouldn't have to tell you how to do *your* job."

"You don't seem to be telling me much of anything," Tyrone said.

"That's because I don't know anything."

"You know more than you think."

"Not about Molly."

Tyrone stared at Frank for a long moment, trying to decipher how
much of his statements were truth. The best lies held some truth. But this
last statement was an absolute lie, wasn't it? Molly was Frank's wife. He
knew plenty about her. The question was, what was he hiding beneath that
lie? Was it murder?

7

MOLLY

Past
February 1

At ten o'clock Molly kissed her children goodbye and got into her silver Mercedes, backing it out of the driveway. Before Frank, she'd never had a luxury car. She hadn't had a car at all. Once they were married, he took her to all the most expensive car lots, allowing her to test drive any vehicle she wanted. She'd felt like a kid in a candy store.

He had her rank each car after she had a chance to drive it on a scale from one to ten. It was so exciting. Right up until she learned he was using the ranking system to choose the vehicle she liked the least and purchased it. A backhanded gift. A way to say *you may think you know what you like, but you're wrong.* Her Mercedes had been that car. She'd fancied herself a Lexus girl, but apparently she'd been wrong.

When she reached the turn off from their long driveway onto the gravel road that led to the highway to town, her phone started ringing. It connected automatically to her vehicle, so the noise encircled her, assaulting her ears. She didn't look at the caller's identification. She didn't have to. She picked up before the second ring. Frank was not one to wait.

"Hi, baby," she said, forcing her voice into the high-pitched lilt her husband liked best.

"You're on your way to the gym." It was a statement, not a question.

"Yes."

"You'll be done by noon." Also, a statement.

"Yes."

"I've scheduled a doctor's appointment for you."

"A doctor's appointment." She repeated his words, resigned. She didn't need to ask what kind of doctor or the location of the office. She already knew the answers.

"It's time to reup on the Botox and what's that..." She could hear him snapping his fingers.

"Juvéderm."

"Yeah. That filler stuff. You were looking old, and I mean *old* this morning."

It wouldn't have anything to do with the marital rape and loss of sleep after learning you stuck your dick into another woman, now, would it? This was a thought she didn't dare voice.

"Your appointment is at three o'clock."

Three o'clock would be a stretch. It took an hour and a half to get to Des Moines from Fort Calhoun, and it took thirty minutes to get from the gym back home. That meant she wouldn't be home until twelve thirty. She'd have to leave by one thirty to get to the plastic surgeon's office on time, which seemed doable to anyone who didn't have two small children at home. But it wasn't. Frank would know that if he bothered to spend a single second around his children.

"Did you hear me?" Frank said. "Three o'clock."

"I'll be there," Molly said. It was the only acceptable answer.

"Great," Frank said, then hung up without saying goodbye.

Rage was building within her. It roiled in her stomach. Useless, pent-up anger that built a little with each passing day. Frank did not love her, he owned her. She was a pet. No, not a pet. A doll. Something for him to shape and move however he liked. She'd behaved for ten years. Ten long, agonizing years, and she'd had enough. She wanted out of this life. She needed out. But how? She didn't know. She had nothing without Frank. She needed him as much as she needed to get away from him.

She flipped to her Spotify account and opened her recent playlist, clicking on the top song. Metallica's *Nothing Else Matters* blared from the expensive speakers surrounding her. No one in Fort Calhoun would take her for a Metallica fan, but nobody in Fort Calhoun knew the true person beneath this Barbie girl façade. They saw what they wanted to see.

To others, she was a trophy, and to Frank, they were right. But she'd grown old and dusty. He was ready for a replacement, and he'd already found one. He'd cast all his past wives aside once they neared Molly's age. There was no reason to think Frank would behave differently this time around. Nothing else about him had changed. He was still arrogant, still a philanderer. He still took without permission. The children weren't even a deterrent. Frank left Vivian when Frankie Junior was small. Vivian had landed on her feet, but Frank hadn't made her sign a prenuptial agreement like he had with Molly.

When Molly arrived at the gym, she pulled into a parking spot near the back of the lot. The gym was almost always busy. She entered through the front door and stepped up to the front desk, scanning her membership card. The kid working was young, eighteen or nineteen with dark hair and a t-shirt two sizes too small so it hugged his small muscles. A nametag pinned to his shirt read *Riley*. He'd been working for Frank for a few months. He was studying a magazine when she entered, and she thought she could make it past without him noticing her, but no dice.

"Oh, hi there, Molly," Riley said, closing his magazine. The front of it read *Wired* with an image of Mark Zuckerberg.

"Hi." Molly gave a halfhearted wave.

"Are you here for the aerobics class at eleven?"

"I'm going to lift first, but yes."

Riley knew why she was there. She came the same time for the same reason every weekday. He was just trying to draw out the conversation. He had a crush on her. Molly could always tell. Men were obvious. She could see it in the way his gaze lingered a little too long and how he repeated her name in their short conversation.

"Are you doing anything after your workout, Molly?"

Yeah, she was going to get Botox and fillers because she had gotten too old for her middle-aged husband even though she was only twenty-eight. She forced a smile and instead said, "Same thing as always. Taking care of the kids."

"That must be hard."

"It is."

Molly started edging toward the workout equipment, a sign that he should allow the conversation to end. To her, Riley's flirtation was innocent enough, but Nolan had different opinions about the kid. Nolan attended the same gym, just at a different time so they could stagger childcare. He said Riley talked about her constantly, even to strangers—that he was obsessed with Molly.

"I better, um, get to it," Molly said, nodding toward the exercise equipment. "There are only so many hours in the day."

"Right." Riley nodded. "Have a good workout, Molly."

Molly finally stepped past the front desk and made her way toward the weight equipment at the back. She could feel the eyes of the other men tracking her as she passed. As often as possible, she met their gazes, waving hello and smiling. It was her way of saying, *I caught you. Stop ogling.* They seemed cowed at first, but only for a moment, not long enough to prevent it from happening the next day.

Sometimes she wondered why she even bothered working out, but she knew the answer. Frank. He'd made her the face of the gym, the model. He hadn't asked her permission, he'd told her. She was expected to be there every day, to be seen, to be kind. She was supposed to make women want to look like her and men want to sleep with her. She had the latter covered, but she had little to no relationship with other women. If they wanted to be like her, they had chosen to do it at a distance.

But that's my life, she thought as she approached the machine used for squats. From the outside, it was picture perfect. From the inside, it was a prison. A gilded prison, but a prison all the same.

8

ANGEL

Past
February 1

"I want to divorce Molly," Frank said. His tone was flippant, casual, as though he was deciding between paper and plastic.

Angel and Frank were still in her office, the thirty-minute time slot extended to allow for the side conversation about Molly.

"Okay," Angel said. She was unsurprised. Frank was incapable of staying. For better or worse did not apply to him. "What has you considering divorce?"

Frank shrugged. "Same as always."

That was code for, *I found someone else.*

"This one is not going to be as easy as the others," Angel said.

"Why not?"

"You've got two kids together, right?"

"Yeah. Matt and Genevieve."

"How old are they?"

"Umm…" He looked at the ceiling, silent for a long moment. "You're going to think I'm a terrible dad, but I don't actually know. They're little."

Angel thought he was a terrible dad long before this conversation. In all the years she'd known and worked with Frank, she'd rarely seen him with his kids. They were only with him at community events or fundraising opportunities as props, not children. She'd never seen him interact with them. This failure, his inability to remember their ages, did not make that any better or worse.

"How about checking social media?" Angel suggested. "I'm sure Molly posted pictures on their birthdays."

"That's a great idea," Frank said, snapping his fingers. He pulled out his phone and started pressing buttons. He was silent for a little while, then looked up. "Genie had four candles on her last cake and Matt had five."

Angel scribbled the numbers down on her notepad. "I don't suppose the pictures give their dates of birth."

Frank shrugged. "I can tell you the dates Molly posted the pictures."

"That won't work," Angel said, waving a dismissive hand. Molly could have waited days or weeks before posting.

"Molly doesn't work, does she?" Angel knew the answer, but she had to verify.

"No. She quit her job when we got married. She was a waitress at one of my restaurants."

"Right."

The marriage had created quite a stir in the community. Frank was married at the time, not to Vivian, but to a different ex-wife. Molly was barely eighteen, and Frank was forty-two. Nobody knew when, exactly, the affair had started, but everyone suspected that it was well before Molly was legally an adult. Molly had remained silent on the topic, so the gossip had died down after a while. In time, they became a couple like everyone else, old news.

"She doesn't have a degree either, does she?" Angel asked.

"She graduated from high school, if that's what you are asking."

"It's not. I'm talking about skills, professional degrees or additional training."

"Does getting her nails done count?"

"No," Angel said, her gaze drifting to her own unpolished nails. A visit to the nail salon sounded nice, but it would never fit her schedule. The thought of spending one afternoon of her life getting pampered rather than embroiled in other people's marital problems was as unreal as a set of fake nails.

"She has a knack for finding the most annoying, absolutely gay au pair on the planet. Does that count as a skill?"

"No. You have a male au pair?"

"Yes. The guy's name is Nolan. He's a real flamer."

Angel blinked several times. "Is there any chance they are having an affair?"

"He's gay."

"Has he told you that?"

"No, but it's obvious. He's a full-time babysitter. A *man* would not do *that*."

"Right," Angel said, shaking her head. She was offended by his stereotyping and his word choice, but she saw no reason to challenge him. Changing Frank's mind would require a shift in his core beliefs, and that was not going to happen. "What are your thoughts on custody?"

"Fifty-fifty right?"

"You are gone a lot. How is that going to work?" Angel said.

"An au pair, obviously."

"Right, Nolan."

"No. A different au pair."

Angel stared at him. He wanted to separate the family, take the kids away from their mother half the time, and sever the tie between them and their nanny, their primary caretaker, the one thing that could be a constant at both houses. Keeping Nolan on would be the best way to promote the children's emotional wellbeing while they adjusted to their new post-divorce lives. It was selfish.

"Don't give me that look. My son has spent enough time around that fairy. He's going to start acting like that, waving his hands around like a kite in a derecho. Do you know what he told me the other day?" Frank continued without allowing space for an answer. "He said his favorite color was pink. *Pink!* And I caught him wearing glitter on his lips. *Glitter!* I wanted to slap it right off his face. Where is he getting that stuff?" Again, he didn't pause long. "I'll tell you where. He's getting his bad habits from that fairy man."

"Habits. Right," Angel said, training her eyes on her notepad, squeezing her pen so tight that her knuckles turned white.

"How much is it going to cost me?"

"A divorce from Molly?"

"Yeah."

Angel turned to her computer. She brought up the child support calculator, inputting Frank's income, an astronomical number, even to her, and Molly's income, which was zero. She chose the "shared care" option and clicked *submit*. The calculator went blank for a millisecond, then filled with numbers.

"This is just a rough amount, mind you, but support will be somewhere in the ballpark of ten thousand per month."

"*Ten thousand dollars!* You've got to be kidding me."

"I'm not."

"But I would have the kids fifty percent of the time."

"You would, but Molly has zero income, no work history, and no education. Her earning potential is minimum wage, at best. The law says that the kids are entitled to the same level of comfort in each home. In the event of a divorce, you are required to support Molly so she can afford the same things that you can."

"That makes no sense."

It didn't make sense to him, sure. Frank thought he was impenetrable. Unbelievably arrogant. If someone came at him with a knife, he wouldn't even flinch, believing the knife would bend away from his skin simply because he willed it.

"It makes plenty of sense," Angel said. "The law does not want kids going from a hovel to a mansion. That's not fair to them."

"What about me? That number isn't fair to me. *I'm* the one who makes all the money."

Angel shrugged. She had no control over the situation. The legislature set the child support amounts. "The numbers don't lie."

"I didn't have to pay any of my other ex-wives this much."

"Well, you weren't as established when you divorced Vivian. She also was close to your age and had a degree. As you know, we can bring Molly back to court in two years to recalculate child support. She could have a job and a degree by then."

"That's too much. I can't pay that much."

"You'll have to if you divorce Molly. And that doesn't even take spousal support into consideration."

"Spousal support?"

"Alimony."

"I'd have to pay *more*?"

"Probably."

"No. No. No." Frank stood and shook his head. "That won't work. I'll think of something else."

"Like working on the marriage?"

"Yeah, sure." His words were flippant, sarcastic.

Angel blinked hard. He either stayed with her or he didn't. Work on the marriage or give up. There wasn't any other legal option.

"I need to get going." He lifted his arm and looked at the Rolex on his wrist. It was a new version with a price tag that Angel didn't even want to contemplate. She was no cheapskate, she had splurged on designer handbags in the past, but his watch was in a whole separate ballpark. A Birken bag to her Coach. "I've got work to do. You deal with Vivian, and I'll worry about Molly."

"Okay," Angel said, standing and coming around the desk. "I'll get my appearance on file in Vivian's modification action later this afternoon."

Angel led him out of her office and to the front door. They shook hands and he left. Angel closed the door behind him and issued a heavy sigh of relief. An hour with Frank Sand tested her patience. She could only tolerate his bigotry and misogyny for so long. Yet, he was a loyal client. He was the type of client that their firm *needed* to continue succeeding. For that reason, she hoped he'd choose to divorce Molly. That would mean another fifteen years of litigation, steady income for the firm. Of the two choices—stay or leave—Frank was only capable of one anyway. Leaving.

9

TYRONE

Present
June 15

Frank had plenty of secrets, Tyrone could see it on the other man. It was in the way his gaze shifted away and his hands fidgeted. But, then again, everyone had secrets. Even Tyrone. A secret wasn't a crime, but it could be if it had a connection to Molly's disappearance and eventual death.

"Everyone knows *something* about their spouse. You can't possibly know *nothing*, Frank," Tyrone said.

"I know that she was good in the sack. So, sure, I do know something."

Was. That word jumped out at Tyrone. Frank had referred to his wife in past tense.

A knock at the door caught Tyrone's attention. Frank didn't even look up.

"Are you expecting company?" Tyrone asked.

Frank lifted one big shoulder and let it fall, his gaze trained on Tyrone.

The door opened and a patrol officer entered. A white kid, young with soft yellow wisps of a mustache forming above his top lip. He was technically an "adult," but he wasn't old enough to legally drink alcohol. Adult enough to go to war or to prison, but not adult enough to rent a car.

"Can I help you?" Tyrone asked.

"I, uh," the kid stammered.

The young guys were frightened of Tyrone. He had no idea why; he'd never yelled or even snapped at any of them. Perhaps it was because of the way he looked, or maybe it was his Chicago roots.

"What is it?"

"She's...his lawyer," the kid stepped aside, leaving a woman in the doorway.

Tyrone's heart sank. The woman was Angel Malone, a local attorney. Her presence virtually guaranteed the end of Tyrone's interview with Frank and would lead to more roadblocks in an already challenging investigation.

Everyone in Fort Calhoun knew Angel or knew of her. Tyrone had dealings with her family that should place him squarely in the former category. He'd been inside her home, spoken with her numerous times and spoken with her husband. Yet, he didn't feel like he knew her. Maybe nobody did.

Not that it mattered to Tyrone. He had come to town for a job. His intent was to get in, get experience, and get out. It would take decades before he'd make it to a detective position in Chicago. The force was cutthroat and there were so many people gunning for the same position. Accepting a small-town detective position in Fort Calhoun was his plan to jump to the front of the line. The change—so far at least—had been positive after ten years as a beat cop in Chicago. Yet, he hoped that change would lead him back home and not stuck in the small towns of Iowa. He didn't belong.

"What's going on here?" Angel said, her voice stern.

She wasn't looking at Tyrone, but he couldn't take his eyes off her. Angel was Tyrone's age with long, dark hair. She was thin, but curvy. Some would say too curvy, but not Tyrone. Her light blue eyes flitted from Frank to Tyrone, settling on Frank.

"I said, what is going on here?" Angel repeated.

"My Angel," Frank said. "You came."

She flinched at the possessive way he said her name, *My Angel*, like she belonged to him. Frank didn't seem to notice. Tyrone, one of the few black people in town, was all too aware of microaggressions. Angel was a female working in a male-dominated field in a good-old-boy town. Like

Tyrone, she was an outsider. Microaggressions were an everyday occurrence.

Frank rose to his feet and spread his arms wide, like he wanted her to rush into them and give him a hug. She didn't. "I'm so happy you're here," he said, lowering his arms after a long, awkward moment.

"You didn't give me a choice," she held up her phone. "You called me seventy-five times. I was at home. My kids are in the car," she hooked a thumb toward the door.

Angel had been the person Frank had been calling. At least seventy-five of the times. But was Angel the person on the line when he'd said, *It didn't work*? He had said he'd spoken to the au pair, but that could have been a lie. And what had he meant by that anyway? Tyrone had so many questions for Frank, but he wouldn't be able to ask them now. Angel was going to shut the whole thing down.

"You brought your kids?" Frank said, irritation flashing in his eyes. "Don't you have someone to help you with that?"

"Yeah, I brought them. They are in the car, and no. I don't." Her tone was flat.

Now that Tyrone was truly studying her, he could see the telltale signs of exhaustion. She was in jeans and a sweatshirt. He'd never seen her in anything other than a suit. There were bags beneath her eyes, and she wore no makeup.

"Right, well, I'm glad you are here, my guardian Angel."

Angel ignored his comment and turned her attention to Tyrone. "What is this all about?"

"He says they found Molly," Frank said.

Angel froze. "What do you mean *found her*? Where is she?"

"She's dead," Tyrone said.

"Dead," Angel repeated, raising an eyebrow. There was a long moment of silence while the information sank in. When Angel finally spoke, there was fire in her gaze and her tone was a low growl. "She's dead, and you've brought my client here to interrogate him without the presence of his lawyer."

"I don't know why he would need a lawyer."

Angel rolled her eyes. "Everyone needs a lawyer. Especially if cops are asking questions about dead wives. Husbands are always number one on the suspect list."

"I'm just trying to keep him informed," Tyrone said, lifting his palms face up, "that's all."

"Don't lie to me." She turned to Frank. "This interview is over. Come on, let's go."

Tyrone had known his explanation was thin, in no way believable to someone like Angel, but it was the best he could come up with on the spot.

"He didn't tell me anything," Frank said as he approached his attorney. "He says he is trying to keep me informed, but he hasn't informed me of anything. He can't do that. He can't lie to me like that, can he?"

Angel ignored the question.

"What would you like to know?" It was Tyrone's last-ditch effort to get the interview back on track.

Angel placed her hands on her hips. "Whatever you are willing to disclose."

"Do you know where we found her?" *Or what was left of her.*

"That's a question, not a statement," Angel said.

"Fair enough. She was in a pig pen."

"A pig pen. Is that a joke?" Angel said. "If it is, we aren't laughing."

"No joke."

Tyrone's gaze flitted to Frank. He did not seem surprised. "But you knew that, didn't you?"

"Don't talk to him," Angel swung around and pointed to Frank. "Do not answer that." Then she turned to face Tyrone. "That was a fucked-up trick. This conversation is over. Come on Frank." She turned on her heel and gestured with her hand for him to follow.

Frank hung back. A man unaccustomed to following a woman's directives.

"I said statements, not questions, and the detective here seems incapable of following that simple rule," Angel called over her shoulder.

Tyrone shrugged. She was right. He didn't intend to follow her rules. They were designed to get Frank out of trouble, Tyrone's goals were the opposite. There was no tie between Molly and that farm, which meant she'd been dumped there. And Angel was right, the husband was always the primary suspect in murder cases.

"Let's go," Angel said, motioning again for Frank to head out the door.

Tyrone did not want to let Frank leave, but he had no tangible reason to hold him.

Frank was hesitating. He stared at Tyrone for a long moment, then he said, "I just want to—"

"Stop," Angel cut him off. "That's enough." Again, she motioned for Frank to exit the room. This time he acquiesced.

Angel gave Tyrone one last look. Her expression had changed, morphing from anger to assessment. She was studying him as though he was a puzzle with pieces that didn't quite fit together.

"I thought we were leaving," Frank said from out in the hallway.

At the sound of Frank's voice, Angel ripped her gaze away from Tyrone's. She exited the room in hurried steps, leaving Tyrone alone in the small interview room.

10

MOLLY

Past

February 1

Frank controlled every aspect of Molly's life, including her workout regimen. She didn't have a trainer. Frank wouldn't allow it. He controlled her, in part, through isolation, and a trainer would be an opportunity to develop a friendship. Instead, he had the trainers come up with weekly workout plans for her to follow. Squats were first on her list of exercises for the day.

She placed twenty-pound weights on each side of the bar and secured them with spring clips. Then she ducked beneath it in a crouching position, so it rested on her shoulders. She lifted the barbell up to remove it from its secure resting spot and dropped into a squat, then rose. She counted to ten before returning the bar to its original position. The first set was done. Two more to go.

"Hi there," a voice said from behind her.

Molly startled and looked up, meeting the person's gaze in the mirror. The entire weight area was covered in mirrors, allowing weightlifters to admire themselves from every angle because one, apparently, wasn't good enough.

Hi," Molly said.

he man was Mike Malone. He was married to Angel Malone, Frank's
ey and confidant. Mike had been coming to the gym for a long time,
only recently started showing up during the time Molly attended.
ne Mike scanned his card, the computer logged the date and time.
When she first noticed his staring, she had Riley check Mike's habits. He
was a late afternoon exerciser until he came in early one day to see Molly
leave at eleven thirty. He'd been there at ten thirty every day since.

"Need a spotter?" Mike asked.

"Umm, sure."

She didn't need a spotter, but she told herself that forming a friendship
with Angel's husband couldn't be a bad thing. Angel was ruthless in the
courtroom, everyone knew that, and she'd represented Frank in all his past
divorces. She was a threat. Every time they argued about Frank's affairs, the
threat of Angel hung there between them, unsaid but present. *Divorce me. I
dare you. I'll go to Angel, and you'll get nothing. Not even the kids.*

Sometimes Molly wondered if Angel was truly capable of all the things
Frank touted—he was always going on about her—or if he was only saying
those things to discourage Molly from leaving him, to keep her caged. She
had never had access to anyone who might know the answer to that question, but Mike would. That was why she didn't turn Mike away like she did
the other men.

"How many sets do you have left?" Mike asked.

"Two."

"Better get to it." He clapped his hands like he was her trainer.

She dropped below the bar, positioning it over her shoulders. She stood
under the full weight of the bar and began squatting, dropping down ten
times. Mike stayed behind her where she could see him in the mirror. He
stood back, arms crossed, staring at her ass the whole time. Suddenly, she
felt exposed, self-conscious, and she lost her balance.

"Woah, there," Mike caught the bar before she fell, easily lifting it and
placing it back in its original position. "Do you think you've got too much
weight? Maybe we should switch you to less weight and more reps."

You'd like that wouldn't you, Molly thought, but instead she said,
"Maybe."

"How about we start training together? Me and you."

"Sure," Molly said, but she was less confident about it than she sounded. There was an intensity in his gaze that was starting to unsettle her. It caught an edge somewhere between interest and fixation.

"Obviously, you don't need a trainer," Mike said, his eyes tracking from her shoulders to her toes, "and neither do I," he turned to the side to admire himself in the mirror, "but it's always nice to have someone else to train with."

"Yeah. Definitely."

For the first time, Molly took a good look at Mike Malone. He was a huge man. It wasn't natural. Was he using supplements purchased from the local GMC or something harder? She guessed the latter. A girl walked by them, her gaze focused on Molly and Mike. Mike saw her in the mirror and turned around and waved.

"Hey, Rebecca," Mike said.

Rebecca. She was the girl from Frank's phone, the messages last night. A mixture of embarrassment and fury flashed through Molly. How long had this girl been sleeping with her husband?

"Hey, yourself," Rebecca said with a flirtatious giggle. She was talking to Mike, but she kept her attention on Molly.

She didn't stop walking. She continued past them, sizing Molly up with every step.

Mike leaned closer to Molly. "Rebecca spends a *lot* of time here."

Molly watched the younger girl as she continued toward the cardio area of the gym, her ponytail swishing from side to side. She was tiny, like Molly, with lighter hair. Molly 2.0.

"He doesn't deserve you," Mike said, his voice low.

Mike was so close to her that she could feel his breath on her neck. Molly had to fight the urge to jump back.

"You know that, don't you?" Mike said.

Molly didn't know what to say.

"Rebecca is a cheap copy. You're the real deal."

Mike knew about Frank's affair. Molly's gaze rose and traveled around the gym, moving from one person to the next. How many of these people knew that her husband was screwing Rebecca? How many of them snickered about it behind Molly's back? She'd never felt more alone than she did in that moment.

Frank's control was absolute. Even when she was in public, she was alone.

11

ANGEL

Past

February 1

Frank Sand had a way of slithering into Angel's life and seizing control of her time, but his grip on her was fleeting. It disappeared the moment he left her office. Frank was only one of the many dysfunctional parents that strolled through Angel's door. Every one of them demanded her attention, and there was no option other than to set the file aside and move on to the next one.

The remainder of the day continued as expected. Several more clients came through Angel's office, some signing stipulation agreements, others signing new petitions. Angel had three separate temporary custody and support hearings that ate up the afternoon, but she was back in her office by four o'clock to wind down the workday.

The late afternoon was reserved for phone calls. There were ten messages by the time she made it through all her meetings and court hearings. It was a daunting number, but only because of the nature of the calls. Clients often called lawyers to vent. There might be a small morsel of a legal question in there, but that wasn't the reason for the call. It was because the client knew their attorney was always on their side. Angel would not hold them accountable for their contribution to the problems in the marriage, like family, friends, and even therapists would.

These types of calls did not require much from Angel aside from an occasional *yeah*, and *I understand*. So, she also used the time to do some internet shopping. Multi-tasking was a way of life for attorneys. Over the years Angel had developed a taste for fine wines and cheeses. She was on the phone, browsing her favorite website with a basket full of goodies when she decided to check the joint bank account.

She grabbed her cell phone while cradling the office phone between her ear and shoulder and logged into her mobile banking application. She typed in her login information and the screen populated with her account information. When she saw the number in the joint account, her jaw dropped.

"What the hell?" she mumbled.

"I'm sorry," Angel's client said.

"Nothing, nothing. Sorry, Marcy." Angel tried to keep the panic out of her voice.

"It doesn't sound like nothing." Marcy was on the upper side of middle age, divorcing her husband of twenty years.

Angel logged out of her bank account, then logged back in, clicking once again on the joint checking account. Again, the number read $99.85. *That can't be possible*, she thought. That account had $40,000 in it yesterday.

"Are you listening to me?" Marcy's whiny voice prattled on, but Angel could barely hear it over the buzzing in her ears.

She clicked on transactions. There was one earlier that day, around ten o'clock, moving nearly all of the cash to her husband's personal account. "Oh no," Angel said, shaking her head. "That mother fucker did not."

"Angel," Marcy hissed.

"Sorry," Angel said, her attention zapping back to the phone call. "I'm going to need to go. Uh, family emergency."

"Oh, I do hope those two little darlings are okay."

Marcy was referring to Angel's children, four-year-old twin girls. They attended all-day pre-school at their daycare. They were not identical. One of the girls, Lily, was recently diagnosed with type I diabetes, but the other twin, Gretchen, was fine. At least so far. One of the benefits and curses of living in a small town was that few things remained secrets, especially something as visible as insulin shots. All of Fort Calhoun knew of Lily's condition within weeks of her diagnosis.

"The girls are fine. My husband, he's about to be in major trouble, though."

"You get him. Men are the worst."

"Thanks," Angel said. She told her client she'd call her the next day and grabbed a nearby post-it notepad. She wrote a reminder note and stuck it to her desk. She would call back first thing in the morning. Then she ended the call and rushed out the door, leaving nine messages unanswered.

It was five-thirty when she burst through the front door. "Mike," she shouted, tossing her designer handbag on the couch as she passed. There was no slowing her down, not when she was in this kind of rage.

She found her husband and their two daughters in the kitchen. The girls were seated at the large, rectangular white-marble kitchen counter. They each had a plate in front of them containing carrot sticks and apples.

"We need to talk," Angel said, striding into the kitchen, her intense gaze boring into her husband.

Mike was a muscular man, he'd always been that way, but over the past year, he'd taken it to the extreme. He obsessed over calories and exercise, and he tried to force his over-the-top eating habits on the rest of the family.

"Mommy," the girls turned around and looked at her in unison.

Her girls, Gretchen and Lillian, Gretty and Lily for short. They didn't have twin names because Angel thought that was dumb. It was cute, but only when they were small. Twin names wouldn't be so sweet when these girls were in their forties. Angel's gaze automatically shifted to Gretty. She was the mouthpiece of the two while Lily was the daredevil.

"What is it, sweetheart?" Angel asked.

"Daddy won't let us dip," Gretty said, jutting her bottom lip out into a pout.

Normally, Angel tried to support her husband when it came to the kids, even with his health obsession. She saw way too much parental undermining through her job. It wasn't good for the kids, but she was too mad to support Mike in anything. Not today.

"What do you want? Ranch and peanut butter?"

"Yes!" Gretty said, a smile warming her soft, white cheeks.

"Angel," Mike said, but his voice didn't hold its usual disapproval.

He saw that she was furious, and he also knew why. She didn't have an overactive temper. She rarely got upset, but when she did, she was explosive.

"No. Don't." She marched over to the fridge, grabbed the ranch, then over to a cabinet, removing the peanut butter and a spoon, setting all three items in the middle of the two girls. "Eat up," she said to them. "I need to speak to your father."

"Thanks!" Gretty said. Lily already had the lid off the peanut butter and was eating a spoonful without bothering to put it on her apple slices.

"Let's go," she motioned for Mike to follow. He did, but reluctantly. She led the way into the home office, waited for him to enter, then slammed the door shut.

"You have two seconds to explain what happened to all the money in the joint account."

"Do we have to do this today? I'm tired from watching the girls."

Angel grabbed her phone and opened the daycare's mobile application. She clicked on Lily's account and her daily activities populated the screen. "Says here that you picked them up at four o'clock. You've had them for an hour-and-a-half. You can't be *that* tired."

"I just don't want to do this," he said with a sigh.

"Yeah, you should have thought about that when you drained the joint account. Now, where's the money?"

"I spent it," he said.

"On what?"

"A boat."

"A *boat*. You've got to be fucking kidding me. We don't live anywhere near water. What are you going to do with a boat?"

"Take it to a lake," he said.

"When? Twice a year? The rest of the time it'll be gathering dust in the garage. Is that where it is? In our garage?"

"No. I rented a storage unit."

"Ohhh," Angel said, a sardonic smile spreading across her lips. "You didn't want to give up the parking for your precious Lexus."

"I didn't want either of us to lose our parking spots."

"You know my spot was never in jeopardy."

Mike shrugged.

"I can't believe you did this. Actually, you know what, I can. You have always been so selfish, and it's only gotten worse. How dare you buy something like that without my permission?"

"I didn't know I had to have permission." His voice dipped low and ended in a whine.

He sounded like a petulant teenager. Angel was nine years away from having teenagers. She was in no mood to placate a giant man-baby as well. "It isn't your money. It's mine. I work, you don't."

"We are a couple. What's mine is yours."

"No," Angel growled. "What's mine, you take. You have nothing to give."

"That's not what you tell your clients."

"What I tell my clients is none of your business."

Legally, he was right. And the worst part was that he knew it. When they were younger and happier, she used to tell her husband all the work war stories. No names or identifiers, but general facts. Spouses who thought that money earned was their own, not shared. Some thought a prenuptial agreement supported that argument, but it didn't. Not in Iowa. A prenup only dealt with property and moneys owned *before* marriage. Everything earned during the marriage was marital property.

"All you do is work. You ignore me."

"So, you bought a boat for *attention*. You really are a man-baby."

"When was the last time you complimented me? When was the last time you told me you loved me?"

"I don't love you right now. I'd rather take a shovel to your face and then use it to bury you in a shallow grave."

"But think about it."

Angel did pause to think. He was right, she hadn't been affectionate toward him for a long time, but he hadn't given her any reason to be. "I have work, and we have kids. That's life. It's not the same now as it was when we were younger."

"You've never been very affectionate."

"That sounds like a you problem, since you married me anyway."

"I thought you'd get over Tom."

Angel froze, then fury surged through her. It took several moments for her to regain her composure. "This isn't about him. It's about you."

"Is it?" He was smirking.

"You're getting rid of that boat."

"No, I'm not."

Angel glared at him, her hands on her hips.

Then she stormed out of the office, headed for the kitchen. She couldn't stand looking at his face anymore. The girls were still at the kitchen island, eating their snacks. Lily hadn't touched the carrot sticks or apples and she had her entire right hand in the peanut butter jar. Gretty had a little peanut butter and a little ranch on her plate and was dipping her snacks into them while chastising Lily about her "disgusting" eating habits.

Angel pulled out a stool and sat next to Gretty. She would have to check Lily's blood sugar once she was finished eating, so she might as well sit down.

Gretty turned toward Angel, her eyes wide. "Are you and Daddy getting a divorce?"

"No," Angel said. Her answer was automatic, but certain.

She sometimes wished she hadn't married him. They'd had a whirlwind romance and quick marriage. Looking back on it now, she knew it was too fast. She'd been running from heartbreak, and she ran straight into Mike's arms. After two kids and a mortgage, she was stuck with him. Divorce was too expensive. She'd already crunched the numbers. She and Frank had that in common. She'd be paying an astronomical amount of support to Mike so that he could sit on the couch and play video games all day.

It was a problem that she shared with many of her clients. As their attorney, she worked off the concept of contingent plans. She would approach a divorce one way but expected hiccups. When something unexpected happened in discovery, she'd switch tactics, moving in a different direction. She was always one step ahead of her opponents.

That was the wonderful thing about practicing law. It was methodical. A game of chess. Real life was not that way. But perhaps she was looking at it all wrong. Maybe she, too, needed some contingent plans in her personal life.

12

TYRONE

Present
June 15

Helpless. The badge wielded a great deal of power, but Tyrone was still helpless to stop them. He had to watch Angel lead her client and his most likely suspect out of the police station. He couldn't force Frank to talk. All he could do was hope that something in the case would break, lead to a tangible clue. It wasn't a positive start to any investigation.

"That didn't go well."

Tyrone looked up to see Jackie leaning against the doorframe, her arms crossed.

"No, it didn't."

"What was your impression?" she asked, coming into the room and dropping into the chair across from him.

Tyrone's gaze shifted to the camera wedged into a corner, just below the ceiling. "Not here." He stood and made a shooing motion. They walked out into the hallway, outside of the intrusive gaze of the camera and the reach of the microphones. "We have enough problems with this case. We don't need to make it worse."

Jackie nodded and walked beside him as they made their way toward their "offices," which were cubicles in the middle of a large office, one room split into four. The police department in Fort Calhoun had grown quicky out of necessity. Crime had been on an upward trajectory for a long time and city council ignored the problem until they couldn't anymore. Only the most senior of officers had solid-walled offices, and Tyrone did not fit in that category. With luck, he never would. He'd be back in Chicago.

"Frank is hiding something." Jackie said it with confidence, then turned to him and said, "Don't you think?"

"Yes. But everyone is hiding something."

"You don't think he did it?"

"Did what? Caused Molly's disappearance, killed her, or desecrated her body?"

"All three?"

Tyrone shrugged. "I have no idea. I *think* he has plenty to do with at least one of those things, but that's only a hunch."

"So, what do we do now?"

"Did you call over to the forensics laboratory?" The people in the case may not be forthcoming, but physical evidence would hold nothing back.

"Yes. They are still testing samples. They've tested ten of the separate pools of blood, all come back as Molly's, but there are fifty more left to test."

Tyrone groaned. That was going to take forever. "What about the pigs?"

"Slaughtered, but nobody has started analyzing the stomach contents. They said they are backed up. It could be a few weeks before they get to it."

The criminalistics laboratory in Ankeny, Iowa, was the only laboratory that tested evidence within the state. Every piece of evidence from marijuana buds to murder weapons passed through their doors for forensics testing. It kept the process centralized but led to long wait periods. A few weeks was actually better than most lead times, but it didn't feel positive to Tyrone.

"I know, it sucks," Jackie said, her voice as dejected as Tyrone felt.

"Do you still have that missing person's file?"

"The one for Molly Sand?"

Tyrone nodded.

"Yeah, it's sitting in my office."

Tyrone gestured for her to lead the way.

Jackie's cubicle was a complete disaster. There were files and documents strewn everywhere. Bags of potato chips, empty wrappers and soft drink cans sat between them. This kind of mess would lead to a reprimand in Chicago. A senior officer would have been on Jackie about it the second one wrapper got close to a case file. But here, in this small town, Tyrone doubted anyone in charge had ever been near Jackie's cubicle. Technically, Tyrone was superior as a detective, but he did not hold a management role over Jackie, so he didn't comment.

"Here it is," Jackie said, holding up a thin file. She handed it to him. "There's not a lot."

The case file couldn't contain any more than a few sheets of paper. It annoyed Tyrone, but that wasn't Jackie's fault. Police departments did not dedicate much time or energy to missing adults. People could move around as they wished, and that included abandoning their families. The problem was that there was no way to differentiate between the people who had chosen to run, and those that hadn't.

Tyrone's mother had disappeared when he was a child. She'd never been found. Tyrone had always believed foul play was involved, but the police waited too long to start an investigation. Now it was too old, too cold, to warrant attention. Whatever had happened to his mother would remain a mystery. One he would not have a chance to solve unless he became a detective in Chicago. Then, he could reopen the case and do what those white detectives should have done all those years ago.

"There wasn't much to go off of," Jackie said, her voice slicing through Tyrone's thoughts. "Molly Sand disappeared on Valentines' Day. Remember the news coverage back then? They called her *The Vanishing Valentine*. I wasn't in love with the name, but it seemed to catch on."

"It was corny," Tyrone said.

"Frank Sand reported her disappearance on the fifteenth."

"Did you meet with Frank?"

"Yes. At his house."

"Did you have your body camera on?"

"Yes, but I didn't pull the footage. I didn't see a point."

Tyrone fought a flash of irritation. The recordings only stayed in the system for thirty days. It was well past then. Without copying it, the recording was gone forever. Jackie had missed the whole point of a body camera. Sometimes it was impossible to know if an interaction would become significant.

She's new to the job. She didn't know better. It was a mantra he had told himself more than a few times already and he felt sure it would continue. She'd been assigned Molly's disappearance as her first case after graduation from the law enforcement academy. She was the very definition of green back then.

"When we are done here, go check to see if the video is in the archives." It probably wouldn't be, but they needed to be certain.

Jackie nodded. "Sorry."

"Don't apologize. Get into the habit of saving that stuff."

"It takes so much time to copy it onto a disk."

She was right about that. Their equipment was old. It was one of the harder adjustments for Tyrone, moving from a large department with a massive budget to a small force with few resources. It often took two or more hours to copy video footage.

All the while, the officer copying the disk had to stand by, watching the tiny bar tick across the screen until the process was complete, ensuring chain of custody of the evidence. Leaving the evidence alone outside of a locked evidence locker for even a moment would leave a hole in that chain. Holes prevented the prosecution from laying the foundation for its introduction into court.

"What do you remember about that initial meeting with Frank?" If he couldn't have the video, he'd get whatever he could from Jackie.

"My biggest takeaway was Frank's attitude."

"Why?"

"Because his priorities seemed...off."

"How so?"

"He was agitated, I remember that. Annoyed with the kids. He'd been left alone with them, and I got the impression that wasn't something that happened often. He seemed overwhelmed by their rambunctiousness."

"Were they rambunctious?"

"Not really. I remember thinking they were relatively calm, quiet kids. They seemed almost scared of their father."

"Was there a sitter there to help him with the kids?"

Jackie shook her head. "He'd said the au pair had taken off."

"What was the guy's name? The au pair?"

Jackie bit her lip, searching her memory. "Nolan."

Tyrone scribbled the name onto a notepad. "Last name?"

"Weise."

"Address?"

Jackie shrugged. "I never got it. I was less focused on the au pair, and more focused on Frank's obvious irritation with the sudden lack of child-care. That was far more important to him than Molly's disappearance. Her loss seemed to be a minor blip on his radar."

She's new to the job. She didn't know better.

"I remember thinking that Molly must not have been as dumb as everyone seemed to think," Jackie said, "because she knew better than to bring another woman into the home full-time."

"Intelligence and intuition are two separate things."

"I suppose."

"Alright, we have our logical next step."

"What's that?"

"We need to talk to this Nolan guy."

"That's the problem. He's missing too."

Just then Jake walked by in his starched blue uniform. "Getting anywhere?" he asked, stopping in the doorway of the cubicle. He looked from Jackie to Tyrone as he raised one eyebrow. The Chief had asked Jake if he would work with Tyrone on Molly's case, but he'd passed on the opportunity, unwilling to tie his name to an investigation without a body. Nobody wanted the case, it seemed.

"We are getting as far as expected," Tyrone said.

"So, nowhere," Jake said, a smile slicing across his lips. "I hope you two enjoy your future as janitors." He was holding an open bag of Doritos. He dropped an orange triangle and crushed it beneath his boot. "Practice. Don't say I didn't do anything for you," he said, before chuckling and turning on his heel and strutting down the hall.

Tyrone and Jackie watched Jake walk away in silence. He wasn't wrong. That was the problem. At this rate, Tyrone would never get back to Chicago and his mother's disappearance would remain on a shelf in the cold case archives growing colder and dustier.

13

ANGEL

Past
February 2

Angel's alarm blared. She scrambled up and whacked her alarm clock, casting the room back into silence. She stared at the time through bleary, tired eyes. *Five o'clock.*

Mike did not stir.

They still slept in the same bed, but it might as well be separate rooms. Their bed was a California King and they never touched, not even by accident. They used to sleep at the very center, pressed together with their arms slung around one another. But not anymore. Over time, they started migrating away, creating space. It started as a sliver and morphed into a cavern.

She slipped out of bed and headed into the bathroom, sliding her feet into a pair of slippers, and pulling a large, fluffy robe over her shoulders. She ran the tap and splashed some cold water on her face. She met her gaze in the mirror, then looked down. She hated seeing herself bare like this, without the armor of makeup. It was when the wounds of the past were visible. The scar that sliced across her cheek had dulled over the years, a lighter, but still stark reminder of what she'd lost.

It was the product of a slick road, screeching tires, the crunch of metal, followed by silence as her first love, Tom, breathed his last breaths into the chill air. That was her happily ever after, her future, gone in an instant. Now he was nothing but a memory. Dust in the ground.

Stop it. She shook the thought from her mind, and patted her face dry, turning away from the mirror, and hurrying out of the bathroom.

The house was silent and still. Nobody else would be awake for hours. Angel made her way down the hallway, her slippered feet *pit-pattering* against the hardwood floor. As she passed the girls' room, she stopped to peek in. The room was eclectic, half messy, a tornado of tossed aside clothing and toys. This was Lily's side of the room. Gretty's side was organized, with books on a shelf, arranged by color.

Angel gazed at their similar, but not quite identical faces, nestled together, forehead pressed to forehead. The house was big enough for each to have their own room, but they had chosen to share. Just like they each had their own twin-sized bed with matching *My Little Pony* comforters, but one always found her way to the other's bed during the night.

They were so peaceful while sleeping. It was hard to believe they would transform into wild children in a matter of hours. These two would always have each other. They wouldn't need anyone else. And who did Angel have? No one. Mike was supposed to be her person, her replacement for what she'd lost, but he was growing more erratic, more distant with each passing day. Intentionally creating conflict by purchasing large items without regard for her feelings.

Angel shook her head and closed the door, turning away. She continued down the hall and into the kitchen. Her laptop sat at the kitchen island. She started a carafe of coffee and settled onto the counter stool in front of the computer. Her life was a balancing act, and she was doing all she could to stay upright. Each segment demanded all her attention—her failing marriage, her children, and most of all her work—but she was never enough. More was always required.

She worked too much, she knew that, but there just wasn't anything she could do about it. Their family needed money. Lily's insulin and doctor visits were expensive, and Angel was the only breadwinner. The mortgage wasn't going to pay itself. Mike seemed to think he could blow large amounts of cash without a second thought. They weren't rich. They were upper-middle class. There was a very big difference. As Frank had so eloquently put it while referring to his first ex-wife, Vivian, Mike lived a champagne lifestyle on a beer budget.

Stop dwelling and get on with it, Angel told herself. Angel poured herself a cup of coffee and returned to her seat, opening a client file. For the next hour, she lost herself in her work.

"Mommy," a small voice caught Angel's attention, causing her to whirl.

"Oh, Gretty," she said, bringing a hand to her chest. "You scared me."

"I didn't mean to." Gretchen looked down at her bare feet. Her pajamas were red with little black reindeer pulling Santa's sleigh. "Lily's hungry."

Lily came to Gretty's side, popping a thumb in her mouth. She was wearing pajamas that matched Gretchen's except hers were green with black reindeer. Angel had tried to get the girls to retire the pajamas a month ago—Christmas was over, after all—but with no success. To them, pajamas were pajamas, and some things weren't worth the fight.

"You girls are up early," Angel said, her gaze shifting to the clock. She didn't know how much time had passed.

It was just after six o'clock, early for them. Naturally, Mike wasn't up. Angel would have to spend the rest of her morning looking after the girls. It was supposed to be Mike's job, but he wasn't very good at anything anymore. She was going to fall behind on work, but the alternative was to wake her husband, and Angel would rather fall behind than deal with him the morning after a fight.

"What would you like for breakfast?" Angel said, rising out of her seat and stretching.

The girls looked at one another, then turned to her. "Donuts."

"How about some eggs?" Angel placed a skillet on the stove.

"And donuts?" Gretty said.

"Do we have any?" Angel asked.

Lily really shouldn't have fried dough for breakfast, not with her diabetes, but she was a child. Angel wanted her to have a chance to be a child. That, too, was a balancing act for her. She spent most weekends searching for recipes that were treat-like, diabetic friendly, but still tasty. It was a task that was as hard as it sounded.

"Yes!" Gretty said as she scurried toward the refrigerator. "You made them last weekend, remember?"

Angel remembered now. She'd spent half of her Saturday morning searching for ingredients at the local health food store and making the donuts. Lily hadn't had a treat like that since her diagnosis and neither had Gretty. Angel had presented them as a surprise, but Mike wouldn't allow the girls to eat them. He said donuts would make them fat. Poor Lily had cried for hours afterward. Angel didn't blame her. She'd wanted to cry, too.

"Alright, get them out," Angel said. "But eggs first."

She cracked four eggs into a bowl and whisked them together, pouring them into the heated pan. When the eggs were scrambled, she poured them onto a plate, placed it between her girls, setting two forks beside it.

"Eat up," Angel said.

As they ate the eggs, Angel removed the small box of doughnuts from the freezer and opened it, displaying the contents to the girls so they could each select a homemade diabetic-friendly donut. She defrosted them in the microwave and set them on the table. The excitement in Lily's eyes when she finished the last bite of egg and turned to that donut was priceless. Then Mike entered the room, yawning and stretching. He didn't look at Angel, an intentional choice, and instead focused on the girls. When he saw their meal, he froze.

"What the hell is that?" Mike demanded, turning his fiery gaze on his wife.

Angel cocked her head. "I don't know."

"Daddy said a bad word," Gretty said.

Mike ignored her. "Those are doughnuts. Where did they come from?"

"They were in the freezer."

Gretty and Lily didn't wait to see who would win the argument. They began downing their donut like their little lives depended on it. Their treat intake certainly did.

"They aren't supposed to eat crap like that." Mike grabbed the container of donuts—Angel had made a dozen—and marched over to the trash can, lifted the lid, and dumped them inside.

"Daddy!" Gretty yelled. "You're mean."

This was not the first time he'd done something cruel to her, but it was the first time he'd done it to the girls. She walked over to the trash can, pressed her foot on the lever to lift the lid. She would dig them out. They weren't dirty; they were still in the box. She reached in to grab it, but stopped when Mike's large hand encircled her bicep, squeezing.

"Mommy said we could have them. She made them special for us. And you threw them away." Tears streamed down Gretty's cheeks.

Lily glared at her father. Sometimes that little girl's facial expressions could be far worse than words. There was hate in those tiny eyes.

"Mommy will get them for you," Angel said, trying to pull her arm from Mike's grip.

"No. She won't," he said through gritted teeth. His grasp tightened around her arm. He twisted, causing her to cry out in pain.

"What did you do!" Gretty shouted at her father.

"Nothing," he said, releasing Angel's arm.

Angel yanked it back, placing a hand over the angry red mark already forming. There would be a bruise.

"She wasn't listening," Mike said, defensive.

"They are zero sugar donuts. Why can't they have them?" Angel said, rubbing her arm.

"You know why."

"No. I don't know why." He may be able to overpower her, but she had righteousness on her side. She marched over to her recipe cabinet, removing her *Cooking for Diabetics* cookbook. She flipped through several pages, then stopped on the recipe with donuts pictured below. She flipped it around and pointed to a line below the caption. "Says here, *safe for diabetics.*" She slammed the book down on the counter. "So, tell me, what is the problem?"

"I don't want them getting fat like you." His words were cold, delivered with cruel intent.

"Fat," Angel scoffed.

She wasn't fat. She was curvy and soft, but certainly not fat. Mike had gotten used to the women at that dumb gym that Frank owned. They were rail thin, Frank's wife included. Toothpicks on legs. Angel didn't see the appeal.

Frank had given Angel's family free lifetime access to the gym. It was supposed to be a perk to her longtime representation of him, one Angel never intended on using. But Mike had jumped at the offer, growing obsessed with weightlifting and muscle mass. Lately she'd started wondering if Mike was taking steroids. He'd always been moody, but he'd grown unstable with a dangerous undertone, a sign that could point toward Roid-Rage.

"Don't call Mommy fat," Gretty said.

Angel hadn't set out to alienate Mike from the kids. She didn't have to. He was doing that all on his own.

"I don't have to put up with this," Angel said. "I'm going to work." She turned to the girls. "I'm sorry. Mommy will be home tonight."

Both twins scooted off their seats and came running to Angel. She hugged them tight, her gaze meeting Mike's. He stared at her with a mixture of anger and disgust. She looked away, then broke her embrace with her girls. Then she checked Lily's blood sugar. It was normal. No insulin needed. Angel hugged both girls one more time, then left without saying goodbye to her husband.

The drive to work was short, but she used that time to clear her mind. The morning had started out tumultuously. She parked outside her office building and went inside. *Parker and Malone, PLLC*, was one of the businesses on the second floor. She took the elevator up and entered through the front door, and then she headed straight into her partner's office.

"Well, Angel," George Parker said, struggling to his feet. "Good morning."

He was thin. All knees and elbows in the way that was only possible in teenagers and elderly men. His white hair was still thick for his age, parted carefully to one side. A style she guessed he'd worn his entire life. He was seventy-five years old but hadn't retired. He'd planned on leaving the firm a year ago, but his wife had died suddenly and unexpectedly, and he needed the distraction.

"I hate Mike."

"A lover's quarrel, eh?"

"No. Not lovers," Angel dropped into the seat across from George's desk. "There is no love between us anymore."

George chuckled. "Give it time. Marriage is work."

"Everyone says that, but it shouldn't be this hard."

"Maybe not, but you've always held Mike at arm's length."

Angel didn't want to have this conversation, not after her morning, but she couldn't get up and leave. George would only follow.

"There has always been a Tom-shaped hole between you two," George said.

"I lost Tom a long time ago," Angel said.

"Have you taken Highway 141 since?"

"No," Angel admitted. She couldn't bear driving by the scene, seeing the cross at the side of the highway with its fake flowers and its reminders of him.

"You need therapy. You've never allowed yourself to heal."

"I healed."

"No. You diverted your attention by meeting and marrying Mike."

Angel shook her head, but she knew he was right. She'd known Mike for all of three months before they got married. He was a replacement for an irreplaceable person.

"But you vowed 'til death do us part.' Your word means something, doesn't it?"

"I do divorces for a living, George."

"Yes, but that makes you less inclined to divorce, doesn't it?"

"Yes." She dealt with her clients challenges every day. If there was any way to avoid going through the same thing, she would do it.

"You know, I used to fight with Beverly, especially when the kids were young," George said. "We'd fight like cats and dogs."

"Yeah?" Angel knew plenty of cats and dogs that got along just fine. She imagined that was the kind of fighting George and Beverly had done. Spats over who was supposed to load the dishwasher, not Beverly buying a boat without his input.

"You'll get through it," George said with far too much positivity.

That's easy for you to say, Angel thought.

George had adored his wife. She was gone now, and it was easier to love the dead. Angel knew from experience. Maybe George loved Beverly so much *because* she was dead. Maybe Angel still loved Tom for the same reason.

Her life was a mess. She never should have married Mike, but it was too late to change that now. The time for regrets was two kids and a mortgage ago. Yet, 'til death do us part' seemed like an impossibility. Unless, of course, death came sooner rather than later.

14

MOLLY

Molly was pinned to the mattress. She awoke to Frank's thick arm slung around her waist, his belly pressed into her back, his leg over hers. She couldn't move. Her eyes shot open, her heart racing.

Let me go.

She was trapped like an animal, desperate for escape.

Let me go.

He was not in peak physical shape—he didn't hold himself to the same standard he demanded of Molly—but he was strong, and he'd been a champion wrestler in his youth.

Calm down.

She took a deep breath, releasing it slowly, in and out, until her heart rate slowed, and her mind cleared.

He's asleep.

She could tell by the steady snores rattling from his chest. She wiggled out of his grip, moving inch by inch, freezing every time his breathing hitched or a snore caught in his throat. When she was free, she stood there for a moment, studying her sleeping husband. She loathed him. He'd kept a physical distance over the past month, sleeping at separate sides of the bed, but he changed after she'd caught wind of the affair, after their confrontation that ended so badly for her. Now he clung to her at night.

It wasn't love; it was ownership. She was pulling away. Something in her mind had flipped, a light that always burned had finally gone black. She still said all the right things to him, portrayed the perfect wife, but her enthusiasm for the role was gone. She was going through the motions with everything but the kids. Frank was dense, but he could sense the change. That was why he clung to her like a precious doll. But there was no affection attached to that ownership. He didn't want to lose her, he wanted to choose when to discard her.

I could pinch his nose, hold a hand over his mouth, and then it would be over. It was wishful thinking. He'd wake up, of course, overpower her, and do something horrible in retribution. Besides, she didn't have murder in her. His death would be the best thing for her, her children, and probably the entire Fort Calhoun Community, but she still couldn't bring herself to go that far.

She turned away from him and made her way into their enormous closet, closing the door and flipping on the light. She'd slept in the same thing since she married Frank, a silky teddy. At Frank's insistence, of course. She had at least twenty of them even though she would have preferred to sleep in flannels, especially in the bone chilling Iowa winters. She slipped a pair of flannels on and shivered with the sudden warmth.

She had convinced Frank to buy the flannels so she wouldn't have to bump into Frankie Junior, his older son from his marriage to Vivian, in the mornings while wearing only a teddy and a robe. Frankie Junior was seventeen, almost a man, with raging hormones. Even Frank understood that Molly should dress more conservatively around him.

Molly stepped out of the closet and made her way out of the room and down the grand staircase, headed for the kitchen. The house was silent, but she sensed that she wasn't the only person awake. She could feel it in the air, a disturbance to the stillness. She found him in the kitchen, his eyes tracking her every movement.

"You're up early," Molly said, forcing a smile.

Frankie Junior shrugged. He was standing next to the island, his cell phone in one hand. His gaze did not leave her, and he did not blink as she approached. It sent a chill up her spine.

The custody arrangement with Vivian was week on, week off. When Frankie stayed with them, he woke up early enough to spend time alone with Molly. It wasn't natural, and it hadn't always been this way. It was a new habit he'd picked up over the last few months. He had to be setting an alarm. Six o'clock was not a time that teenagers naturally awoke.

Molly trudged past him and over to the counter, popping a pod into the Keurig. She pressed start and forced herself to turn around and face him. "What do you have going on today?"

He shrugged again. "School."

The Keurig made a gurgling sound, then coffee began splashing into her mug. "Any after-school activities today?"

She couldn't stand the weirdness that had developed between them. It thrived in silent moments, causing her to fill them with conversation. She'd met him when he was only seven. He'd been standoffish back then, as expected. Few people liked their first stepmom, and Molly was Frankie Junior's fourth. He probably knew better than to get attached. And he remained disinterested until recently.

"I'll come home after school. You'll be here, right?"

"Probably. Why?"

"I thought we..."

He trailed off when he heard little footsteps pattering down the staircase. Molly didn't know what he was about to say, and she didn't want to know. She grabbed her coffee and headed out into the entryway in time to see her daughter and son sliding down the stairs on their bottoms while holding hands. They were the light in her darkness.

"Hi, Mommy," Genevieve called.

"Shhhh." Molly lifted a finger and placed it before her lips. "Don't wake your father."

When her two kids reached the bottom of the stairs, she bent to their level and gave them each a hug and a kiss.

"Would you like some breakfast?" she asked, looking both her children in the eyes.

"Yup," Genevieve said. Matthew nodded.

Molly took a child's hand in each of hers and led them into the kitchen. Frankie Junior was still seated at the counter. His lip curled when he saw his younger half-brother and half-sister. He'd never taken to his siblings.

"Say 'good morning' to your brother," Molly said, kissing Genevieve, then Matthew on the tops of their heads.

"Good Mo—" they started to recite in unison, but Frankie Junior cut them off.

"I need to get ready for school," he said, shoving a counter stool out of his way and stalking out of the room.

"What's wrong with him?" Matthew asked.

"Nothing," Molly said, producing what she hoped looked like a genuine smile. "Woke up on the wrong side of the bed, I guess."

"He always wakes up in the wrong bed," Genevieve said with a snort. "And he wears perfume."

"What?" Molly asked, scrunching up her nose. "He wears perfume?"

"Yeah," Matthew agreed. "He wears *your* perfume."

"No, he doesn't," Molly said, but her mind was whirring. She had noticed a bottle of Chanel No. 5 missing.

"He's weird," Genevieve said, pulling Molly out of her thoughts.

Matthew nodded agreement.

"That's enough of that, you two. He is your brother." *Like it or not.* "What will it be for breakfast? Omelets?"

"Yes," Matthew and Genevieve said in unison.

Molly handed the kids their iPads and headphones and turned to the stove to fix their breakfasts. She was halfway through when she heard Frankie Junior's heavy feet stomping their way down the staircase. When he reached the front door, he opened it and slammed it closed behind him. The sound echoed off the high ceilings of the entryway.

Shit, Molly thought, holding her breath. *I hope he didn't wake his father.* She stood there, frozen to the spot, gripping the spatula like a weapon for a few long, tense moments, then she relaxed.

Molly had woken Frank up once, and she had never done it again. It was in their first month of marriage. She'd been young and impulsive, and oh so naïve. They weren't in this house yet, they were in the small apartment he'd rented to avoid his last ex-wife. All she'd done was turn on the television. It was too loud. He'd come tearing out of the room, roaring like a bear. He didn't say a word to her. He went straight for the TV, picked it up, and threw it at her. She dove out of the way, but it smashed to the floor, the screen shattering into a thousand jagged shards.

Molly shook her head, dispelling the memory. If Frank had been disturbed by Frankie Junior slamming the door, he'd be downstairs by now. But why had Frankie Junior done it? He was fully aware of his father's temper. She wasn't the only one who'd woken Frank before noon. He, too, had been on the receiving end of that wrath a time or two. Was he trying to drive a wedge between Molly and Frank? If so, there was no need. That wedge was already there, caught beneath the skin like a splinter, festering.

She turned back to the stove, focusing on the omelets as her two children watched cartoons, blissfully ignorant of the anxiety wrapping itself around Molly. There were too many stressors in Molly's life. *Only four more months of this*, she reminded herself. Then, Frankie Junior would be off to college, and she could stop worrying about flannel pajamas, disappearing bottles of perfume, and slamming doors.

Or so she hoped.

15

TYRONE

Tyrone's cell phone rang. He was still in Jackie's cubicle. He set the missing person paperwork on her desk and removed the phone from his pocket, looking at the name flashing across the screen. *Harper Jenkins.* She was the first assistant in the prosecutor's office, the person who handled the most serious crimes in the Fort Calhoun County Attorney's Office. She had been assigned to Molly's case. Prosecutors didn't always get involved in cases this early, but they did in major felony offenses, like murder investigations.

The local prosecutor's office was small by Tyrone's standards. There were only five attorneys, one of which was the elected county attorney. Yet, prosecutors all seemed to be the same no matter where he lived. Ambitious, controlling, and intelligent. It was important for Tyrone to keep every one of them on his good side. They'd be his best—or worst—references when it came time to return to Chicago.

Like other law enforcement, prosecutors were organized on a tiered scale. They just used different names. The county attorney was the chief of police, the first assistant the captain of the force, and everyone else was a beat cop. In larger offices there would be second assistants and department heads, but none of that existed in a town of 20,000 people.

"Who is it?" Jackie said.

"Harper."

"Better pick up."

Tyrone accepted the call and pressed speakerphone, holding the phone midway between himself and Jackie. "Gully here. I've got you on speakerphone. Jackie's here, too." He tried to keep his tone casual, but a hint of anxiety clung to his words.

"Hi," Jackie said, shifting her weight and shoving her hands in her pockets.

"Where are you with the Sand murder investigation?" As always, she cut to the chase.

Nowhere. "We've had a few leads, but they haven't been fruitful. We'll keep shaking branches and see what falls."

"So, you've got nothing," Harper said.

"We still have a lot of interviews left. There are several ex-wives, Frank's older son, and the current and former au pairs. The former au pair is missing, but we'll find him."

"I hope he's not dead, too. The only way to make this case more sensational is to add to the body count."

Her delivery was deadpan. Not because she didn't care, but because death was a part of her job. Prosecutors, like law enforcement, saw horrible crime scenes and worked with terrible, dangerous people. It was no place for emotion. Those who couldn't compartmentalize, couldn't separate the cases from the people, didn't last long. It was too painful.

"I hope he's alive, too," Tyrone said.

"Well, you'd better get moving because you're running out of time."

Every moment mattered. Investigations grew colder by the second, but Tyrone got the impression that Harper was referring to a different timeline. "Did something happen?"

"Yeah. The local news station caught wind of the story. We tried to keep it quiet, but no dice. The story is too sensational."

"How did that happen?"

"It doesn't matter. I'd guess that Frank Sand or his attorney leaked it. They're the ones who will benefit from chaos."

Jackie pulled her phone out and started scrolling through social media. Her thumb ran across the screen, flicking from post to post.

"I don't see anything about it on social media," Jackie said.

"Yeah, well, you wouldn't," Harper said. "I convinced them to hold the story until the morning. I wanted more time, but you know reporters. They all want to break the news."

"Tomorrow," Tyrone repeated. "That isn't enough time."

Media coverage meant scrutiny. Scrutiny made witnesses shut down. Sometimes they'd even disappear until after the trial was over, choosing anonymity over involvement. Tyrone had enough disappearing parties, he didn't need more.

"That's all the time you're going to get. Nothing draws eyeballs like a beautiful woman eaten by pigs. People do not like when their food eats them."

Harper was right, of course. Molly was beautiful, young, and she was white. She was the picture of the wholesome Midwest mother. All key elements to traction in a news story. In Tyrone's experience, media attention was only helpful after a case went cold. Tyrone's mother's disappearance and likely death hadn't garnered any attention. Not then, and certainly not now. She had been a mother, too, but she was an inner-city, black mom.

He missed her still. People always said, "time will heal your pain," but that hadn't happened for Tyrone. He'd grown up passed from one distant relative to the next, always hoping for even a fraction of the love his mother had provided. His family had been good to him, that wasn't the problem. The problem was that his mother had loved him so fiercely. Nothing could replace her.

Jackie swatted him on the shoulder, tearing him out of his thoughts. "I'm sorry, what did you say?" Tyrone asked, recovering his composure.

"Is there anything else?" Harper said.

"Have you heard any more from forensics?" Tyrone asked. "Knowing more would be helpful."

"Not yet, but I'll call over there after I'm done talking to you. I need to light a fire under their asses as well. We are running out of time."

"Okay," Tyrone said.

"Keep me updated," Harper said.

"Will do."

Tyrone hung up and lowered the phone to his side. Anxiety was building within him, growing more intense by the second.

"What now?" Jackie asked, staring at him, wide eyed, waiting for directions. She was excellent on patrol, but she would never become a detective. At least not until she learned to think for herself.

"We keep pushing forward. We've still got a long list of witnesses to interview. At this point, I think it is best for us to split up. I'll start talking to potential witnesses with ties to the family. I need you to track down that missing au pair."

"Nolan?"

"Yes."

"What if he's dead?"

"Then you won't find him alive," he said flatly.

"Then what?"

"We'll play it by ear."

"Alright," she said, but she didn't sound convinced.

"I'm going to go visit Frank's first ex-wife." He glanced at his watch. It was late morning. "I'm hoping she can give me some background on the family."

Jackie looked down at her notepad. "Vivian?"

"That's her."

Tyrone left Jackie in her office to begin her search. They had to keep working every angle, something had to break free. He needed to solve this case. It was brand new with fresh witnesses. If he couldn't find the answer in Molly's case, he'd never solve his mother's case. Not even if he was tapped for the next available detective position in Chicago. Her case was long cold, witnesses dead or gone, and no trace of her had ever been discovered. If he couldn't bring Molly's killer to justice, Tyrone's mother had no hope.

16

MOLLY

Nolan was her lifeline. Without him, she'd be lost. He was her only adult confidant. If he ever betrayed her or turned his back on her, she didn't know how she'd make it through life.

"Morning, my family," Nolan said, as he entered the kitchen nodding. He stopped and stared at Molly as she finished the kids' omelets, sliding them onto plates. "How do you look like that," he gestured to her, "in the mornings, when I look like this. It's not fair. It's not fair, I tell you."

Molly forced a smile. "Just lucky, I guess." He knew something was off with her and he was trying to make her feel better. She didn't actually look good. She placed the kids' breakfasts in front of them and turned back to Nolan. "Can you hold the fort for a bit. I'm going to run upstairs and get dressed."

"Yeah, sure," Nolan said, yawning again as he popped a pod into the Keurig. "Go do your hot girl stuff. I'll watch the little monsters." He winked as the coffee started to trickle into his mug.

"Thanks." Molly went upstairs to shower, dress, and get ready. Most days she took two showers, one before the gym and one after. If she had her way, she'd wait until after the gym, but Frank expected her to look stunning every second of every day.

She was putting the final touches on her makeup when Frank came into the bathroom, bleary-eyed, hair disheveled. He was wearing a white under-shirt and grey boxer shorts. He said nothing to her when he entered, then went straight to the toilet and started peeing. Molly cringed at the sound of his urine hitting the water. She hated it. He would never tolerate her peeing in front of him, not that she had any desire to do it.

"Ahhhh," Frank said when he was finished. Then he turned around to face her. The bleariness was gone from his eyes. He was fully awake now.

Molly met his gaze in the mirror much the same way as she had done with Mike at the gym the day before. Unlike Mike, Frank wasn't ogling, he looked mad. But how could he possibly be angry? He'd just woken up.

"I need to talk to you," Frank said.

Then talk.

"There are a lot of rumors flying around about you lately."

"Me?" Molly placed a hand on her chest. "What are you talking about?"

"When I came to the gym to check on it yesterday evening, I got a call from one of my daytime employees. Riley. You know him?"

"Yeah. I know Riley."

"He told me he saw you and Mike Malone getting cozy."

"Cozy?" Molly repeated. "He asked to spot me. I said yes. I didn't realize safety translated into coziness."

"Well, it does. I watched the video."

"You what?" He was spying on her using the gym's cameras. She should have expected it—nothing was beyond Frank when it came to power and control—but it hadn't occurred to her he'd go that far.

"Yeah. Of course, I did. When someone tells me that Mike Malone, my attorney's husband, is on the prowl and he's prowling after *my* wife, I'm going to look into it."

His focus on Mike's behavior rather than Molly's was somewhat settling. It eased the concern that Frank was mad *at* her, but she still felt violated.

"So, I looked at the tape. That man watched you the entire time you lifted. He drooled over you. He didn't even try to hide it."

"Everyone watches me." She'd never spoken to Frank with such venom, but something inside her was crumbling. She didn't have the energy for meekness and apologies. She wanted to fight.

"Isn't that the point of looking like this?" She gestured to herself. Her tiny, barely there waist and her large, fake breasts. "The fillers, the surgery, the diets, the cosmetics. Isn't that the point? To be attractive? That's what you want in a wife, isn't it? And now you're complaining because you have it."

"I want my wife to be attractive *for me*, not for everyone else."

"Well, that is something I can't give. I have to exercise to fit into the clothing you buy. If you start buying size four or six, I can stop going to the gym and do less intense, at-home workouts without all the equipment and the aerobics instructor."

"No. You need to go to the gym."

"Okay. Then expect men to watch me."

"Just stay away from Mike Malone."

"And what about all the other guys?"

Frank's eyes narrowed. "What other guys?"

"Every other person that attends that gym. They all watch me, including Riley." *The little tattle tale.*

"They aren't like Mike Malone. I watched the tapes from weeks and even months before yesterday."

Molly blinked several times. She didn't know how to react to that. Frank's businesses didn't keep recordings for more than twenty-four hours. They didn't have the storage. Instead, their surveillance system recorded over itself. For Frank to have recordings dating that far back, it meant he'd manually gone into the system and saved the time slots that she'd been at the gym.

"Mike was watching you. Every. Single. Time. His eyes stayed glued on you. He tried to approach you so many times but turned around at the last minute. This guy, Molly, I'm telling you, he's obsessed with you."

Suddenly, she was very tired. Everyone, it seemed, was obsessed with her. Including her husband, who had been saving recordings of her. "What do you want me to do about it, Frank?"

"Stay away from him."

"I'll try. But we attend the same gym. You could kick him out. You do own the place." Getting rid of Mike would be a power move, for sure, but Frank would also be admitting that he was willing to take a personal and potentially social hit for Molly. It wasn't a grand gesture of love, but it was something.

"I can't do that. He's Angel's husband."

"Right," Molly said, crossing her arms. "And you need Angel in case you decide to get rid of me."

"I didn't say that. Angel helps me out with a lot more than divorces."

"Like what? Prenuptial agreements?"

"Among other things."

"Right. Well, then, I'm out of ideas. I'll try to stay away from Mike, but I can't make any promises. You are running a business. Your wife cannot be rude to a customer, can she?"

"No."

"Great. Glad that's settled," Molly said. "I'm going to go downstairs and check on the kids." She left Frank alone in the bathroom to shower and get ready himself, heading down the stairs into the kitchen, still fuming from their argument.

"What happened?" Nolan asked when she reached the kitchen. Molly had never had much of a poker face.

Molly's gaze flicked to her children. They were both at the counter, watching their iPads, ears covered in headphones. "Frank. We had an argument."

Nolan guided her over to the small table in the breakfast nook, pulling a chair out for her. "Sit. Sit, sweetheart. Let's have a chat. What did he do this time?"

They both sat down and got situated, then she launched into the full story, keeping her tone hushed so Frank wouldn't overhear if he happened to come downstairs.

"You've got to be kidding me," Nolan said, his eyes narrowed. "Frank is one to talk."

"Why do you say that?" Molly agreed, but it sounded like Nolan knew something she didn't know.

"Oh, honey, I hate to be the bearer of bad news, but you know I go to the yoga class at night. Obviously, since you are at home with the kids when I go. Anyway, Frank follows Rebecca like a West Hollywood wife follows their plastic surgeon's Instagram account. Checking it out. All. The. Time."

Molly's heart sank. "She's the girl he was texting with."

"Yeah, well, honey, they've been doing a lot more than texting."

"They have?" Molly already knew it—she'd seen the texts—but she didn't know Frank had been flagrant enough for so many others to notice.

"Umm hmm. He's been drooling over her the same way he says Mike's been watching you, honey."

That explained why Frank had been so agitated by Mike's attention to Molly. He knew Mike's intentions because he shared the same for Rebecca. *It takes one to know one.*

"I've never seen it personally. I mean, I would obviously tell you if I had, but I have lots of friends at that gym."

Molly didn't doubt that. Nolan was personable and outgoing. People flocked to him.

"I've been told by more than one person on more than one occasion that Frank takes Rebecca back to his office, locks the door, and closes those blinds. I know I probably should have told you sooner, honey, but this is all gossip and I've got no hard evidence."

Molly's face grew hot. She had evidence. She found it on his phone.

"But," Nolan leaned closer and lowered his voice even further, "I heard a new rumor last night."

"What's that?"

It was almost too much to bear, but she had to know. Burying her head in the sand would not solve her problems. And they weren't her problems alone. Frank's choices affected their children. She had to be vigilant; she had to be aware. If not for herself, then for them.

"Rebecca, that basic bitch, is saying that Frank is going to file for divorce. Can you believe that?"

Molly gasped. "He's going to leave me?"

What would she do? She had no way to support herself or the kids. No family to lean on. No friends with any money. If she was out, so was Nolan. They'd have nowhere to go. She'd be unstable. She could lose the kids. That couldn't happen.

"It's hearsay within hearsay," Nolan said, back pedaling. "So, don't get too worked up about it, honey. If it's true, and that's a big *if*, that doesn't actually mean Frank is leaving you. It just means that Frank is telling Rebecca that he's leaving you. I mean, seriously. Who would leave you for *her*? She's got nothing going on upstairs," he tapped his head, "and she's barely an adult. She can't even legally drink alcohol. He's probably manipulating her."

Molly nodded. Frank was not one to tell the truth. He told people what they wanted to hear. Over the years, she'd learned how to read between the lines and garner at least a small nugget of honesty within his lies, but that had come only after years of marriage. Rebecca didn't know that yet. The only person Frank was ever honest with was his attorney and Angel had to keep his secrets. It was her job.

"I'm guessing Angel knows Frank's true intentions."

"Probably," Nolan agreed.

"But she'll never tell me anything."

"Oh, no, not Angel, darling. She'll take his secrets to the grave."

It was aggravating. Molly had poured her heart and soul into this marriage. She'd altered her body. She'd given up her dreams. She'd given Frank two beautiful children. And still it wasn't enough for him. He had to have more. And he would use Angel Malone to get it. It made Molly want to get even with Frank and Angel, and she thought, perhaps, she might know one person who could make that happen.

17

ANGEL

Work was Angel's safe space. The farther she and Mike drifted from one another, the harder she clung to her job. Mike might not want her, but her clients needed her. When she left home in the mornings, low and defeated, she could forget about her own problems and focus on someone else's. She became her own person, rather than the girls' mother and Mike's babysitter.

When she left George's office, she hadn't felt all that much better. Mike was on the verge of filing for divorce. Their marriage was on life support, and Mike was poised and ready to pull the plug. She'd done enough family law work to sense the end. Yet, she still had some time. He would have roadblocks that didn't exist for others.

Mike's primary barrier would be finding an attorney who didn't know Angel. It was not a small bridge to cross. She'd practiced all over central and northwest Iowa. He'd have to go far east or far west to find someone who didn't have a conflict with Angel or her partner. It would buy her some time.

For what? Why was she buying time? That was a question she couldn't answer. At least not yet.

She stepped inside her office and took a deep breath, pushing the thoughts of Mike out of her mind. Her focus needed to be on her clients. Their problems were as real as hers. She removed her laptop from its bag and placed it on her desk, settling into her office chair. The first thing on the agenda for the morning was drafting a response to Frank's ex-wife's petition for modification of child support and custody of their nearly eighteen-year-old son.

The document was called an Answer. Angel responded line by line, paragraph by paragraph, addressing the issues raised in the petition. Both documents were formal, completely devoid of details, so it didn't take long for Angel to finish the response. She basically wrote, "The respondent DENIES this paragraph of the petitioner's petition," repeatedly.

When she finished, she emailed a draft copy to Frank attached to an email with the subject line "Meet me tomorrow eight-thirty sharp." He would need to sign the Answer before she could file it. They wouldn't get a court date until the response was filed.

Once that was done, she made a few phone calls to clients. Her caseload was high, and her clients insisted on regular communication. It was nearing noon when she finished her last call. She locked her computer, stood and stretched, then made her way back toward George's office.

"I'm going to leave for a little while," Angel said as she pulled on her coat. She'd remained in the doorway, choosing not to enter his office. She didn't need permission to take lunch, but she and George had a habit of letting one another know their comings and goings in case a surprise client showed up without an appointment.

"You don't usually leave for lunch."

That was true. She almost always worked through lunches, eating an energy bar rather than a proper meal so she could make the most of every second of the day. Time was money, and she wasn't going to waste it on lunch.

"Are you meeting someone?" George said, a sparkle in his eyes.

Angel paused. Was he insinuating she was having an affair? "I, uh…"

"I knew you could work it out," George said, coming around the desk and leaning up against it. "Marriage is hard, but you can get through this. Lunch with Mike is a great start."

"I, uh, yeah," she finally said. "I'm going to meet Mike for lunch."

"Of course, you are." He came over to her and patted her on the shoulder. "You take as long as you need. Take the afternoon off. Maybe you two can get the flames going again."

That was impossible. Not only because Angel was *not* going to see Mike, but also because she couldn't stand him. He was probably at home playing video games. That, or at the gym ogling Molly Sand. Angel had been Frank's first call when he caught Mike, "pawing his wife," on the gym surveillance system.

"Your roided-up husband won't leave my wife alone," Frank had said.

Angel had pinched her nose, trying to keep the frustration at bay. "What do you want me to do about it?"

"Make him stop."

Fat chance. Rage flared in Angel's chest. Mike was spending their money, calling her fat, ignoring their children, and now he was messing with her client's wives. He was damaging her business. And why? Because he wanted to screw a life-sized Barbie.

"I'll take care of it," Angel had said.

"You'd better," Frank said and ended the call.

She immediately regretted her words. She'd made a promise to a client that she wasn't sure she could keep. Mike didn't give a shit what she thought. She'd have a better chance if she approached Molly, which was the last thing she wanted to do. What would she say? *Hi, Molly. I'm the person who will screw you over in your divorce if your husband decides to file. Oh, and he's definitely thinking about filing—sorry about that—but could you do me a solid and stay away from my husband?*

Mike was no prize. She'd be doing Molly a favor by warning her away, not that Molly would see it that way. Mike was supposed to be a stay-at-home Dad, watching their girls as he had promised back when she was pregnant. Instead, he spent his days running around a fictitious world holding an assault rifle, shooting everything in sight, working out, and flirting with married women. He had his priorities straight.

Angel supposed that's what she got for marrying a musician. He had promised that he was going somewhere, perfecting his music. That was the whole reason they'd put the girls in daycare. He'd lasted three months as a stay-at-home dad before insisting that they get an au pair.

"Is there something you needed?" George said, pulling Angel out of her thoughts.

"Sorry, no," Angel said, heading for the exit.

"Good luck," he called after her.

Angel lifted an arm in acknowledgement. It was not luck that she needed. She exited the building and headed toward the bank across the street. It was a local bank, one her firm had used since she moved to town. Stepping inside, she hurried to the front desk.

"Good afternoon, Ms. Angel," the teller said, flashing a bright smile. This was one thing Angel loved and hated about small towns. Everyone knew her.

"Good afternoon."

"What can I do for you?"

"I need to, uh, open a new account."

"A new account?" The woman's sculpted eyebrows lifted.

"Yes."

They both stood there for a long moment, the teller waiting for further explanation, Angel unwilling to provide it.

"Right, well, a banker should be able to assist you with that." She looked up and waved a hand to a man across the room. "Miles, Angel here needs your help."

Angel fought the urge to cover her face with a hand.

Miles scurried across the marble flooring, stopping in front of her. "What can I do for you?"

She repeated the same spiel about opening a new account. Again, there was a long pause as he waited for an explanation. She again refused to give it to him.

"Alright," he said after a long, tense moment, clapping his hands together. "Follow me."

They made their way toward a small office in the corner.

"What kind of account are we opening today?"

"A checking account."

"Business or personal?"

"Personal."

"Will you and your husband's names both be on this account?"

"No."

He cleared his throat. "Was that a 'no'?"

"My husband is not going to be on the account."

"Are you sure?"

"Yes." How many times were they going to make her repeat herself?

"You have five thousand in your joint account."

Her paycheck from the last few weeks had automatically deposited into that account, posting that morning.

"Would you like to use some of that to open the new account?" Miles said.

"Move all of it."

"We have to leave at least $100.00 in the original account."

"Okay, then leave $100.00."

Mike had somehow transferred all the money to his own personal account, an account that didn't have her name on it, leaving less than one hundred dollars in the joint account the day before, so it was possible, but she didn't press the issue. Some battles weren't worth fighting.

"I can do that." He paused and gave her a judgmental look over the top of his glasses before turning to his desktop computer.

She didn't care. She would not allow this man to make her feel guilty for protecting her money. If they'd known what Mike had done, if anyone knew he'd used *her* money to buy a *boat*, by God, a boat. It was absolutely insane that he would even consider purchasing something so completely asinine. He'd done it specifically to piss her off. Mike had known she'd be furious.

"Are you sure you don't want to leave a little more in the joint account? For groceries or other expenses?"

"I'm sure."

Mike had no expenses. She paid for everything. She shopped online for the groceries, and they were delivered to the door after she paid for them online. She paid the mortgage and all their other bills. The daycare costs were all covered by her. Mike literally had no need for money, and she would no longer allow him to blow through hers.

It was nearing one o'clock when Angel finished at the bank and hurried back to the office. She'd have to settle for another energy bar as lunch, consumed as she dashed across the street to court. But for now, she was back in her safe space, surrounded by the life she'd created for herself. She could spend the afternoon calm now with the knowledge that her money was safe as well.

18

TYRONE

Frank's first ex-wife, Vivian, lived on the only golf course in town, in an area called *Whispering Pines*. The community was gated, like many of the affluent suburbs of Chicago, but there was no guard at the gatehouse and the gate was open. Tyrone got the impression that these homeowners wanted it to *look* like they had money, but it was a ruse.

His mother used to say, "You don't know if someone is rich until you see their bank account," and this community was a good example of that. Nice things did not mean "rich." Not if you were mortgaged to the hilt, barely treading water. When one wrong domino could bring the whole house of cards crashing down.

Tyrone drove his unmarked police vehicle through the open gate, following his GPS as a robotic female voice gave him instructions to *turn right on Willow Lane*. He had obtained Vivian Sand's address from dispatch and punched it into his phone, allowing it to guide him there. He continued for a quarter mile before he heard, *your destination is on the right*.

The house was a two-story, white-washed brick with a large entryway and well-manicured lawn. Flowers spilled from planters posted like sentries outside the front door. The driveway was new, a bright white with no cracks or blemishes. Vivian's house was better maintained than those nearby, which all showed signs of decay—crab grass, dents in garage doors, peeling paint. Perhaps Vivian wasn't pretending quite as much as the rest of the neighborhood.

He parked in the driveway, got out, and knocked on the front door. After a few moments, the door swung open. A woman stood in front of Tyrone. She had long, bleached blond hair, too thick to be natural. Her lips were full to the point of bursting and there wasn't a line on her face. Which was odd because Tyrone had checked her information before arriving at the residence. She was fifty years old, yet her skin was tight, completely unlined. It felt wrong, false, yet he couldn't look away.

"Can I help you?" the woman asked.

"I'm here to visit with Vivian Sand."

"I am Vivian. And who might you be?"

"Tyrone Gully, ma'am. I'm with the Fort Calhoun Police Department."

"Where's your uniform?" Her tone had turned playful, brimming on flirtatious.

"I'm a detective. I don't wear a uniform."

"Ohh, a detective." She opened the door wide and moved to the side. "Come on in, detective."

He stepped inside. "Is this a good time? I don't want to keep you from your day."

She was dressed in a white high-waisted pant suit with a bright pink top. Formal for someone that wasn't going anywhere.

"It's as good a time as any." Vivian led the way down a long, well-lit hallway. The flooring was blond wood, freshly waxed and gleaming. "Go ahead and have a seat," she said, when they reached a formal dining room.

He sat in a chair near the end of the long dining table. A large chandelier clung to the ceiling, casting light around the room. She chose a seat right next to him, far too close for comfort, but Tyrone couldn't think of a polite way to create distance.

"So, detective," Vivian said, threading her fingers together, "what brings you to my humble home?"

Humble was not the word Tyrone would use to describe it. They'd passed a living area on their way to the dining room with a baby grand piano. Humble people did not have anything "grand" in their homes, even if it was baby-sized.

"I'm here to talk about Frank Sand."

"Frank?" Vivian said, pressing a hand to her chest. A gesture of mock concern. "What has that man done this time?"

"I'm not saying he's done anything, ma'am—"

"Call me Vivian."

"Okay, Vivian. I'm not saying he's done anything. I'm just gathering information."

"Because of Molly?" She said, leaning forward with a hand cupped around her mouth like a child telling a secret in the schoolyard. Except this wasn't little-kid gossip. This was a murder investigation.

"When was the last time you spoke to Frank?"

Vivian shrugged. "It's been a while. It's felt like a vacation, to be honest."

So, Frank hadn't warned her that the Molly Sand investigation had morphed from a missing person to murder.

"What is your relationship with Frank?"

Vivian shrugged. "Distant but cordial. Aside from Molly, I'm the only one of his wives that had a child with him. Frankie Junior. He's eighteen now."

"Where is Frankie Junior?"

"Oh, he doesn't live here anymore. He turned eighteen and whoosh," she made a flying gesture with her well-manicured hand, "he was gone." Her nails were the exact shade of pink as her shirt.

Tyrone made a note to get Frankie Junior's address from Vivian before he left. "How long have you and Frank Senior been divorced?"

"It's been years. Frankie Junior was only three at the time. Frank Senior doesn't like children much. He likes the idea of them—so many men do— but he isn't much of a father. Are you a father?"

"No."

Tyrone did some quick math in his head. If Frankie Junior was three at the time, then the divorce would have been fifteen years ago. Frank had three ex-wives and he'd been married to Molly for ten years. That meant he had three failed marriages in less than five years. *Busy man*. And not in a good way.

"Why not?" Vivian asked, leaning forward with her elbows on the table and placing her chin in her hands.

"Why not what?"

"Why don't you have kids?" Vivian asked.

Tyrone shrugged. "I just don't."

He didn't like the conversation turning to his personal life. He didn't have kids because the loss of his mother had cast a long shadow over his life, his career geared at solving her disappearance. There was no space for dating or an eventual wife and children. Not until he solved his mother's murder, and her soul could rest in peace.

"That's not a real answer," Vivian said, yanking Tyrone back into the present.

It was the only answer she was going to get.

"What happened to Frank's other ex-wives?" Tyrone asked.

"They moved after their divorces. They weren't from here. There was nothing tying them to Fort Calhoun, so they all flitted away. Truth be told, I envy their freedom. Frank can be a real pain in the backside if you know what I mean."

Tyrone thought back to his interview with Frank. He knew exactly what she meant. "Do you know if any of them have been back recently?"

Vivian shrugged a bony shoulder. "I don't keep track of them."

Fair enough. "What was your divorce settlement like? If you don't mind me asking."

"Oh, I don't mind. It is public record, after all. I made out pretty well," she gestured around herself, "obviously."

"You work, though, don't you?"

"Yes. And it's a thorn in Frank's side. I'm a very sought-after realtor. I don't make the kind of money that Frank does, but I do well for myself. Plus, I've got all the businesses I inherited through the divorce. I don't have to do much with them, and I still get paid as a partial owner."

"Which businesses?"

In Tyrone's research, Frank Sand owned a lot of businesses. Restaurants and bars, convenience stores, and hotels. He even owned a chain of gyms called *Frankly Hot and Heavy*. There was one in town. It was one of those places where everyone owned a membership, more of a club than a place to exercise.

"The restaurants. That's all he had at the time of our divorce."

"Do you still maintain ownership in his restaurants?"

"Yes. Frank keeps begging me to sell to him—he likes control, you know —but I don't see the point. What's in it for me? They're making money and I only pop in to look around once or twice a week. It's a win-win scenario for me." She leaned forward as though imparting another secret. "To tell you the truth, it makes me feel a bit like Lisa Vanderpump. Who wouldn't want that? Right?"

"I don't know who that is," Tyrone said.

"Do you watch reality TV?"

"No." He didn't have time for television, reality or otherwise.

"Well, you should."

"Sounds like it." Tyrone tapped the end of his pen against his notepad. "What kind of husband was Frank?"

"The worst kind. A philanderer. Controlling. Self-centered. He expects perfection. He's very hard to please. My mother used to say—she's passed now, God rest her soul—but she used to say that Frank would take his slice out of the middle of the cake."

"He doesn't sound easy to live with."

"He wasn't."

"Was he ever violent?"

"No. Not with me, but people can change."

"Has Frank changed?"

Vivian shrugged. "I don't know."

"What about Frank's wife, Molly?" Tyrone asked.

"Molly was a dimwitted moron."

Was. Tyrone's mind snagged on that word. Vivian couldn't know of Molly's death unless she had already talked to Frank, and she'd already said she hadn't talked to him in a while. It was a thread he needed to pull, but not yet. He wanted to keep her talking and calling her out on it now would only cause her to lawyer up and end the interview.

"Frank only married her because she was young and beautiful."

There was that word again, *was*.

"But beauty fades." She gestured to her face. "I was young once, too, you know. And beautiful."

Vivian still was beautiful. Tyrone could only imagine what she'd looked like when she was young. She was probably a knockout.

"It truly is best that she died young. What's that saying *only the good die young?* That phrase is used when referring to men. For women, it should be *only the beautiful die young*. Because think about it, Molly will always be remembered as this stunning twenty-something with perky breasts and flawless skin. She'll never grow old and wrinkled."

That was one way to look at it, Tyrone supposed, but he doubted that Molly or her children would agree. "How do you know Molly is dead?" At this point, she'd spoken too directly to skirt the question anymore.

"It's a deduction," Vivian said, waving a dismissive hand. "That girl has been missing since February. And you know what the weather is like in February. Dreadful."

Tyrone had assumed Iowa weather would be better than it was in Chicago, but he'd been wrong. It was bitter cold in winter, often dipping down to negative temperatures and negative double-digit wind chills. There were days that a person could get frostbite by standing unprotected in the cold for five minutes.

"I understand that," Tyrone said, "but Molly doesn't have to be outside. She could have taken a long vacation to Florida or Arizona."

"Oh, sure she *could* have, but she didn't. Like I said, Molly was a dimwitted moron. There is no way she could possibly devise a plan to leave without a trace. Where's she getting her money? Where did she go? Who is she with? She's beautiful, but she's no mastermind."

"Maybe someone else was the mastermind. Maybe she ran off with a lover."

"I see what you mean. You are right about a lover. She was having an affair."

Tyrone blinked. "Molly was having an affair. With who?"

"Mike Malone."

"Angel Malone's husband?"

"The one and only."

Angel's husband was missing, too. His missing person file was probably even thinner than Molly's. The Chief hadn't even assigned an officer to the case. Nobody seemed to be worried about the guy, so law enforcement wasn't worried either.

"Could they have run off together, Molly and Mike?"

"Doubtful. Mike doesn't have Frank Sand money. And Molly likes money." She paused, pressing her full lips together. "But it's possible."

Tyrone knew that Molly was no longer off honeymooning somewhere with her new lover, but that didn't mean it hadn't started that way. Molly could have run off with Mike, expecting happily ever after. The excitement and newness would eventually wear off, and the relationship might have soured, causing Mike to get rid of her. But then where was Mike? Was he a murderer on the run, a potential victim, or unconnected?

"Then there are the children. I have exactly zero respect for Molly, but she did seem to love them. I don't think she would leave without them."

Tyrone's thoughts strayed to his own mother. He, too, was a child when she disappeared. A memory of her reading to him at night, kissing him on the top of the head, and telling him to *nighty night, sleep tight, don't let the bedbugs bite* drifted to the forefront of his mind. A faded memory, but it was all he had left of her. She had loved him. She wouldn't have left him.

"Motherhood was all she had," Vivian said, cutting through Tyrone's thoughts.

"Right, okay," Tyrone said shaking his head. "So, you're assuming Molly is dead."

Vivian had sounded far more confident than someone who had merely deduced a fact. It seemed like Vivian *knew* of Molly's death. He could have grilled her about it, but he decided against it. He still needed information from her and alienating her would not further his investigation.

"What about your son, Frankie Junior. What's his relationship with Frank Senior?"

Vivian pursed her lips again, holding them together for a second before she allowed them to pop back out. "Frankie's relationship with his father is complicated."

"How so?"

"Frank has not been there for Frankie. Then he had those two little brats with Molly, and he's around even less. Frankie hadn't thought it possible for his father to become worse, but he did. After the birth of those two, Frankie was nothing but an afterthought, if that. But he is Frank's namesake. Frank should be paying him all the attention."

"I see," Tyrone said. "Do you have an address for Frankie Junior? I would like to talk to him about his father."

"Sure," Vivian picked up her phone. It was the newest edition iPhone with a crystal encrusted case. She pressed a manicured figure against the screen a few times, then recited Frankie's address.

"Thank you," Tyrone said, rising to his feet. "I think that's all I'll need for now. I might be back with more questions, but you were very helpful."

"Anytime, officer," Vivian said, twisting a lock of hair around her finger.

He wasn't an officer, he was a detective, but he didn't correct her. Instead, he thanked her again for her time, then left through the front door. Once in the car, he inputted Frankie Junior's address into his GPS and backed out of Vivian's driveway. The kid lived in Ames, a nearby college town.

As Tyrone made his way through the winding streets of Whispering Pines and past the empty gatehouse, he thought about his interviews with Frankie Junior's parents. Neither of them seemed like genuine or honest people. He wondered if Frankie Junior would be like his parents, smoke and mirrors, or if he would be willing to divulge all of Frank Sand's darkest secrets. There was only one way to find out.

19

MOLLY

Molly didn't live life. She wasn't an active participant. Her days were planned, prepared in advance by Frank. She had a schedule and she stuck to it, day after day after day. A hamster caught in a wheel, running because it wouldn't stop spinning, spinning because she couldn't stop running. She arrived at the gym at her regular time, stepping through the front doors at ten-thirty sharp.

Riley was working the front desk. She scanned her card, and the computer issued a loud *beep.*

Riley smiled, a bright toothy smile aimed at her. "Good morning, Molly."

Molly looked at him, wondering how this child had the gall to speak to her in the same chipper way as always, as though he hadn't gone to her husband and told on her. He was a snitch. A phrase from her childhood, her old life, came back to her. *Snitches get stitches.*

She wasn't one for violence, and she'd never understood why her old neighborhood took the saying so seriously, but she did now. Riley deserved punishment. He had betrayed her confidence. But she wasn't that same girl. She was somehow more and less than she'd been back then.

"Is everything alright?" Riley asked. A bead of sweat formed on his brow.

Anxiety wafted from him. It was an intoxicating feeling, the power that came from another person's anxiety. She'd caused it. A week ago, she would have felt bad, but not anymore. She was tired of men. Tired of labels. She was eye candy to them. A thing to watch, not a person with feelings and emotions.

Riley tugged at the collar of his Under Armour t-shirt. "Have I done something wrong?"

Molly turned and walked past him without saying a word. He knew what he'd done. She wasn't going to explain it to him, and she wasn't going to give him an opportunity to apologize. He could fuck off with his apologies. In fact, all men could fuck off with everything. She set her keys and bag in the locker room and headed for the free weight equipment, ignoring the eyes that tracked her as she passed.

She selected two ten-pound dumbbells and took a couple steps back from the mirror, but before she could start on her first set of curls, she saw Mike Malone approaching her from behind. She met his gaze in the mirror and held it. An invitation. A sly smile spread across his lips. He stopped directly behind her, close enough that she could feel his breath on her neck. She didn't flinch.

"You started without your trainer," Mike whispered in her ear.

She shrugged.

"That was bad. You're a bad girl."

"Maybe I need punishment."

Mike's smile grew wider. "Maybe you do." He licked his lips, then took a step back. "But first, we work out."

"First things first."

Their banter was both dangerous and freeing. It transported her back to her teenage years, before Frank, before children. Back before she'd traded freedom for security. When she had complete autonomy over her body, over her life. They stood side by side and started a lifting regimen with free-weights. Mike used fifty-pound weights; she kept the tens. As they got into a rhythm, she turned the conversation to something more practical.

"What is it like to be married to a lawyer?" she asked.

"Solitary confinement." He started Arnold presses and she followed.

"What do you mean?"

"I'm stuck. I can't get out of the marriage because all the lawyers within a three-hour radius know my wife. I've tried sitting with four already. As soon as they learned my wife's name, they were out."

"Wow. That sucks."

"Yeah."

They finished the first set of Arnold presses and set the weights down for a few minutes of rest.

"Why solitary? What's so solitary about it?" Molly asked.

"Angel is gone all the time. Her whole life is work and the children. And she's turning the girls into tiny versions of herself, which means they're starting to hate me."

"Oh."

It was kind of genius, Angel's ability to control her husband without micromanaging his movements. To centralize control, Angel had to be meticulous, ruthless, and cunning, all things that made for wins in the courtroom, but did not translate into happiness in the home life.

"Plank rows," Mike said.

He dropped into a plank position, and she did the same. The mirror that low was blocked by two rows of dumbbells, and Molly was thankful for it. The position would have given Mike a perfect view down her workout top. Exercise clothing was already so tight that it didn't leave much to the imagination, there was no need for a bonus view.

"Have you learned anything about divorce proceedings from her? I know you aren't a lawyer, but..."

This line of conversation was a bit of a long shot for Molly. Frank didn't discuss his businesses with her—he didn't discuss much of anything with her—and theirs was the only marriage she had as a reference.

"Angel doesn't talk to me anymore. Not about anything."

They had that in common. Molly stopped rowing and pushed herself up so that she was on her knees with her backside resting on her heels. Their marriages seemed to have quite a lot in common.

"In the early years, though," Mike said as he continued rowing with one hand, then switched to the other, "we talked all the time. I picked up a thing or two. What do you want to know?" He finished his set and moved into a seated position.

They were side by side and too low to see one another in the mirror. She doubted the cameras could pick them up at this angle either. It was sheltering, a respite from the eyes that constantly followed her.

"If I divorced Frank, would I really get nothing?"

"Do you have a prenup?"

"I knew it." Molly's heart sank. "Yes, and Frank has always said I would get nothing, but I thought maybe he was just saying that to keep me where he wants me."

"He is."

"Wait, what?" Molly turned to face Mike. He was looking at her with an intensity that she couldn't decipher. It sent a chill up her spine, part excitement and part trepidation. "What do you mean?"

"Prenups don't mean you won't get anything. How long have you been married?"

"Ten years."

"You can't touch anything he had before you were married, but anything purchased with marital assets, meaning money made while you were married, is subject to a fifty-percent split. That includes all income made during the marriage. Arguably, you'd get more because you rely on him."

"Oh."

"And he'd have to pay you spousal support."

"Spousal support?"

"Alimony. I don't know how long he'd have to pay, but it would have to be long enough for you to get back on your feet. I would guess it would be at least five years."

"But what about the kids?"

"What about the kids?"

"Can he take them?"

"Who takes care of them now?"

"I do."

"Then I wouldn't worry about that," Mike said, pushing himself to his feet. "Courts prefer a fifty-fifty split, if the Angel from five years ago can be believed, and she was pretty honest back then, but a traditional marriage like yours would likely have the kids placed in your care."

"If it is fifty-fifty, would he have to pay child support?"

Depending on the amount of spousal support, she would likely be able to support herself and the kids on a budget, but she'd need some help with childcare, at least during the days when she was taking classes. Because she *would* go back to school. She was good with people—when Frank allowed her around people—and she wanted to do something helpful. Nursing might be a good option.

"Unless Frank got the kids—and he wouldn't in your scenario—he would have to pay you *something* in child support. Even with shared care. It would be less than if you had full custody. I don't know how much less, but I know it would be less."

"Oh."

A torrent of emotions passed through her. Anger. Frustration. Embarrassment. Relief. Frank had been lying to her, and she'd simply accepted his lies as though they were truth. But he'd never been truthful with anyone if there was a benefit to lying. She could file for divorce, and she would get something. She'd get a lot more than something. She'd get rid of Frank, and she could still survive and take care of the kids. Divorce was a win-win scenario for her.

"Are you thinking about filing for divorce?"

Molly shrugged, her shoulders lifting and lowering. "Maybe."

"You shouldn't have the same problems finding a lawyer. Most of the attorneys around here hate Angel. They're all chomping at the bit to get back at her for wins she's had in the past."

Molly hoped he was right because Angel would be in her husband's corner. "So, why wouldn't they take you on as a client?"

"Conflict of interest. They have pending cases against Angel. They don't want Angel to take her anger out on them or their clients for representing me."

A bell started to chime above their heads. It was the five-minute warning for Molly's aerobics class. But she had one more thing to do before class started. She'd come to the gym with a plan to get back at Frank. Knowing the information that she knew now about divorce almost made her change her mind. She had other forms of recourse with Frank, but Mike had given her all this information at no cost. He deserved a reward.

"I have this friend," Molly said, swallowing hard to push down the butterflies flitting around her chest. "He has an empty house, a townhome."

Mike raised an eyebrow.

She reached into a side pocket of her yoga pants and produced a slip of paper. "This is the address. Meet me there. Four-thirty today?"

A smile spread across Mike's face. "I wouldn't miss it for the world."

They both stood, coming out of their cave of privacy, and moved to return their weights to their proper location. Molly set the weights on the rack and then turned to see eyes locked on her. It was Vivian, Frank's first ex-wife. She didn't look away or even attempt to pretend she hadn't been watching Molly and Mike. A flash of irritation ran up Molly's spine. She hadn't done anything wrong—at least not yet—and still she was under strict scrutiny by everyone in town.

Look all you want. Molly didn't care anymore. Frank's threats of destitution after divorce were all lies.

Instead of breaking Vivian's gaze and running to the aerobics room with her head down, she held it. *Let her tell Frank.*

A small smile formed on Vivian's lips. They stood like that for a long moment, then Vivian nodded. A gesture of approval or a challenge? Molly didn't know, but she was certain she'd find out.

20

ANGEL

Mike was going to retaliate, Angel knew it, but when? She'd spent the afternoon wound tight, waiting for a response. He would be irate when he learned she'd moved the money to a private account. She'd expected him to call and shout *where's the money*, but her phone didn't ring. There were no texts either. Nothing. She was prepared for the fight. But this, this radio silence, she didn't know what to do with it.

She grabbed her phone for what felt like the hundredth time that afternoon. The screen lit up. Still, nothing. There were no new notifications. *What is he doing?* She had no idea.

Pulling up the messaging app, she clicked on her husband's icon. It was still labeled *Hubby* with a picture of the two of them together during their honeymoon, back in the days when she'd believed she was in love.

What a joke. She had never been in love with Mike. He was her silver medal, plated and flaking, now baring the ugliness beneath. She sighed and ran her hand along the scar on her cheek, the physical reminder of the true love that she had lost. Tom.

She'd been in the car with Tom that fateful day. They'd been on their way back from visiting a friend at the *Flat Tire Lounge* in Madrid, Iowa, a small town along the popular High Trestle Trail bike path. They'd had a few drinks each, but she wasn't drunk, and neither was he, or so she'd thought. The autopsy report had showed something very different. Antidepressants. She hadn't known he'd been taking anything like that, but he was. It interacted with the alcohol, increasing his intoxication level.

Tom was driving. Why hadn't she insisted on driving? She was fine. Why hadn't she noticed his condition? She should have been more aware. A good person would have seen, understood the situation before it was too late. She was not a good person. Why did he have to die, he was such a good man, when men like Mike and Frank went on living their lives? This was the dark game she often played inside her mind. The *what if, what if, what if,* thought patterns that threatened her sanity.

The girls, she reminded herself, pulling her thoughts back to the present. She had to move forward. She couldn't shrink into the depths of despair. Her girls relied on her to take care of them. Mike wouldn't do it.

Angel's gaze refocused on Mike's icon on her phone. She clicked on it and erased "Hubby," replacing it with "Steroid mother fucker." She'd never found anything illegal like performance enhancing drugs in the house, but she wasn't an idiot. Nobody gained that kind of weight that fast with only whey powder.

She next deleted the picture of herself and Mike, leaving an empty circle with SMF in the middle. *There.* It was a bit of an electronic tantrum, but it made her feel a little better. She went back to the meager thread of messages between her and her husband. They didn't communicate often. When they did, it was mundane information delivered icily. Things like, *There are no band-aids. Gretty cut her finger and needs one. Why didn't you get them last time I asked?*

Angel navigated to the empty message box, clicking on it. The curser blinked, ready for her to write *something*. But what would she say? Should she create an excuse for him to look at the bank accounts? She couldn't think of a reason to guide him there without simply coming out and telling the truth. She didn't want to do that either.

"There's no point," Angel said to herself, lowering the phone and placing it back on her desk. She would wait him out. Either he knew and he was intentionally ignoring her, or he didn't know, and the fight was yet to come.

At five-forty-five, her cell phone began to ring. It was a local number; one she didn't have saved. That usually meant a new potential client who had received Angel's information from a former or current client recommending her services.

She clicked the green icon and brought the phone to her ear. "This is Angel Malone."

"Hello, Angel, this is Katrina from Future Academy Learning Center."

"Oh." It was the girls' daycare. "Is everything alright?"

"Yes and no."

A shot of fear ran up Angel's spine. "Did something happen?"

"No."

Relief spread through her, but it was short-lived. The school was calling for a reason. "What's wrong then?"

"Your husband has not come to pick up the girls. The center closed fifteen minutes ago. He's the primary phone number on the account, so I've been calling him. He isn't answering."

"I am so sorry," Angel said, shooting to her feet and grabbing her coat. "I'm on my way. Give me five minutes, I'll come get them."

"Thank you. Get here in five minutes and we can waive some of the late fee."

"Thank you, thank you," Angel said, hanging up and running toward the door.

"Why the rush?" George said, coming out of his office.

"Mike didn't pick up the girls. They are stuck there, and daycare charges $50 for every five minutes a parent is late."

George whistled. "That's bad. I hope something hasn't happened to Mike."

"Bye," Angel said, leaving through the door and trying not to slam it behind her.

If something hadn't happened to Mike, it was about to. This was his response to her moving the money. The answer to his silence. He would simply rack up bills in other ways. Bills *she* would have to pay. It was a power move, one designed to cut her to the core. She arrived at the school within the allotted five minutes, coming inside to find Gretty and Lily sitting at the front desk with Katrina, coloring. They all looked up when she entered.

"Mommy," Gretty shouted, running to her, and throwing her arms around Angel's legs.

Lily said nothing, but hugged Angel on the other side. Both girls' eyes were red rimmed and puffy from crying. Angel's blood boiled. Mike could do what he wanted to her, but his behaviors were harming the girls. Maybe that's what he wanted.

"Daddy forgot us," Gretty said, stepping back and looking up at Angel. "Maybe you should start picking us up."

"Daddy and Mommy will discuss it, but that's probably what will happen."

Angel would have to move some things around in her schedule to make a five-thirty pickup time work, but it was for the best. If Mike did file for divorce, she would want primary care. She needed to start gathering evidence to prove that she could juggle a high-powered job and single motherhood. Otherwise, she'd lose the girls to Mike. At least from the outside, he appeared to be the primary caretaker.

"Is Mike okay?" Katrina asked. "This has never happened before."

"He's fine. He's just caught a touch of the flu." A little white lie never hurt anyone. "You know how men are when they get sick. *Such* babies. He fell asleep and didn't wake up until a few minutes ago."

"Oh, good. I was worried," Katrina said, placing a hand to her chest. "Well, considering the circumstances, I'm willing to waive the late fee this one time."

"Thank you, thank you," Angel said. "That is so kind."

"Yes, well, your girls were not all that much work. I'm just glad something more serious didn't happen."

Something more serious hadn't happened. At least not yet, but Angel was ready to kill him once she got home. She pushed the thought from her mind and looked down at her girls. They were still clutching her legs.

"We better get moving. We shouldn't keep you any longer. The girls need dinner anyway, and you've got your own family to care for." Angel forced her voice to come out smooth as honey all while rage ripped through her. After saying goodbye, she rushed the girls out to the car and clicked them into their car seats.

"Did you bring a snack?" Gretty asked.

"No, honey. Daddy was supposed to pick you up, so I wasn't prepared."

"Do you have our iPads?"

Angel started the car and backed out, gripping the steering wheel tight. "Again, same answer, honey."

"Daddy better be in trouble," Gretty said.

Angel glanced in the rearview mirror to see Gretty cross her arms and look out the window, a pout on her lips. Lily mimicked her sister's behavior, but she looked more sad than mad. As Angel drove, she called Mike over and over again. His phone rang the first few times, then started going straight to voicemail.

That mother fucker is ignoring my calls.

Then she saw it. There, on the side of Main Street was Mike's car. It was parked at a duplex. The place was crappy. It couldn't be worth more than one hundred thousand dollars. There was no mistaking the silver Lexus with a vanity plate reading *MUSCLE*.

Who lives there? Angel wondered, staring at her husband's vehicle parked in an unfamiliar driveway.

A horn sounded behind her, pulling her out of her stupor. She was on a busy road, moving at a speed barely above a crawl. She pulled off to the shoulder and grabbed a legal pad, writing down the address. Then she snapped a picture of Mike's Lexus in the driveway.

Angel would find out who lived there, and she would find a way to use it against Mike. The other shoe was about to drop, but this time, she would be prepared. She would wait until the best time and place to cause the most damage. If it was games he wanted to play, he would soon learn she was no amateur player.

21

TYRONE

Summers in college towns were disturbingly quiet. They were like a corpse at an open casket funeral, lifelike, but unnaturally still.

Tyrone couldn't help thinking of tumbleweeds and ghost towns as he drove through the empty streets of Ames, Iowa, headed for the address Vivian Sand had provided for her son Frankie. He pulled into the driveway for a large house with six different mailboxes out front. A once grand home broken into separate apartments. It was typical of college towns, and it was common in Chicago. A splash of normalcy in the unnerving silence.

He got out of his unmarked cruiser and stepped onto the front porch. There were two mailboxes to the left of the front door, one right beside it, and a third mailbox to the right. The mailboxes to the left had an arrow indicating that the entrances were to the side of the house. The one mailbox on the other side had an arrow pointing the other direction.

Tyrone shuddered at the thought of using the narrow path between the side of the house and the homes beside it. He was claustrophobic and he had no idea what he was walking into. Frankie Sand could be a psychopath and a killer.

Apartment three, Vivian said apartment three, Tyrone thought, scanning the numbers on the mailbox. The middle mailbox contained a large number three on it, and Tyrone exhaled heavily. It looked like he wasn't going to have to shimmy around the building.

He stepped up to what had once been the front door to the residence and knocked three times. Then he waited. A rustling sound came from within. Someone was home. He was just about to knock again when he heard a voice.

"Coming, coming."

Tyrone lowered his hand and waited. A few moments passed and then there was the sound of a chain sliding out of place and a deadbolt clicking. The door swung open, and a young man stood in front of Tyrone. He looked far too young to be living on his own.

"Umm, hi," the kid said.

"Are you Frankie Sand?"

"Depends on who's asking."

"I am," Tyrone said.

"Alright, yeah." Frankie chuckled. "I've always wanted to say that." There was a dull look in the kid's eyes and a cloud of smoke drifted out the door.

"I figured."

"Why are you looking for me?"

The kid had the door wide open. Tyrone could see past him and into the residence. The place was small, but fully furnished. There was an L-shaped brown leather couch sitting atop an expensive looking Oriental rug. It was furniture far better than the standard college kid had. Tyrone guessed Frankie's mother had everything to do with that.

"I'm a detective with the Fort Calhoun Police Department," Tyrone flashed his badge. "I was wondering if you had some time to speak with me about Molly."

"I, uh," Frankie's eyes darted from left to right and a thin sheet of sweat formed along his brow line.

"If you're worried about the smell, I'm not here for that. I don't even have jurisdiction."

The kid visibly relaxed. The place reeked of marijuana.

"How about we talk on the porch. Will that make you more comfortable?"

Frankie nodded and stepped out, pulling the door closed behind him.

There was a set of mismatched patio furniture at one side of the large front porch. "Can we sit over there or does that belong to someone else?"

"We can sit there. One of the neighbors set it out to encourage 'communication.'" He used air quotes around the word *communication*.

"I take it you aren't into communicating," Tyrone said, making his way toward the furniture and sitting in the least dusty chair.

"I mean, I'm not against it. I'm just not good at it." Frankie's hair was short, but it was longer in front so a lock of hair kept falling over his eye, causing him to brush it aside. He shoved his hands into his pockets and walked over to Tyrone, sitting in the chair across from him.

"You're awfully young to be living on your own."

"I'm eighteen."

"Most eighteen-year-olds live with their parents until the start of the school year."

"I'm not most eighteen-year-olds."

"I can see that."

There was a short silence, then Frankie sighed heavily. "I don't have a home. At least, I've never really felt like I had a home. You've met my mom, right?"

Tyrone nodded.

"And my dad?"

He nodded again.

"They are obsessed with themselves and with money. Nobody paid attention to where I was going or what I was doing. When I was barely a teenager, I rebelled, but I quickly realized there was no point. Nobody would punish me. If I got into real trouble, they'd swoop in and solve the problem, but they weren't doing it for me. They did it for themselves, their image."

Tyrone nodded, an acknowledgement he was listening, but he did not interrupt.

"There was no point in rebelling, so I focused on school instead. I kept my head down, worked hard, and finished with straight A's. Now I'm here," he gestured around him, "and I don't have to worry about them anymore. I'm invisible by choice, not by circumstance."

"You chose to live in an apartment, not the dorms."

"I couldn't move into the dorms until school started, and like I said, I wasn't going to wait. I found this apartment and took it."

"How do you plan to meet people?"

Frankie shrugged. "I don't care."

"Do you have a job?"

"I have better. I have a trust fund." There was a short pause. "You said you were here about Molly," Frankie said, his eyes flashing when he said his stepmother's name.

"Yes."

"Is there any news?"

"I'm new to the investigation. I'm here to learn what I can about the case." It wasn't a lie, but it wasn't exactly the truth, either. Tyrone didn't like it, but intentional omissions and occasional fibs were necessary tools for some investigations. "Can you tell me a little about your stepmother?"

"Don't call her that."

"What?"

"Don't call Molly that. She's only ten years older than me." The kid's hands tightened at his sides, rolling into fists.

"That bothers you," Tyrone said.

"Well, yeah. We are far closer in age than my dad and her."

Tyrone lifted his eyebrows.

"The age difference is disgusting. She was eighteen when they got married. Eighteen. My age. He was already an old man by then."

Frank Sand had been thirty-eight when he married Molly, not much older than Tyrone was at that moment. Tyrone did not like to consider himself an "old man," but he supposed he probably did seem old to a kid Frankie's age. He certainly had no interest in eighteen-year-old girls. Like Frankie, they seemed like children.

"And she had worked for him. He was her boss. He sexually harassed her. That's what we would call it these days. Back then, they just called it business."

"You think your dad harassed Molly before they were married?"

"Harassed her *into* marriage is more like it."

"Why do you think that?"

"I don't think it. I know it."

"How?"

"Molly told me."

Tyrone blinked several times. "You're telling me that your stepmother confided in you, her stepson, about her marriage with your father."

"Stop saying that. My Molly confided in me, yes."

"*Your* Molly?"

"Yes." Frankie crossed his arms, looking the picture of the petulant child. "My dad wanted her only for her body. I wanted more. We had a connection. I cared about her mind, her soul."

"Okay..."

"You've seen pictures of her, I'm sure," he met Tyrone's gaze. "Everyone has. She's been splashed all over the news for months now. She's beautiful. Every inch of her is a piece of art. It's like, I can't explain it, but when I look at her, I see perfection."

The kid had a problem. He was far past infatuated. He was obsessed.

"And it isn't just her outward beauty," he continued. "She is a genuine person. She has a kind heart. My mom thinks she's stupid, and maybe she is, but she didn't get to go to college or learn past high school, thanks to my dad."

"You and Molly weren't," Tyrone paused, trying to think of the least offensive way of saying it, "involved, were you?"

"Involved?"

"Sexually involved."

"No," Frankie said, but he would not meet Tyrone's gaze.

Tyrone's mind flashed back to when his mother was still alive. A white man, probably close to Frankie's age had come by their apartment on several occasions. He worked in a building somewhere near Tyrone's mother's job. Tyrone was too young for his mother to confide in him, but he could sense her anxiety every time he knocked on the door, bringing her back some item she hadn't remembered losing. He'd told the police about the man, but they'd never questioned him. They'd never even learned his name. Was Frankie and Molly's relationship like that?

"Molly would never have done something like that," Frankie said, cutting through Tyrone's thoughts.

Tyrone raised an eyebrow.

"She isn't a cheater. My dad is the cheater."

"How are you so certain?"

"I just am."

"Have you heard anything from Molly since February?"

Molly was dead and officers recovered her cell phone out on that farm, discarded near the pig pen. It was in evidence, the data being downloaded by someone in the criminalistics laboratory as they spoke, so Frankie couldn't have received anything within the last day or two. But Molly had been missing for a long time. If Frankie had heard from her at some point, it would help pinpoint her time of death, whether it was before or after she was tossed in with the pigs.

"I haven't heard anything," he crossed his arms and rolled his shoulders into a deep hunch.

Is that evasiveness or sadness I'm sensing? Tyrone couldn't tell.

"You know what happened to her, don't you?" Frankie asked.

The silence hung in the air, stretching long between them, exposing the questions and doubts wedged between them. It was a question posed in a way that exposed nothing of Frankie's knowledge but placed Tyrone directly in the hotseat. Tyrone had underestimated the kid. He was not a naïve child. Child, perhaps, but not naïve.

"I don't know what happened to her," Tyrone said. Again, it was not a lie or the truth. Frankie hadn't asked if Molly was dead. That, Tyrone knew. But he *didn't* know how or when her murder had happened. Which meant his answer to Frankie's question could easily and honestly be *no*.

"Do you know what happened to her?" Tyrone asked. They had entered a sort of dance. Like boxers, they were parrying around one another, looking for an opening to strike.

Frankie flinched. "No. Why would you ask that?"

There was genuine hurt in his eyes. Or at least something that resembled genuine pain. Tyrone had learned long ago that people, even kids, could be actors of Oscar-winning proportions when necessary. "I just want the truth."

"If you want the truth, you should talk to Nolan."

"The au pair?"

"The old au pair. He disappeared at the same time as Molly. Find him and you'll find her. I guarantee it."

Wrong, Tyrone thought.

At least he hoped the kid was wrong. They hadn't found much of Molly. Blood, hair, her purse, her cell phone, a high-heeled shoe, and her identification, but the rest, that had been devoured by pigs. If Nolan was in that pig pen with her, the swine had left no trace of him. That would be a tragedy and a mystery that police would never solve.

"Nolan is obsessed with Molly."

That sounded rich coming from this kid. But the phrase *it takes one to know one* wasn't a completely off base childhood retort. Many sayings like that were rooted in truth, that's why they carried on generation after generation.

"He was always with her. She could hardly breathe without Nolan rushing to her side asking if she needed something."

That didn't sound all that bad to Tyrone, but the way Frankie had said it, you'd think he was describing a bout of domestic violence.

"Where can I find Nolan?"

"I don't know." Frankie ran a hand through his hair. "Dad fired him the same day Molly disappeared."

"He fired him?" Tyrone repeated. That would indicate that Frank senior knew that Molly would go missing and wanted to get rid of the person closest to her as well.

"Well, I don't know when, exactly, he fired him. It could have been after he stopped showing up to work. I just know that after Molly was gone, I never saw Nolan again."

"What do you know about the new au pair?"

"Rebecca?"

"Yeah."

"She looks like a younger version of Molly, but she is no Molly."

"What do you mean by that?"

"Nobody can replace Molly."

That wasn't a helpful answer. "How are they different, Rebecca and Molly?"

"Molly is kind. She's a good person with a beautiful heart. Rebecca is just like everyone else."

"What is 'everyone else' like?"

"Assholes."

Most people *were* assholes, but Tyrone tried not to curse. White people could use words like that to emphasize a point, but if he cursed while on the job, he'd be the angry black man.

"I'll try to track Nolan down," Tyrone said.

Frankie nodded, seemingly satisfied.

"That's all I have for now," Tyrone said as he stood and stretched. "I'll be in touch if I have any more questions." He slid his business card across the table. It was off-white cardstock with his name, cell phone number, his position, and a picture of the Fort Calhoun Police Department Badge. "If you think of anything more you want to tell me, go ahead and give me a ring."

Frankie Junior accepted the card and slipped it into his back pocket. "Will do."

He left with Frankie still standing on the porch, watching his retreating form. Tyrone didn't have to turn around, he could feel the kid's intense gaze boring into him. Frankie had referred to Molly in present tense the entire interview, which was the opposite of his mother. Tyrone wondered if it was an act. The kid's obsession with his stepmother was alarming.

Frankie was highly intelligent, that was certain. The question was whether a sleeping killer lurked beneath that childish frame, waiting to reawaken, much like the sleeping college town he currently inhabited. If so, Tyrone had a month to solve this case before the college students returned and Frankie found another girl to obsess over and kill.

22

ANGEL

Past
February 2

The nightly routine was Mike's one and only obligation. He had never enjoyed caring for the girls, but he had cared about them. That had shifted. It was like he'd woken up and decided, *I don't want to be a dad anymore.* And that was it. He was done.

Was he going through a midlife crisis? He wasn't old enough for that. They weren't even forty yet. Mid-life was fifty, wasn't it? Crisis or not, caring for kids after a full day of work was her reality, her new normal.

"Dad doesn't let us have peanut butter," Gretty said. Her eyes were locked on Angel's hands as she spread the thick butter-like substance across a piece of keto-friendly bread.

"Dad's not here," Angel said.

They had stopped at the small neighborhood grocery store on the way home, zipping down the health food aisles, shoving anything diabetic friendly and easy to make into her cart. That list included all kinds of Mike non-approved items, like Lunchables, peanut butter sandwiches, and high protein chocolate bars. If he wasn't around to help, his opinion didn't matter.

"Where is Daddy?" Lily asked, joining her sister at the island. Her voice was always softer than her sister's, more subdued and introspective.

"That's a good question." Angel's gaze strayed to the ornate clock mounted on the kitchen wall. It was beautifully crafted with roman numerals, but it was more art than function. The thing was damn near impossible to read. She shook her head and looked at her Apple watch. It was just shy of seven in the evening.

"Is Daddy in trouble?" Gretty asked.

Angel thought of the mountain of work waiting for her attention. She couldn't start on it until both girls were tucked into bed. First, they needed to finish eating and then take baths. She would check Lily's blood sugar and give her an insulin shot, if needed. She'd have to read several bedtime stories and wait in the rocking chair until they fell asleep. The evening seemed endless. She wouldn't be getting much sleep herself.

"If he isn't, he should be," Gretty added.

"Oh, he's in trouble," Angel confirmed. "He's in very big trouble."

"You're not going to kill him, are you?" Lily asked, her voice small. "You'll go to jail if you do. I don't want you to go to jail."

"What?" Angel was leaning up against the counter picking at her nails, she stopped and met her daughter's gaze. "Why would you think that?"

Lily shrugged her little shoulders. "Because you fight a lot."

"Fighting doesn't lead to killing."

"It does on TV," Lily said.

Angel was going to have to stop watching the news around them. "Listen, honey," Angel slid onto the stool beside Lily, "everything is going to be fine. You don't need to worry about anything."

Lily nodded.

"Why not?" Gretty interjected.

"Because you are kids, and we are parents. All you need to worry about is eating your dinner, getting a good night's sleep, and learning as much as you can at pre-K tomorrow."

"I already know a lot," Gretty said.

"You can always learn more. Now," she gestured to the girls' plates, "finish up and we'll start a bath."

Angel stepped out of the room while the girls focused on eating, bringing her cell phone along with her. She dialed Mike's number on repeat, trying and failing to get him to answer. It rang and eventually went to voicemail on the first ten or so times, then switched to immediately going to voicemail. His phone was off. Again. She didn't leave any messages. Voicemails were digital records, and she couldn't trust herself to keep her temper in check.

Minute by minute as the clock ticked forward, her fury grew. By eight, baths were finished, and the girls were dressed in pajamas, but still no Mike. By nine, the girls were in their beds, and she was irate. She couldn't sit back and do nothing anymore, twiddling her thumbs, waiting for him to return.

If he wants to play games, then so be it, Angel thought. *I'll play games, and I aim to win.*

Once the girls were finally asleep, she stepped out of their room and pulled the door shut behind her. Then she settled down at her laptop at the kitchen island, pulling out the notepad where she'd written the address to that dingy duplex. She opened the Iowa land records website and searched the address. A name popped up, *Bernice Weise*. She didn't recognize it, and the last title transfer was in the sixties.

That doesn't make sense. Why would Mike visit an old lady? Unless...

Angel googled Bernice's full name. A news article popped up, showing an old woman holding up a pie. The article was from six months ago, and it announced Bernice as the winner of the local retirement home's bake-off. She was in a retirement home, so she wasn't living in the duplex anymore. In the image, there were two other people standing next to Bernice, one on each side. Molly Sand and Nolan Weise.

Bingo.

Angel did not *know* what Mike was doing with Nolan or Molly. But after years in family law, watching families bend until they broke, she had a pretty good idea of what was happening. She grabbed her phone and googled "Fort Calhoun Police Department," looking for the non-emergency line to call. She had it within seconds and clicked the number.

The line rang two times, then a female voice answered. "Fort Calhoun Police Department. How can I help you?"

"Yes, hello," Angel spoke in her most innocent voice. "I'm calling to report a missing person."

"A missing person, you say?"

"Yes," Angel said. "My husband, Mike Malone."

"Is Mike short for Michael?"

"Yes."

"How old is Mr. Malone?"

Angel thought back to his last birthday. It was only a couple months ago. "He is thirty-one."

He was five years younger than her. When they'd married, people made jokes that she was *robbing the cradle*, but compared to Frank, who probably never got snide comments like that, there was barely an age difference.

"When did you last see him?"

"This morning, before I left for work."

"Is it possible he's out somewhere with friends?"

"No. He handles the nightly routine for our four-year-old twins. He failed to pick them up from daycare tonight and he hasn't been home at all. This is completely out of the ordinary for him."

"I'll send someone over," the woman said. She asked for Angel's address, and they ended the call.

Angel moved to the living room to wait for the officer to arrive. She'd meant to focus on her actual job once the girls were in bed, but she couldn't help herself. Mike was antagonizing her, and she felt weak if she didn't respond.

Everything about the evening had gone haywire. What was another couple of hours dealing with a cop? It would be worth it when the officer hauled Mike through the front door. He'd be furious. Probably angrier than she'd ever seen him, but she was fine with that. He'd pushed her and pushed her, and she'd allowed it. Not anymore. Her husband had chosen the wrong opponent.

23

TYRONE

Twenty-minutes had never seemed so long. The drive back to Fort Calhoun from Frankie Junior's apartment felt like an endless vortex of wasted time. Thoughts twisted through Tyrone's mind, a poisonous vine spreading with each passing moment.

His only assignment was Molly's murder, but every interview led nowhere, Frankie Junior's included. The kid was obsessed in an *if I can't have her, nobody can*, sort of way. It was motive, but for what? Did he truly want her dead? Maybe he had made an advance that was rebuffed. It could have been enough to set him off. But it was all conjecture. *What ifs* when criminal investigations spoke in certainties.

Tyrone's phone started buzzing on the seat next to him, causing him to jump. He picked it up. "Gully, here."

"Hey, Tyrone, it's Jackie."

"Tell me something good."

Jackie hesitated.

Tyrone sighed heavily. "No luck finding this Nolan guy?"

"I found some information."

It was not what he had hoped, but it was better than nothing. "What have you learned?"

"His last name is Weise. A lot of people think he's gay, but that's not strictly true. I found an ex-girlfriend and an ex-boyfriend, both from neighboring towns."

"He dated a man and a woman at the same time?"

"No. Different times."

"So, he's bi-sexual?" Tyrone said.

"Something like that. Nobody put a label on it, so I didn't either. I only dug up the two relationships. He's possibly had a few more, but they weren't significant enough for anyone to remember."

"Okay."

"I spoke with both of Nolan's exes."

"You did?" Tyrone straightened in his seat. "And..."

"One of them is Naomi White. Do you know her?"

"No." Tyrone wasn't new to Fort Calhoun anymore, but he didn't have a lot of free time. His only local connections were through work.

"She's a home health nurse," she said, pausing in a, *ringing any bells,* sort of way.

"I don't know when I would have come across a home health nurse." Tyrone was getting irritated.

"She volunteers at a lot of the local blood drives."

Tyrone did not like needles.

"Still nothing?" Jackie asked.

"No."

"Okay, well, never mind then. Naomi and the other ex is a guy, his name is Adam, they both described their breakups with Nolan as amicable. They remained friends and would talk often."

"Did they mention Nolan and Molly's relationship?"

"They both did." She paused.

"Don't leave me hanging here. What did they say?"

"They said Molly was nice, and Nolan liked her, even felt an obligation to her, but they were only friends."

Tyrone hated the term *nice*. It was not a personality trait. People tried to seem "nice" based on societal standards. It wasn't something they *were*.

"He wasn't interested in her as more than a friend?" Tyrone asked.

"They didn't seem to think so."

If Nolan's exes weren't jealous of Molly and Nolan's relationship, then there probably wasn't anything going on. Which meant that Frankie Junior had exaggerated, or he was trying to divert Tyrone's attention. Either way, it brought him higher on the suspect list.

"Do either of the exes know where Nolan is now?"

"They don't. They were both concerned."

"Why?"

"They heard from him regularly. Both said they'd talk on a weekly basis. But he hasn't made contact since Molly's disappearance. They've tried calling, but his phone goes straight to voicemail."

"Meaning it's dead." Tyrone hoped Nolan wasn't in the same condition.

"Yeah. Or it is off."

"Why didn't they report him as a missing person?"

"That's the thing," Jackie said. "They claim that they did. Nobody would talk to them about it."

Fury shot through Tyrone. It was so typical. Molly's picture was everywhere, but his fellow officers hadn't even cared about the bisexual man that disappeared along with her.

"They both mentioned that Nolan was afraid of Frank Sand," Jackie continued. "He didn't want to keep working there, but he loved the kids, and Molly was like a sister, so he couldn't leave."

Frank Sand was arrogant and overbearing, but this was the first time Tyrone had heard anyone describe him as physically frightening. "Did either of them tell you why Nolan was afraid?"

"No. They just said he hated being there when Frank was around, but he felt as though he had to be there."

That wasn't helpful. Tyrone needed specifics.

"Did you believe them?" Tyrone asked. He couldn't think of a motive for either of Nolan's exes to lie, but he still had to ask.

"I think so. Naomi was busy at work, so she was a little short with me, but I still believed her."

"Okay," Tyrone said.

"I'll keep working on tracking Nolan down." There was little hope in her voice.

Tyrone was thinking the same thing. *This is a bad sign.* Nolan was afraid of Frank Senior. He and Molly were inseparable. He went missing around the same time as Molly. Molly was dead. Nolan could very easily be the next body that they found. That, or the pigs ate every bit of him and he'd forever be one more name scrawled across the missing persons list.

"Any social media activity?" Tyrone asked, but he already knew the answer.

"No, not under his name, but he could have created new accounts."

"Okay. Keep looking on your end. I'm going to go to Frank Sand's house to see if I can talk to the new au pair, Rebecca."

"Alright. I'll keep you informed."

"Likewise."

They ended the call just as Tyrone was nearing the outskirts of Fort Calhoun. He'd input Frank Sand's address into his GPS before leaving Ames, and the thing was squawking at him, telling him that he was near. Then, he saw it.

The house was ostentatious. A huge monstrosity, built on an acreage just outside of town. It was a three-story brick structure with a main house and a separate structure to the side, connected by a breezeway. Tyrone had passed the place on the many trips home, but he'd never known who had lived in it. Now he knew. Frank Sand.

There was no gate or structure preventing Tyrone from taking the long driveway all the way up to the mansion. So, that's what he did. He turned off the gravel road and onto the smooth, paved driveway, never taking his eyes off the home. When he parked, he removed his keys from his vehicle and stepped out.

As he approached the front door, his cell phone buzzed. He stopped and looked at it. It was a text message from an unknown number.

Do you know what happened to her yet? The message read.

Tyrone assumed the texter was referring to Molly since that was the only case he was working, but it could be anyone, and they could be referring to anyone.

You'll have to be more specific. Tyrone typed back.

Molly. Do you know? The response came almost immediately.

Who is this? Tyrone sent the message, then waited. The response didn't come. He took a screen shot of the messages and texted them to Jackie, saying, *track this number. Let me know who it is.*

Okey Dokey, Jackie typed back.

He stood there and waited. Tracking numbers was one of the easier tasks for law enforcement so long as the person used a major cell phone carrier. Burner phones were far more complicated, but he hoped that wasn't the case here. It wasn't. A moment later, his phone buzzed with a message.

The number belongs to Vivian Sand.

That meant it could be Vivian or Frankie Junior. He doubted that Frankie was paying for his own phone line. Tyrone opened his notebook and flipped back to his notes from his meeting with Vivian. She'd given him her phone number—eagerly with a coquettish smile—and the texts had not come from it. That meant it was Frankie Junior or Vivian had a second number. But there was no reason for Vivian to go through the trouble of obtaining a second number for cryptic texts if she was going to use an account with her name on it.

What's the deal with the messages? Jackie texted.

I don't know, Tyrone responded. It could be innocent interest in the case, or it could be a killer trying to determine if it was time to skip town.

I thought you were meeting with Rebecca, Jackie typed.

I am, Tyrone responded. Then he pocketed his phone and refocused his attention back on Frank Sand's home.

The front door was inset with large, white columns wrapped in white-washed brick holding up the roof like two strong arms, the Greek myth of Atlas holding the sky. Two large windows stood on either side of the gleaming, wood front door. Tyrone considered ringing the doorbell but decided to knock instead.

A few moments passed, then two faces appeared on each side of the door, looking out the windows. A little boy and a little girl, possibly a year apart in age. Tyrone smiled and waved. They giggled and waved back. He suspected this was a game they often played with visitors.

"You two, get away from the door!" A female voice called from somewhere deeper within the house. The woman must have come closer, because she dropped her voice to a lower volume and Tyrone could still hear her. "What did I just tell you?"

"Someone's here," the little boy said.

"Get away from the door. Pretend we aren't home."

"The man already saw us," the girl said, her tone indignant.

"We aren't home," the woman called.

Tyrone fought the urge to roll his eyes. His gaze shifted to the camera mounted above his head, nestled between the roof overhang and the side of the house. Then he sighed and removed his badge from his back pocket. He was a detective, so he was in plain clothes. To that woman inside, he was just some black guy on her porch. No way was she opening the door.

He held the badge up to the camera and said, "I'm with the Fort Calhoun Police Department."

"Where is your uniform?" the woman called. She was closer, just on the other side of the door, but he couldn't see her. She was using the door as a shield.

"I'm a detective. I don't wear a uniform like beat cops."

The woman was silent for a long moment, then Tyrone heard a lock click and the door swung open. A beautiful girl no older than twenty stood in the doorway. She didn't look exactly like Molly Sand as Frankie Junior had suggested, but Rebecca did have some similarities. Her attractiveness was in a plastic, made up way. She wore lots of makeup and her lips were unnaturally full. Her hair was lighter than Molly's, but it was the same length and fell down her back in waves.

"Why didn't you announce yourself as a police officer?"

"I'm not an officer, I'm a detective."

"So, you don't have to knock on the door and shout *Police* like they do on TV?"

"No."

Tyrone thought of his conversation with Vivian Sand, how she had described Molly as unintelligent. He hadn't known Molly, but he would guess she wasn't quite as dense as this girl. If this was Frank's replacement for Molly, and all signs pointed to *yes*, then Vivian wasn't going to like her any more than she'd liked Molly. Probably less.

"Do you have a few minutes to talk?"

Rebecca looked uncertain. "Mr. Sand isn't home."

That was what Tyrone had hoped. Frank Senior would send him packing the moment he saw Tyrone. "It'll only take a few minutes."

"Okay." She opened the door wide, gesturing for him to enter. "I don't see the harm in that."

There was plenty of potential harm if you looked at it from Frank Sand's perspective, but Tyrone was not going to point that out to Rebecca. She could be a treasure trove of information. He could only hope, because they were running out of time. The news of Molly's death would break tomorrow. Then the torrent of tips would come flooding in. Ninety-nine percent of them would be bogus, but he'd still have to check. Today his investigation was his own. Tomorrow, it would become a circus. He needed to solve this thing, and now, but he was nowhere near finding the truth.

24

ANGEL

Past
February 2

Lights entered the driveway, two wide beams pulling off the road, arching their way toward the house. Angel glanced at her watch. She'd called the police department less than five minutes ago. Did they respond to non-emergency calls that quickly? Or was it Mike returning home?

What if they both show up at the same time? She'd look like a complete idiot. Her chest constricted and her breath caught. Mike would win and the officer would think she was hysterical. Or worse, investigate her for false reports. It was a false report. Mike was not missing at all. She knew he was at that duplex. But she was an attorney; she didn't think she'd get caught. At least not this soon.

The engine to the vehicle cut and a man stepped out. When the porch light caught his features, her heart stopped then started again. This time even faster. The man moved with confidence, his shoulders back and his head held high. It wasn't Mike, but it wasn't a uniformed officer either.

The man had dark skin and he wore a dark jacket with a patch on the shoulder. Maybe it said *Fort Calhoun PD*, but it was too far away to read. He was powerfully built, but not in an obsessive over-exercised way, like Mike.

He was near Angel's age, in his mid-thirties, and far better looking than anyone she'd met in Fort Calhoun. Angel watched him through the front window until he looked up, his gaze meeting hers.

Shit, she stepped out of the window and behind the solidness of the wooden door. It was too late. He could see her far better than she could see him. And she had seen him well enough to identify all his features, right down to his neatly trimmed goatee.

There was a light knock at the door.

She hesitated, trying to gather her wits.

The man cleared his throat, then said, "Fort Calhoun Police Department."

Angel took a deep breath, steeling herself for the lies she was about to spew, then threw the lock and opened the door. At close range, it was obvious the man was law enforcement. There was a vigilance officers carried when responding to calls. No other person appeared on another person's doorstep unflinching as they studied the homeowner. He was completely present in the moment, taking in all his surroundings.

"Hello there," Angel said, extending her hand. "I'm Angel Malone."

He shook her hand. "Tyrone Gully. I'm a detective with the Fort Calhoun Police Department."

Angel opened the door wider, motioning for him to enter. "Are you new? I've never seen you before." She didn't know all the officers by name, but her clients dealt with law enforcement often enough complaining about late custody transfers and requesting protective orders that their faces registered as familiar.

"Just moved from Chicago."

He stepped inside and she closed the door behind him. Angel's home was open concept with a formal seating area directly to the right of the door and a dining room and kitchen to the left. Angel led the detective toward the kitchen. It was the more comfortable place to speak.

"You have a very nice house, Mrs. Malone," Tyrone said.

"Call me Angel. And thank you." She didn't have enough disposable cash to hire an interior designer, so she'd decorated herself in a modern country fashion. It wasn't perfect, but it looked fine. "Would you like some coffee or tea?"

"Coffee would be great." It was late at night, but he was obviously assigned to the night shift. Officers in Calhoun County worked twelve-hour shifts, from six to six. They rotated every few months, the day shift moving over to the night shift and vice versa.

She placed a coffee mug beneath the Keurig, replaced the pod, and pressed start. The machine whirred to life and began spitting steaming coffee within seconds. Once it finished, she removed the cup and handed it to the detective, motioning for him to have a seat at the Island.

"I would offer you cream or sugar," Angel said, her tone apologetic, "but my husband is a health nut. We might have some soy milk in the fridge, though."

"No, thank you," Tyrone said, lifting his hand. "This is great."

"Okay." Angel stood awkwardly at the other side of the island. She didn't know how to segue into the conversation. She had never called law enforcement to report anything before.

"Are you an attorney?" Tyrone asked. His gaze snagged on the stack of files at the other end of the island, sitting next to her work laptop.

"Yes," she said. She had to find time for work. "I do family law."

"Oh, good," he said, a smile pulling at the corners of his lips.

"Why?"

"You've got one hell of a poker face. I can't get a read on you. I would hate to go toe-to-toe with you as a defense attorney."

"You can normally 'read' people?" She was skeptical. She understood intuition, she had plenty of that herself, but she would never claim she could read people.

"Usually, yes."

There was a short, awkward pause. Angel didn't fill it. Silence had never bothered her.

"You called about your husband, right?" Tyrone said. He took a drink of coffee, his intelligent eyes remaining on her, studying, assessing.

This was it. The moment of truth—or untruth—when she botched the whole thing, or she sent this attractive detective on a hunt for her husband who was probably hooking up with a gym rat at a trashy duplex.

"Yes." Her gaze shifted down, her eyelashes fluttering.

"What has you concerned?"

"He was here this morning when I left for work."

"What time was that?"

"Around six-thirty or seven o'clock."

"What was the mood in the house when you left?"

They'd been fighting. He was once again on her about the kids' diet. And then there was that damn boat. The very thought of it made her blood boil. She hadn't even seen it yet, but she sure as hell paid for it. Anger flared, but she tamped it down. She had to play this right. She waited a beat, allowing her agitation to settle. Then she met the detective's gaze and said, "Everything was fine."

"When did you discover things were amiss?"

"When I got a call from daycare. He didn't pick up the girls. We have twin girls. They are four years old."

"And he is the one who usually picks them up?"

"Yes. He's never forgotten to get them. Never."

"What is your husband's name and date of birth?"

"Michael Scot Malone."

"And his date of birth?"

That was more problematic. "He's thirty-one," she said, grabbing her phone to check Facebook. "April fifteenth."

"You are sure that's right?"

"Yes."

"Does your husband have any friends that he might be spending time with?"

"No. Or at least I don't think so. He works out at Frank Sand's gym, Frankly Hot and Heavy, all the time. He could have friends there. I don't have time to exercise, so I wouldn't know any of them."

He wrote something on his notepad. "Have you tried contacting him?"

"A million times."

"Alright," he stood. "I'm going to go see if I can track him down. Missing person cases are often difficult to solve."

"I understand."

"But I take these cases very seriously. Other officers might not, but I lost someone when I was young. I believe she could have been located, but nobody even tried until it was too late."

"Oh, I'm sorry. Is she…" Her voice trailed off. Was it a girlfriend? A wife? A mother? How young had he been? Questions flitted through her mind, but she didn't ask.

"I'm sure she's dead. She wouldn't have chosen to leave."

A pang of guilt hit Angel. She knew Mike would come home eventually. He was a philanderer, or so she assumed, but he wasn't dead. She was only doing this to get back at him. Yet this detective was all because of his own loss, his tragedy.

But this was positive, for her purposes. It would fuel him to work hard, which was good for Mike's embarrassment. Detective Gully was going to find Mike, hopefully in a compromising position. She would get what she wanted which was the end goal, so she pushed all thoughts of guilt aside. Her husband was about to learn not to fuck with Angel Malone.

25

TYRONE

Present
June 15

Horror masked with opulence. That was what Tyrone thought as he stepped inside Frank Sand's home. The entryway towered over him, opening like the giant maw of a monster. Tyrone's gaze darted around, starting with the crown molding lining the high ceilings like gleaming, white teeth, and the giant, glittering chandelier, hanging from the ceiling like an eyeball dangling from its socket.

You are not intimidated, Tyrone told himself. He'd never been inside a home like this. His upbringing was modest, at best, and his current lifestyle remained the same.

"Pretty cool, huh?" Rebecca said, her gaze fixed on the chandelier.

"It's...something, that's for sure."

A tug at his pant leg caught Tyrone's attention. He looked down into the bright curious eyes of the little boy. "Hello there."

The boy blinked, a slow, long, movement, a windup to a burst of questions.

"Who are you?"

"Tyrone."

"Why are you here?"

"To talk to Rebecca."

"Why?"

"Adult stuff."

"Are you a police officer."

"Sorta."

"Do you have a badge?"

"Yes."

"Can I see it?"

Tyrone removed his badge from his back pocket and showed it to the little boy.

"Can I hold it?"

"No."

"Do you have a gun?"

"Not with me."

"I thought all police officers had guns."

"I'm a detective."

"Are you looking for my Mommy?"

Tyrone opened his mouth to speak, then closed it. It was not his place to tell this child that his mother was dead. Frank knew and he would have to decide how to inform his children. Tyrone had little respect for the man, but he was not going to overstep that boundary. "I'm trying to find answers about your Mommy."

"I miss her." The child's eyes glazed. "I want her to come home."

Tyrone's heart twisted. That look in the boy's eyes. The longing. He understood all too well. He, too, had wanted his mother to come home. But like Tyrone, that was something that would never happen for this child.

"That's enough questions, Matthew," Rebecca said. "Get Genevieve and go play while I talk to this nice man."

"He's a detective," Matthew said, placing his hands on his hips. "That doesn't make him a nice man. But I think he is a nice man anyhow."

"Right, detective." Rebecca rolled her eyes and mimicked the child's body language, hands on hips, leg jutted out.

It was childish, the way she antagonized a boy hardly more than a quarter of her age. What would she do next? Stick her tongue out at him?

"I don't want to play. I want to stay and talk," Matthew said, pushing his lower lip into a pout.

"Well, you can't." Again, Rebecca mimicked him.

"Yes, I can."

"No, you can't."

"You can't stop me."

"Yes, I can. I'll lock you in your room," Rebecca said.

"I'll escape."

Tyrone had little knowledge of kids, but even he knew this was not the way a nanny should interact with children. He wouldn't trust her to care for a cat, let alone two small children traumatized by the loss of their mother and their beloved au pair, Nolan.

"How about this." He dropped into a crouch so that he was eye level with the little boy. Tyrone didn't care to help Rebecca win against the children, but he needed to interview her without Frank present. This might be his only chance. "If you are really good while I speak with Miss Rebecca, I'll let you hold my badge for a few minutes before I leave."

"Oh. Cool," Matthew said, nodding.

"Can I hold it, too?" Genevieve said. She was younger than Matthew and she had a slight lisp. With that high-pitched voice and her blond ringlet curls she might be the cutest little girl he'd ever met.

"You have to be good, too. Do you promise to be good?"

"I swear," she said, dragging her finger cross her chest. "Cross my heart."

Thankfully, she ended the statement there. Tyrone didn't think he could bear to hear that tiny, beautiful voice say, *and hope to die*. Not after what had happened to her mother.

"Then, yes," he said. "You can hold my badge, too."

The kids ran off and Rebecca issued a heavy sigh of relief. "They are bad kids. They never listen."

He nodded, but he didn't agree. These kids weren't *bad*. They were unique, she just had to learn to connect with them on their level.

"How long have you been working with the family?"

"Since February."

It didn't seem like Rebecca and the children had much of a connection. He would have guessed she was new to the job.

"Let's go to the formal dining room," Rebecca said, leading Tyrone through the large, spacious home.

It was open concept with the dining table not far from the large kitchen area. An enormous table stretched the expanse of the area, long enough to seat ten people. A chandelier hung above the center of the table, a smaller replica of the one hanging in the entryway.

"Sit wherever you'd like," Rebecca said.

Tyrone chose the seat at the end of the table. Rebecca sat across from him. Just as they were sitting, the two kids rushed over to play in an area nearby. They were close, but not close enough to overhear the conversation.

"So, you're here to talk about Molly?"

"Sorta," Tyrone said. "I am trying to get an understanding of the family. You said you were hired in February?"

"Yes."

"When, exactly, were you hired?"

"Oh, I don't know an exact date. Somewhere near the middle of the month."

"Did you know Molly?"

"Not really. I'd see her at the gym sometimes, but I never talked to her."

"Why not?" Tyrone asked.

"Because she didn't like other girls. She acted like she was better than everyone. She'd hold her nose up in the air and walk by all, *I'm rich, I'm hot, I don't need you.* You know what I mean?"

Not really.

"She never talked to anyone but Mike Malone. If you ask me, those two probably ran off together. They were, like, all over each other. And then poof," she opened her palms and circled her hands in the air, "they were gone. I don't know what all this fuss is about her disappearance. She left her husband. She left her kids. She's terrible. Bye. Get out of here. *Bye.*"

"What happened to the other au pair," he looked down at his notes, pretending he didn't know the name by heart, "Nolan."

Rebecca opened her mouth to speak, but Matthew piped up before she could respond.

"Dad fired him. He said he's a fairy. But I like fairies. I don't see why that's a reason to fire anyone."

Had Matthew heard what Rebecca said about his mother? Tyrone hoped not.

Rebecca swung around and leveled the boy with an icy glare. "That's not true, Matthew."

"You weren't here. You don't know. Dad wanted to get rid of him. Them."

Them.

"Then my mom was gone and so was Nolan." The kid's voice hitched at the end.

"You don't know anything," Rebecca snarled, "And I'm going to tell your father if you don't get out of here right now."

Matthew and Genevieve both jumped up and dashed out of the room. Tyrone didn't like how quickly they ran with the mention of their father. He hoped Frank wasn't using corporal punishment. He'd hate to think his visit might lead to a beating.

Once the kids were gone, Rebecca turned back to Tyrone, a false smile spreading across her lips. "Kids," she said with a sigh. "They have such imaginations. It can cause them to confuse facts."

In Tyrone's experience, kids were the more truthful ones. It was the adults that tended to "confuse facts."

"The previous au pair left without notice. He was not fired."

Tyrone nodded. "How do you know that?"

"Umm, Frank told me." She unwrapped a piece of pink bubble gum and popped it in her mouth.

"Do you remember the exact day when you started?" He looked down at his notepad. "You said it was somewhere in the middle of the month of February. I know that was a long time ago, but exact dates can help form a timeline."

"Ummm," Rebecca looked up at the ceiling, biting her lip. Then her gaze flickered down, meeting his. "I know. I remember now. It was February sixteenth."

"You sound pretty certain of that date."

"I am. It was a few days after Valentine's Day. I broke up with my boyfriend on the fourteenth because he didn't buy me anything. Can you believe that? Nothing." She made a slashing motion in the air. "Not even a measly box of chocolates, so I broke up with him."

"Okay." Tyrone wrote the date in his notepad. The affair with Frank probably had something to do with the ending of her relationship as well, but Tyrone didn't raise the issue. At least not yet.

"The next day, I went to the gym. I was angry and I needed to work off some steam."

"Frank's gym?"

"Umm, yeah. Duh." She blew a bubble, opened her mouth and popped it.

"I just needed to make sure." Detectives could not make assumptions. He needed facts.

Rebecca shrugged and blew another bubble.

"Is that where you met Frank? The gym?"

"Yeah. He's there a lot. He doesn't work out, but he talks to people."

Yeah, sure. Talking. I doubt Frank spends a lot of time "talking" to the men.

"While I was there, he came up to me and asked if I needed a spotter. I didn't, I wasn't lifting *that* much weight, but you don't say 'no' to Frank Sand. Nobody does."

Tyrone didn't like the sound of that.

"We got to talking, and he was all, *I need someone to watch my kids.* That Nolan dude had run off. Can you believe that? I started the next day."

"Do you have a lot of experience with children?" Tyrone asked.

"No. None at all. I'm an only child and I didn't babysit when I was younger."

"Frank has an older child, right? Frankie Junior. Do you know him?"

Rebecca wrinkled her nose. "Yes. I know him."

"Why are you making that face?"

"I went to school with Frankie, and he used to come to the gym all the time. He's a couple years younger than me. He's a freaking weirdo."

"How so?" Tyrone asked.

"He's, like, crazy about Molly. He talked about her all the time at school. In, like, the grossest way. People started calling him *Mother Lover.*"

"They called him that to his face?"

"I mean," she scrunched up her nose, "not really. They'd shout it at him during passing periods, things like that, but that wasn't, like, what they called him instead of his name."

High schoolers were cruel, and Frankie Junior was an introverted child. He had probably been victimized by bullies most his life.

"You said Frankie Junior came to the gym?" Tyrone asked.

"Yeah. He only came on weekends, and it was only when Molly was there. He didn't even work out. He'd follow her around like a little puppy. It was gross and pathetic."

Like father, like son. "Why only weekends?"

"Umm because he had school. Duh." Rebecca popped another bubble.

"Did Frankie Junior's interest in Molly bother her?"

Rebecca shrugged and tossed a strand of hair over her shoulder. "I don't know. I never talked to Molly. But she probably liked it. She was an attention whore."

Was. "Why didn't Frank have Frankie Junior watch his younger siblings?" Tyrone asked.

"Same reason Frankie didn't go to the gym during the week. School."

Tyrone fell silent, his gaze traveling around the room. Toys were everywhere, tossed into corners and tucked under tables. "This job must be a challenge for you."

"Oh, it is, but I, like, need the money and Frank pays good." She sat back, her head rising high. "I am going to be an actress and model one day, but I need to get out of this dirty old town first. Which means I need cash." She rubbed her fingers together.

"Do you have any training in either area?"

"I've taken some theater classes, but I need more. That's also why I need this job. It's crappy. I hate kids, but my boss is cool, and he pays well. It's worth it."

"Molly used to work for Frank, back before they were married. She probably thought her boss was cool back then, too. Now she's dead."

Rebecca gasped, placing a hand over her mouth. The reaction felt genuine in the moment, like she had no idea that Molly was dead. Yet, it was overkill. Molly had been missing for months. Many people presumed she was dead. It shouldn't be *that* big of a surprise. Besides, Frank knew.

Rebecca, his current girlfriend and child minder, was who he'd claimed he'd called after learning of his wife's death. At least that was what he had said during his interview. Perhaps Rebecca ought to spend more time in acting classes.

There was a long pause, then she leaned forward, placing both hands flat on the table. "How do you, like, know? Did Frank go look at the body?"

Tyrone narrowed his eyes. "No. There wasn't a body."

"Then how do you know she's dead?"

"DNA." *And the massive amount of blood.* That pigsty was coated in it. Nobody lost that much blood and lived.

"Oh." Rebecca sat back, disappointed.

"How does Frank treat you?" Tyrone said.

Rebecca shrugged. "I told you he's a good boss. He pays well."

"I mean personally." Tyrone leaned forward. "If you think your romantic relationship has stayed between you and your boss, you're sorely mistaken."

Rebecca blinked several times. "He's fine. Everything is fine." She crossed her arms.

Fine was the passive aggressive word for "terrible."

"Is that so?" Tyrone asked.

"Yes," Rebeca said, widening her eyes. "Can we talk about something else?"

Rebecca was deeply unhappy. Yet she hadn't left this job. Was it because of the money? He looked around. They were surrounded by it. Frank's kind of cash could be as intimidating as the giant chandelier clinging to the entryway ceiling. It could buy loyalty. It could buy blood. Rebecca had plenty of reasons to want Molly dead, personal and financial. Was she keeping Frank's secrets or was she keeping her own?

26

MOLLY

Past
February 2

She couldn't stop drinking. In the first hour at the duplex with Mike, they drank an entire bottle of wine. It was nerves. The anxiety started when Molly pulled into the driveway. The first thing she noticed was Vivian's face on a *For Sale* sign posted at the side of the drive.

A bad omen.

Nolan hadn't mentioned that the attached duplex was for sale and Vivian was the selling agent. Vivian's assessing eyes seemed to follow her as she drove up the driveway and into the garage. Molly almost lost her nerve. She had never done anything so reckless.

Should I go through with it?

But she reached up and pressed the button to the garage door opener that Nolan had given her, listening to the heavy door as it trundled closed, ushering her into darkness. She'd already gone this far; she might as well go inside. Then the drinking started. It was muddling her mind. But as time stretched, Molly forced herself to slow down with the alcohol.

"What time is it?" Molly asked. She didn't wear a watch and she didn't have her cell phone. She'd left it at the house with Nolan so Frank couldn't track her movements. If her phone didn't move, he would assume she was right where he wanted her.

Mike's phone rested on the table in front of him. It had been lighting up with calls that he kept declining. He tapped the screen. The screensaver was an image of Mike flexing in front of a mirror.

"Nine bells," he said.

"Oh, okay." Frank wouldn't be home until late in the evening, if at all.

"I can't believe I'm here." Mike blew out a heavy breath. "Alone. With *you*." He leaned forward, placing both elbows on the table and resting his chin in his hands.

Molly avoided his gaze, looking from the flimsy Formica table to the laminate countertops. She couldn't believe she was here either. Nolan's grandmother's duplex was inexpensive, but cozy enough, and it felt like freedom. It was the first place she'd been by choice in over ten years.

"I've been into you for so long," Mike said.

"You have?" Molly took another large gulp of wine before meeting his gaze. She quickly looked away. There was so much intensity there. He wasn't looking, he was staring. Was he even blinking?

"Oh, yeah. I've wanted you for five years."

"Five years?" Molly wine caught in her throat, but she forced herself to swallow. He'd only just started appearing at the gym during her workout time. She knew he watched her, and he was interested, but it hadn't occurred to her that he'd been stalking her. For *years*.

"My marriage has been bad for a long time." He ran a hand through his hair. "It continues to get worse, but it was bad even before the girls were born. It's over now."

Listening to him talk about his marriage while he drank sips of wine, she wondered if Frank was having similar conversations with Rebecca. It was surreal to think that she was in the very same situation with a different man. The thought was so odd that it, coupled with wine, made her giggle. Laughing was inappropriate for the heavy conversation, she knew that, but she couldn't help herself.

"What's so funny?" Mike's smile dropped. He was suddenly serious with an edge that hardened into something more dangerous.

She covered her mouth with her hand. "Nothing. Sorry. Nothing."

"I didn't say anything funny."

"I know." Molly suddenly realized her vulnerability. She was in a strange house with a strange man without a phone to call for help. He could easily harm her, and nobody would know for hours. "I'm sorry."

A flash ignited something behind Mike's eyes, and he opened his mouth to say something, but he was interrupted by a knock on the door.

They both froze.

The sound came again. *Crack. Crack. Boom.* The sharp snap of knuckles followed by the pound of a closed fist.

Mike lifted an eyebrow. "Are you expecting someone?"

"No," Molly said, shaking her head. "Are you?"

"No." Mike stood and went to the door, taking long, determined strides.

Molly couldn't see the door from where she sat, and she was thankful for that. She had no idea who it might be. She hoped it wasn't Frank. How could it be? Unless...

No. She shook her head. *Nolan would never rat me out.* She held her breath, waiting in silence. The door creaked open. Then Mike spoke.

"Good evening, officer, what can I do for you?"

"Are you Michael Malone?" It was a male's voice, deep and authoritative.

"Yes. Why?"

"You should go on home. Your wife is looking for you."

"My wife." Molly had never heard the word *wife* spoken with such derision.

"Yes."

"She called the cops because I was out? And you took it seriously? Of course, you would. Angel gets everything she wants." He was getting agitated again, his volume increasing.

"She reported that you were missing." The officer's voice was muffled, but he didn't sound intimidated by Mike.

Molly was.

Mike scoffed. "A missing person. You've got to be fucking kidding me."

Molly leaned forward, wrapping her arms around her shoulders. *What have I gotten myself into?* She was going to be sick.

Nothing sexual had happened between them yet, and she was thankful for that. She didn't want anything to do with this man. His temper was feral. A wild, untamed beast. She wanted to cover her ears, stop the sound of his harsh voice, but a part of her needed to know. Who was this man? But as the conversation outside grew more heated, Mike stepped out onto the porch and closed the door behind him, muffling the voices. She could hear the rage, but not the words.

A few minutes passed. She sat in a dark kitchen listening to Mike's muffled shouts and the officer's calm replies. It brought her back to her childhood, to her parents' drug deals. Sometimes they didn't go as planned. Sometimes people shouted. Sometimes there were threats. Sometimes there were gunshots.

What am I doing? Molly covered her face with her hands.

Frank was a philanderer, and he was possessive, he always got what he wanted when he wanted it, but he'd never displayed even a fraction of Mike's temper. In these few moments alone in Nolan's grandmother's kitchen, she was reminded of why she'd chosen Frank in the first place. Security.

Mike reentered the duplex and stomped into the kitchen. Molly rose to her feet. The last fifteen minutes had been sobering.

"Is everything okay?" Molly asked.

"No. My bitch wife sent the cops after me."

"Oh." Faced with the full force of his rage, Molly thought it best to play dumb.

He grabbed his coat and stomped back toward the door.

"What are you going to do?" Molly asked, trying to keep her voice from shaking.

"I'm going to take care of her. She wants to fuck with me, she's going to find out what happens. Fuck around and find out." He opened the door and slammed it so hard the walls shook.

Molly bit her lip and watched him go, standing frozen to the spot. She heard his car start and back out of the driveway. She went into the attached garage and got into her own car. She had no idea what Mike planned to do to Angel, but Molly was not about to stay at the duplex and wait for him to return. She opened the garage and backed out of the driveway. On the drive home, she was careful to maintain the speed limit. She would not pass a breathalyzer test.

It was ten o'clock when her car made the long trek down the paved driveway to her home. As expected, Frank's car wasn't there. He was usually at one of his bars partying until two or three o'clock in the morning. That, or he was having a sleepover somewhere with Rebecca. Either way, he hadn't caught her. She parked in the garage and stumbled into the house.

She found her two children downstairs in Nolan's room, all three snuggled together fast asleep. Wrappers were strewn across the room and light flickered from the television. They must have fallen asleep while watching a movie. Molly crawled into bed with them, into safety, and snuggled in closely with her children. They were safe. She was safe. At least for now. She finally felt calm enough to allow herself to close her eyes.

27

ANGEL

Past
February 2

Angel could not focus. She tried to work after Detective Gully left, but she wasn't getting anywhere. She'd sit down at her computer, stare at the screen for several minutes, then hop back up and pace.

What is happening out there? Her plan had seemed infallible hours ago, but now she was questioning it. Would the detective even find Mike?

As she paced, she tried not to look at her computer with each pass. She was wound too tightly to work, but work guilt had her wishing she could get *something* done. Then she heard the front door slam. It was ten minutes shy of ten o'clock.

"*Angel!*" Mike's voice reverberated through the silent house, careening toward her, as angry and intense as a shotgun blast. "*You'd better have a Goddamn fucking good reason for sending the cops after me!*" His last few words were slurred. Had he been drinking? As a health psycho, he rarely drank. *Food is fuel*, he'd say. *Alcohol*, he'd sneer. *You might as well drink gasoline.*

For a moment, she was frozen in place, unsure if she should laugh or hide. Her plan had worked. Tyrone had found him, and he was not happy about it. She'd never heard this kind of anger from him before. A shiver ran up her spine. She didn't know what to do.

Mike entered the room, his hands balled into fists. "There you are."

His gaze met hers, paralyzing in its callousness. There was no love there, no kindness, no compassion.

"Why would you send the cops after me? What the fuck is your game?"

She was speechless, her mind numb. What was her game? It had been a game, he was right, but in that moment, it didn't seem wise to admit it.

"What is wrong with you?" He took a slow, deliberate step toward her. He was still several feet away, but it was not enough space.

"Keep your voice down." Angel finally forced herself to say something. "The girls are sleeping."

"I don't give a fuck about the girls."

Heat shot through her. How could he say something like that? "They are your children."

"They're bitches, just like you."

"Take. That. Back," she said through clenched teeth.

"Why would you call the cops?"

"Where were you?"

His nostrils flared and he took another step closer. "Where's the money?"

"Money?"

"Don't play dumb. The joint account, fucktard. What did you do with the money?"

In all the excitement, Angel had completely forgotten about her lunch hour rendezvous with the bank. "I moved it. You have demonstrated that you are too irresponsible to be trusted with it."

"This is about the boat." He took another step closer.

"Uh, yeah."

"You moved the money to get back at me."

"Ding. Ding," she mimicked ringing a bell. "We have a winner."

"And you called the cops to punish me for leaving the girls at school."

Angel leaned forward and lowered her voice. "Check. Mate."

"*Fucking cunt!*" He dropped his shoulder and ran at her tackling her to the floor.

Her back hit the hardwood with a thump and a cry tore from her throat.

"Did that hurt? That's just the beginning." He was on top of her, straddling her. Then he leaned back, snatching something off the counter.

"Get off me."

He placed his knees on her elbows, pinning her to the ground. In seconds, he'd completely immobilized her. This was not his first time doing something like this. But who else? Who had he done this to? Not Angel. Maybe other girlfriends. Were there other girls?

"You're hurting me." Angel's elbows felt like they were going to snap in two.

"Good," he said as he displayed the item he'd taken from the table. A steak knife.

She stared at the small, serrated knife in disbelief. She'd used it earlier to scrape peanut butter from a jar.

"Now," he leaned forward and pressed the knife blade to her neck. "Apologize."

Panic. Sheer, animalistic terror flooded through her. She'd gone too far this time. He was far bigger than her. If he wanted to kill her, she was dead. She struggled to get free, throwing her legs up to kick him in the back, but she couldn't reach.

He applied pressure to the knife, his expression calm. "I wouldn't do that if I were you."

There was a sharp twang, and she could feel the heat as a drop of blood rose to the surface and slipped down the side of her neck.

He leaned closer, looking her straight in the eyes. "I can do it. I will do it."

"Don't."

"Beg."

"Please, Mike." She didn't know what else to say. She couldn't appeal to him by referencing the girls. He'd called them *bitches like her.*

"I own you. Do you know that?"

Her breaths were shallow. His heavy body on her chest wasn't allowing her to take a full breath. Darkness seeped in from the corners of Angel's vision. This was it. She was going to die. She would never see her little girls again. Had she told them how special they are? Had she done that when she tucked them in to sleep? She couldn't remember anymore.

"Are you having trouble breathing?"

"Yes." The word came out in a gasp.

He leaned back, setting the knife back on the island. Then he leaned back forward, pressing both hands around her throat. "How about now."

She couldn't get a full breath before, but at least she could inhale half-way. His large, muscled hands had put an end to that.

"Tell me I own you. *Tell me!*"

Angel couldn't speak. She only nodded, the movement ever so slight, but it was apparently enough to appease him because he removed the pressure and stood. Angel rolled over, coughing and sputtering, gasping for air.

"Get up," he said, his tone cold.

Angel slowly rose to her feet.

"You're going to move all that money back into the joint account. Got it?"

Angel nodded, pressing a hand to her neck, feeling for the knife wound. It was only a nick.

"And you are going to remember who owns who in this relationship. I don't want you pulling any of that shit again." He paused, waiting for her to respond. When she didn't, he said, "Right?" His voice was low, dangerous, a threat.

"Right." The word ripped through her throat.

"I'm going to sleep in the guest room tonight. I don't want to see your fucking face. I don't want to accidentally touch you."

Angel was not going to argue with him about that. The very thought of him near her made her skin crawl. He stormed out of the room.

He hated her. There was no love to be rekindled in their relationship. Yet, divorce wasn't an ideal option either. Domestic violence would virtually guarantee her primary custody, but Mike would still get visitation. He was their father. One incident of violence toward Angel wasn't anywhere near enough to terminate his parental rights.

She'd seen it countless times throughout her career. Men who beat their spouses but still got to see the children. Sure, they had to jump through some hoops for social services, but they never changed. Abusers never did. And that was one reason why so many victims of domestic violence never left. They stayed to protect their children. If he had parental rights, Mike would see them, and that would mean that the girls would be alone with him. She couldn't allow that. Not after the violence she saw tonight.

But what could she do?

28

TYRONE

Present
June 15

Tyrone wanted to spend another hour questioning Rebecca, teasing out her secrets, but he was out of time. It was past six in the evening. Frank Sand was bound to call or return home soon, and Tyrone didn't want to be there when that happened. Frank would get Angel involved, and Tyrone was in no mood to deal with her. He was exhausted, running on fumes. He needed a good night's sleep.

Within moments of leaving the Sand home, his phone began ringing. He grabbed it off the passenger seat. "Gully here."

"What did Rebecca say?" It was Jackie.

"How do you always know when to call?" She had called him within minutes of leaving each interview.

"I'm psychic."

"No, really."

"There is a location device on your car. It's on all city vehicles. In case its stolen, or something happens to an officer in the field. I saw that the locator was moving and figured you were in your car."

"Okay." He didn't like the idea that anyone at the station—including

Jake—could click a button and find his cruiser, but he also understood the officer safety angle. Freedom was often the currency paid for safety.

"I've got bad news on my end," Jackie said.

"No good news to soften the blow?"

"Nope."

"Alright. Out with it," Tyrone said with a sigh.

"I can't find Nolan. I've checked his social media. There's no activity. I've tracked down his family members. There aren't many, but the closest seems to be a grandmother that lives in a nursing home nearby. She has dementia. She wasn't much help, but the staff says they haven't seen Nolan since the middle of February. They said that before February, he visited daily."

"That's not good."

"No. It isn't. I found his mother in Arizona. She moved there a year or so ago. She said she tried to get Nolan to come with her, but he wouldn't. He felt he had an obligation to Molly and her children. She thinks Nolan was the victim of a hate crime."

"Did you believe the mother?"

"I did. I recorded the conversation so you can check for yourself."

"No, no. I trust you." Tyrone didn't trust anyone, but he had to loosen the reins somewhere. He couldn't do everything himself. There was no place for micromanagement in law enforcement. It was a team environment. If Jackie felt certain about this, he needed to follow her lead. There wasn't time to do anything else.

"Is there anywhere in town that Nolan could be hiding?"

"When he worked for the Sands, he lived with Molly and Frank. He doesn't have any other residences."

"So, that's a dead end," Tyrone said.

"Not quite."

"What do you mean?"

"The grandmother, the one in a nursing home, she has a property here in Fort Calhoun. It's a duplex. By all accounts it should be empty."

"Nolan may be staying there," Tyrone finished for her.

"Exactly."

"What's the address?"

Jackie recited it. It sounded familiar, but Fort Calhoun was barely a city. Everything sounded familiar.

"You're not planning to go over there now, are you?" Jackie asked.

Tyrone yawned. "No. I need to get some sleep. I want to do a little research on the property before checking it out anyway."

"I want to go with you."

"That's fine. We'll do it together," Tyrone said.

Jackie was probably antsy to get out in the field. She'd been shut away all day tracking a person who seemed no more real than a phantom. Now that they had a potential lead, it was only fair that he brought her along.

"Alright. Get some sleep. We'll start fresh tomorrow," Tyrone said.

They both hung up. Within seconds of ending the call, Tyrone's phone rang again.

"What now?" Tyrone grumbled. He glanced down at the screen and saw the name *Harper Jenkins* on the screen. It was the assistant county attorney. "This is Gully," he said, bringing the phone to his ear.

"Tyrone. How are things going with the investigation?" Harper said.

"Slow."

"We've got some lab results."

She fell silent, her voice replaced by the rustling of papers. Tyrone waited, tense.

"All the blood samples came back as Molly's."

It was the expected result, but still somber news.

"I talked to the Medical Examiner today. She said she'd testify that the amount of blood indicates that Molly was murdered right there next to the pigs. She can't say whether Molly died instantly or not, thanks to the pigs, but she does feel comfortable testifying that nobody would survive losing that much blood."

"I know there wasn't much left, uh," Tyrone cleared his throat, "but did the ME say anything about potential causes of death?"

Harper sighed. "She said the best she can do is speculate, which isn't good."

"What is the speculation?" Speculation was educated guessing, and it could not be presented at trial. But Tyrone still wanted to know.

"She thinks a head wound because those bleed a lot, or her throat was slashed."

Tyrone paused a moment, allowing that horrible fact to sink in. "Did the ME have any thoughts on date of death?"

"She guesses shortly before Old Pete found her, minus the time it takes for a pig to eat a person."

"Which is..."

"I don't know. I'm not a farmer."

Tyrone had hoped for more, but he hadn't expected it.

"But Old Pete can testify that the blood wasn't there the night before and it was there in the morning. That sets a solid timeline."

"Does that mean what I think it means?" Tyrone asked.

"Someone kept her alive between February and June," Harper said.

Tyrone sucked in a long breath. What was happening in that time? There had to be evidence wherever her abductor had been holding her, but he didn't know where to start looking. "Anything else?"

"Not yet," Harper said. "The lab is still running tests."

"But why kill her now?" Tyrone asked.

"I don't know," Harper said with a sigh. "That's a good question."

"It seems like every time I learn something new, this case gets harder to solve."

"You think this is bad? Wait until tomorrow when the murder hits the news. You're about to get inundated with hundreds, maybe even thousands of pointless tips."

In cases like Molly's, all kinds of people came out of the woodwork with "tips." The crazier the person, the more often they called. Yet, there was no way to tell which was an honest lead and which was completely bogus. Law enforcement had to follow up on them all. Or at least as many as they could.

"Can't wait," Tyrone said.

They ended the call, and he tossed his phone on the passenger seat. Every bone in his body ached with tension and anxiety. The corners of his eyes were heavy, like they were drooping with the weight of the day. It was time to call it quits, head home, and get some sleep.

Every moment was precious in an investigation. He was more than willing to burn the candle at both ends, but there came a time when the mental exhaustion was too much to overcome. He was far too tired to make sense of anything, and Harper was right, tomorrow would be an investigative nightmare. One thing he knew for certain was that there would be lots of lying over the course of this investigation. But blood, it didn't lie. Someone, somewhere, had kidnapped Molly and held her for months on end.

29

ANGEL

Past
February 3

Angel spent the night in the girls' room. After the assault, she'd taken her work laptop and her files and slipped into the dark room. The girls were curled up sleeping together in one of the two twin-sized beds, like always, so Angel took the other. She'd locked the door and placed a chair in front of it. Just in case.

Everything precious is here. My girls. My work. Myself. Angel dropped onto the bed and opened her laptop. The screen lit up, but she didn't type her passcode. She sat there staring at it, eyes losing focus.

Embarrassing. Mortifying. Horrifying.

Those were just a few of the words she would use to describe her evening. She was a lawyer, and she'd allowed Mike to assault her. It wasn't a new concept, domestic violence. Plenty of her clients had domestic disputes during the tumultuous months preceding their divorces. Yet, somehow, she'd always thought of herself as better than that. It wouldn't happen to *her*. She was a lawyer for God's sake, not a victim.

But it did, it did happen. And now she was paralyzed with indecision. She could take pictures of the small cut on her neck, but that was the only proof. She would need far more evidence. She could testify on her own behalf, but Mike would testify to the opposite. It would be a *he said, she said* case, not the kind of odds any attorney would want to take to a jury.

Then there was the gossip. A divorce was bad enough, but domestic violence was a whole separate issue. She'd spent years cultivating an image of strength as an attorney. Many people saw her as a villain. A vicious woman who came after them in their divorces, leaving them with little to nothing. It would weaken her career if people knew what Mike had done to her. And finding an unbiased jury would be nearly impossible.

Gretty moved, pulling Angel out of her thoughts. Angel's gaze shifted to her daughter's small figure, watching as she settled back down, nuzzling closer to her sister. Angel closed her laptop and set it on the floor beside her. She wasn't going to find a solution to her marital problems tonight. What she needed was sleep. She thought it would elude her, but when she laid her head on the pillow, she fell into a deep, dreamless sleep.

Angel was the first to wake up. When she opened her eyes, she was disoriented. *Where am I?* Then, her gaze fell on her two daughters, sleeping together in blissful ignorance of the events of the night before, and it hit her. Mike had assaulted her, threatened her with a knife, and choked her until she nearly blacked out.

She grabbed her phone and checked the time. In the stress of the night before, she hadn't set an alarm. It was nearing seven o'clock. She rolled out of bed and stood, padding over to the other bed, and placing a kiss on each girl's brow.

At least these two have each other. No man would threaten to stab her daughters and get away with it. Mike shouldn't get away with it either. *But he might.*

Before leaving the room, she looked around in search of something she could use as a weapon. But there was nothing. All the girls' toys were plush or foam. It was the first time Angel cursed modern manufacturer's safety concerns. Then, her gaze fell on an angel figurine. A woman holding two infant daughters, one nestled in each arm. It sat perched on one of the higher shelves above the dresser. A gift from Angel's law partner when she'd given birth.

She had to stand on her tiptoes to reach, but she grabbed it and headed out the door. It wasn't the best weapon, but it would do in a pinch, and this was a pinch.

Angel opened the door and crept slowly down the hallway, heading for the main bedroom. *I hope he's not in there*, she thought. She'd have to get dressed for work and she didn't want to do so in complete silence, terrified that Mike would wake up. The main bedroom was the third door on the left. The first was a bathroom, then a guest room.

She stopped outside the guest bedroom and slowly opened the door. A loud snoring sound filtered out. She peeked in to see Mike sprawled across the bed, fully dressed, and lying on top of the covers. He hadn't even removed his shoes and socks.

How drunk was he? She wondered, but then forced that thought out of her head.

It did not excuse his behavior. He had called their little girls, "Bitches like her." They were kids. Small children who weren't even in kindergarten yet. He was already using such horrible language to describe them. What would he do when they were in high school, and he caught them sneaking out?

Don't even think about it. Angel shook her head as though she could forcefully dispel the thought from her mind. She had to solve the problem long before then.

She gently closed the door to the guest bedroom and hurried the rest of the way down the hall into the main bedroom, pulling open drawers, dressing as quickly as possible. A shower left her too vulnerable, so she'd have to go without one. She shoved some makeup and hair styling tools into a bag, then rushed back down the hall to the girls' room. She gently shook each one into consciousness.

"What is it, Mommy?" Gretty asked.

"We need to go."

"Why?" Gretty rubbed her fists into her eyes.

"Because."

"Because why?"

Angel issued a heavy sigh. How was she going to get the girls motivated to get out of the house before Mike saw them? Then she had an idea. "Because we are playing a game. That's why."

Both Gretty and Lily popped up. They loved games. "What kind of game?" Gretty asked.

"It's a race."

Gretty scrunched her nose. "Who are we racing?"

"Daddy. We are trying to get up, dressed and out of the house before he wakes up. Do you think we can do it?"

Gretty turned to her sister, they exchanged a look, then she turned back and said, "Uh, yeah." The two girls rocketed out of the bed, rushing from one corner of the room to the other, gathering their school supplies.

There were no questions about their father's behavior the night before. Children had short memories. Angel was thankful for that. But they were making a lot of noise, and that was a problem.

"Shhhh," Angel said, placing a finger over her lips. "You're going to wake him and then we lose."

"Oh, yeah," Gretty whispered back.

When they finished changing and getting their stuff together, Angel ushered them out into the hallway, grabbing two packages of keto pop tarts, and Lily's diabetes testing kit as they passed the kitchen. School would have to check Lily's sugars after breakfast.

Angel didn't pause or allow her thoughts to dwell on the kitchen, she couldn't. Her mind would replay the assault, the fear. The girls grabbed their coats, and she helped them push their arms through each sleeve. Then they were out the door and headed to her car. She buckled them both into their car seats and then issued a sigh of relief as the garage door trundled open.

They'd made it out. At least for today.

The drive to daycare was uneventful. The teacher gave Angel a concerned look when she saw her, not Mike, dropping the girls off, but she dashed out before questions could follow. Her marital issues were private. She wasn't ready to share them with anyone. Especially a nosy daycare teacher.

When Angel finally got to work, she stopped in the bathroom before heading into the office. She didn't bother with makeup at the house, and she took a few moments to apply it. The lighting was terrible, it would be a sloppy application, but it was the best she could do. She lifted her head and studied her neck in the mirror. There was a small nick, barely even noticeable.

She lowered her head and met her own gaze in the mirror. The scar on her cheek stood out, as always, another unwelcome reminder in her haggard-looking face. Her eyes had a tinge of blue beneath them. She looked haunted, like an actor in a Tim Burton movie. It was exhaustion, both physical and emotional. What was going to happen next? What was she going to do? They couldn't go on living like this.

Get your shit together, Angel told herself. *You've got a full day of work.* She would worry about Mike later. When she finished with her makeup, she grabbed her files and headed down the hallway and into the suite with *Parker and Malone, PLLC*, embossed on a silver placard beside the door.

Angel took a deep breath and stepped inside the office. She was doing the only thing she could in the moment. She was getting on with it. The work wouldn't do itself. Luckily, she was the first one in the office. She didn't have the energy to chit-chat with anyone. It was seven-thirty in the morning and her first appointment was at eight-thirty. Frank Sand. He was coming to sign the Answer to Vivian's petition for modification of custody and support.

She removed her laptop from its bag and plugged it into the monitor on her desk, doubling the number of screens. She settled into the work, losing herself in the familiar rhythm. She didn't know how much time passed when her cell phone started buzzing. She grabbed it. The screen read *unavailable*. If she wasn't a lawyer in private practice, she wouldn't answer the call, but it could be a new client.

"This is Angel Malone," she said, bringing the phone to her ear. Her eyes settled on the clock on her computer screen. It read one minute past eight o'clock.

"Good morning, Miss Malone. This is Detective Gully."

"Oh, hello." Surprise morphed into anxiety. He hadn't returned the night before. She had assumed that was because her husband came home, investigation closed. She hoped he wasn't calling to accuse her of false reports. She was too wrung out this morning to parry with a detective.

"I was at your house last evening about your husband," Tyrone said.

"Yes, yes. I remember." She shook her head. "It was a long night."

"I found him."

Obviously. "I guessed that when he returned home. Where was he?"

"I'm not at liberty to say. I was just calling to tell you that I'm closing the investigation," he paused as though debating his next words, "and to check on you."

Angel's hand drifted to her throat, the cut that had come from such violence. She could hardly believe something like that had happened to her, Angel Malone, attorney at law. It was humiliating.

"Why would you need to check on me?" Angel asked.

"I just wanted to make sure your husband didn't, uh," he cleared his throat, "do anything to, uh, harm you, when he got home."

Yeah, he nearly killed me. Angel thought of those moments where she couldn't breathe. Mike, sitting on her chest with that knife pressed against her throat, looking her straight in the eyes as she fought to breathe. The helplessness was terrifying.

"I'm fine," Angel finally said.

"I didn't ask if you were fine. I asked if he hurt you." This was why Tyrone was a detective rather than a beat cop.

Angel sighed. "I'm too tired for this."

She couldn't confirm or deny. She was in a no-win situation. If she said *yes*, then he would open an investigation. Mike would get arrested, and she'd have to pay for his attorney. He wouldn't qualify for court appointed counsel, thanks to her income. Mike would use that attorney for defense work, but also to file for divorce. She didn't have the money for any of that right now.

"I get it. You aren't ready to discuss it," Tyrone said. "Let me give you some information about the domestic shelter in town."

"Domestic shelter," Angel repeated. "Why would I need a shelter?"

"It's a place to go if you and your children are in danger."

"There's a place he can go," Angel shot back.

"And that is..."

Angel almost said, *straight to hell,* but she somehow found the strength to rein in her emotions. "Thank you, detective, I truly appreciate your phone call. As I said, I am fine. No further assistance is needed."

"Let me give you my direct number. Just in case you ever need it."

"I hope I don't."

"I hope you don't either. Are you ready?"

Angel grabbed a pen and paper. "Yes."

Tyrone recited his cell phone number, then they ended the call and Angel sat back with a heavy sigh. *What am I going to do?* She wondered. Then Frank Sand walked into her office, smiling and whistling like he hadn't a care in the world.

30

TYRONE

Present
June 16

Tyrone's alarm pierced his sleep, quick and sharp, like a knife through flesh. He startled, his eyes shooting open. He rolled toward the noise. *Beep. Beep. Beep.* He reached out, striking his phone, knocking it to the floor.

"Shit," Tyrone said, leaning over the side of the bed to grab it. He silenced the alarm and rolled onto his back. The TV remote lay in the empty spot in his double bed. He grabbed it and turned on the news.

"There was a grim discovery in rural Calhoun County. The remains of—"

Tyrone changed the channel.

"The mystery into the missing mother of two comes to a sad—"

He hit the power button.

Molly's murder was the top story of the day. Both Des Moines news stations were running it. He grabbed his phone and opened the Twitter application, navigating to the accounts of the smaller newspapers and radio stations throughout Iowa. As he clicked on each outlet, he found the same result. *Molly. Molly. Molly.*

"Great," he said with a sigh.

Molly's death was everywhere. Some headlines said, *Vanishing Valentine found dead.* Others said *Pigs devour evidence in Molly Sand Murder investigation.* Still others said, *Pigs eat Molly Sand.* All were true. All were attention grabbing. That was the point.

Law enforcement had a love-hate relationship with media. Reporters could be intrusive, but there was no more reliable way to get information to the masses, which was sometimes necessary. The coverage would complicate Tyrone's investigation, and that was annoying, but it also poked at old wounds that had never healed. This was the second time Molly's face was top news, but Tyrone's mother, her disappearance was not even given a spot at the back of the paper, below the fold. It wasn't fair, but life wasn't fair. Neither was death.

Tyrone got up and dressed quickly. As he drove to work, he flipped from one radio station to the next. They were all discussing Molly. It didn't matter if the station was primarily music, the radio personalities were still dedicating songs to Molly's memory and pausing for moments of silence. Everyone wanted a piece of the story.

When Tyrone arrived at the Law Enforcement Center, the building that housed the police department, sheriff's department, and county attorney's office, there was a line of reporters standing out front. He parked in the back so he could enter without questions shouted at him.

Once inside, he poured a cup of coffee and headed to his cubicle, settling onto the chair in front of his computer. He stared down at his case notes, forcing the negative thoughts of the morning from his mind. Every investigation had a key witness, a key piece of evidence, something *key*.

Nolan was that key, he felt certain of it. His gaze stuck on the address to Nolan's grandmother's vacant townhome. It looked extremely familiar. Yes, every location in a small town felt familiar, but this one tugged at some memory buried deep within his mind. Had he responded to a call at that location? Maybe. He'd have to check calls to service. But first, he wanted to find a picture of Nolan.

Jackie had said there was no recent social media activity, which meant Nolan did have social media pages. Tyrone tried Facebook first. It wasn't hard to find Nolan's page. Tyrone started with Frank's business page and followed it to Molly's personal account. Molly had one friend named Nolan.

Tyrone clicked on the name and the screen filled with an image of a man in his mid to late twenties, with his arms around Molly's children, smiling at the camera. *Bingo*.

As Tyrone stared at the picture, a memory dislodged itself and came to the forefront of his mind. He'd seen this man before. The same clean cut, well-dressed, dark-haired man had been on his way out of Angel Malone's office when Tyrone had been up there to check on her. He remembered it like it was yesterday.

It was February fourteenth. The same day Molly Sand had disappeared, but she hadn't been reported missing yet. He knew that for certain because he was part of the initial search for Molly. Tyrone wouldn't have been randomly stopping by an attorney's office to check on her if he was needed elsewhere to search for a missing mother.

He thought back to how that meeting had gone, and why he was at Angel Malone's office that day. His first phone call to her about domestic violence did not go well. He was going to try again. If not for Angel, then for her two small children. He had been hesitating outside her office, debating whether to go inside, when a man stepped out. The man now staring out from his computer screen. Nolan.

Why was Nolan at Frank's attorney's office the same day Molly disappeared?

Angel Malone represented Frank Sand. So, Nolan couldn't be there on Molly's behalf. Angel was a family law attorney, and Nolan did not have a spouse or children of his own. There was no reason for him to visit Angel. Yet, he'd been there.

Tyrone shook his computer mouse and clicked on the browser icon. He typed the address for Nolan's grandmother's unoccupied duplex into the search bar and pressed the magnifying glass. The computer whirred, then spat out web pages. *Zillow, Trulia, Redfin*. He clicked on the top result. When the page populated, he had to blink several times to make sure he was seeing it right. This was what he had been missing.

He had knocked on that door in response to a call back in early February. A call from Angel Malone reporting her husband missing. That felt like ages ago, and it was a very short investigation, but he still remembered it. Not because of the nature of the investigation, but because of the things Mike Malone had said to him.

It was the first time he had met Angel. He'd heard of her, but they'd never spoken. After meeting with Angel, Tyrone had left her residence to look for her husband. He'd issued a BOLO, be on the lookout, for Mike's vehicle, which Angel believed he had been driving. Another officer quickly responded with an address to a residence. The residence Tyrone now knew belonged to Nolan's grandmother. Based on Jackie's research, Nolan's grandmother would have been in the nursing home well before the incident with Angel and her husband. So, who was at that residence? Nolan would be the only local person with access.

Tyrone had gone to the property, found the silver Lexus parked out front, and knocked on the door. Mike Malone had answered, reeking of booze.

They'd had a conversation that quickly grew heated. Mike had stepped outside and closed the door behind him during the worst of it. Tyrone suspected that someone else was there with Mike and he didn't want that person to see his explosive temper. Was it Nolan? Was it Molly?

When the door had clicked shut behind him, Mike's demeanor had gone from bad to worse. A switch flipped. All semblance of calm evaporated, replaced by rage. His eyes grew fiery, then settled into something flat, dull, and murderous.

"My wife doesn't give a shit about me. She only cares about money."

"Well, she seemed pretty concerned to me," Tyrone had said.

"She's a damn good actress."

Tyrone shrugged. "You ought to go home."

"I'm going to fucking kill her." Mike was not speaking to Tyrone, he had muttered the words to himself, but Tyrone had heard them clear as day.

"Excuse me."

"Nothing."

"I heard you," Tyrone said. "I better not wake up tomorrow morning and learn something has happened to your wife. Yours will be the first door I'm knocking on. Got it?"

"I didn't say—"

"Before you finish that lie, you should remember I wear a body camera. There's evidence. If you harm a single hair on Angel's head, this," he tapped the front of his shirt next to his body camera, "is an admission."

Mike's expression did not change, but he nodded. And that was the end of the conversation and the investigation.

That threat had been the whole reason he'd called Angel the next day, and then stopped by her office on February fourteenth. He suspected she was the victim of domestic violence, and she was too proud to admit it. He had been checking on her wellbeing. Shortly after that night at Nolan's grandmother's duplex, Molly disappeared and so had Mike Malone. Then Tyrone saw Nolan leaving Angel's office.

Where did Mike Malone go? Into hiding?

Mike could be a vital witness, or suspect, in this investigation. Finding him could provide answers to some critical questions. Was Mike living in that duplex? Was Nolan? Had Molly been there with them up until her demise? Only Mike and Nolan knew the answers to these questions, but they were both missing, and Molly was dead. There was only one person who might have some information and that was Angel Malone.

It seemed like Tyrone needed to pay the attorney another visit.

31

ANGEL

Past
February 3

Frank entered her office in the same way he walked through life, without invitation or apology. Every other client waited in the waiting room until Angel informed the office manager, Chloe, that she was ready to meet with them. But not Frank. He rarely waited for anyone. Or perhaps the better term was, he waited for no *woman.*

"Good morning, my Angel," Frank said, striding into the room. When his gaze settled on her, he stopped short. "What happened to you?"

"I don't know what you mean," Angel said, rising to her feet.

"You look like you've been run over by a tractor and then backed over again."

"You always seem to know what women want to hear, Frank."

"You know me." He made finger guns, and pointed them at her, Shooter McGavin style.

"I have the Answer to Vivian's petition ready," Angel said, motioning for Frank to take a seat.

"Great." He removed his coat and tossed it onto one chair and sank into the other. "Where do I sign?"

Angel pushed a stack of documents toward him, twisting it around so the words were upright. "There are three pages." She placed Vivian's original petition next to it. "Each paragraph," she pointed to the first numbered paragraph on the Petition and the same numbered paragraph on the Answer, "corresponds."

"I know," Frank said, picking up a pen and spinning it around his middle and forefinger. "This isn't my first rodeo."

It wasn't his second, third, fourth, fifth, or even sixth rodeo.

"If everything looks right, go ahead and sign on the signature line above your name on the third page."

Frank did not read anything. He flipped the documents over, found the signature line, and signed. "I want to talk to you about Molly," he said, sliding the stack of documents back to Angel.

Nothing like talking about divorcing your current wife while dealing with a modification with your first wife, Angel thought, but she kept her expression neutral, betraying none of her true thoughts.

"I don't like the numbers you quoted the last time."

"What numbers?" Angel threaded her fingers together and placed them in front of her on the desk.

He stared at her for a long moment. "Are you sure you're alright?"

"Yes."

"I have the number for a good plastic surgeon. He's the guy Molly uses."

"I am fine," Angel said. "I didn't sleep well last night, but that's all." She wished that was all.

"Right. Well, I've got that number if you change your mind." Finger guns again.

Frank's phone vibrated. It was sitting on the edge of her desk where they both could see the screen.

Your wife is a stuck-up bitch, the text read.

Angel raised an eyebrow, but she didn't comment. It was none of her business. At least not yet.

Frank grabbed the phone and flipped it over. "That's Rebecca." He didn't elaborate.

"She seems..." Angel trailed off. There was nothing halfway decent to say about that message.

"Anyway, back to what we were talking about," Frank said. "I'm not paying you to read my text messages." He issued a nervous laugh.

That was not strictly true. Frank often handed Angel pages of text messages to use as exhibits in hearings or trials.

"I don't want to pay Molly that much in child support."

"The child support guidelines are the guidelines, Frank. You know I have no control over that. At least she signed a prenuptial agreement, so she can't touch the businesses."

"No kidding. Vivian took me to the cleaners." He tapped the Answer that he'd just signed. "And now she's back to finish the job."

"Speaking of the businesses, have you thought of what you might do with them in case something happens to you?" Angel said.

"Happens to me. What do you mean?"

"A succession plan, Frank. If you are hit by a bus tomorrow and spend two weeks in a coma—or worse—who will take over your businesses?"

"I don't' know," he paused. "I guess Vivian. She annoys the shit out of me when she comes to the restaurants, but she does have good business sense. My businesses are my legacy. I want them to survive."

"Well, you'd better set that up, then. The only businesses Vivian would be able to control right now are the early restaurants."

"How do I do that?" Frank asked. "Is that something you'll do for me?"

"No. You can talk to my law partner, George, about it. He does all the estate planning and whatnot."

"Okay. When can I do that?"

"I'll check with him when we are done here," Angel tapped a finger on her desk. "Now, what about the children?"

"What about the children?"

"Who will care for them if something happens to Molly and you?" Angel asked.

"Nolan. He's soft, but the kids like him."

"Nolan is an employee, not a family member. It would be highly irregular for you to appoint an employee as a guardian."

"Okay, then Vivian again."

Angel sat back, threading her fingers together. "Why Vivian? Aren't you irritated that she's bringing you back to court, *again*?"

"I mean, yeah, I'm irritated," Frank said, twirling a pen around his fingers, "but I have to respect it on some level. Vivian's a go-for-it type of person. Just like me. I want the kids to be raised by someone like me."

Angel doubted Frank was doing much in the way of "raising" his children, but she didn't contradict him. "What about Frankie Junior? He's going to be an adult soon. Could he be the kid's guardian?"

"Oh, hell no," Frank said. "Frankie Junior hates his brother and sister. I mean *hates* them."

"Okay. So, Vivian it is." Angel shook her computer mouse and opened the folder housing all her forms. She selected the correct form and added Frank's information, and the information about the kids. Then printed it. "Look this over and sign it."

Frank looked down at the document. "It's that easy?"

"Yup," Angel said.

Frank uncapped his pen and signed above his name.

"I'll have Chloe and George sign as witnesses," she said, indicating the two witness lines below Frank's signature line.

"Why can't you deal with the businesses, then? Why do I have to talk to your partner?" Frank said. "Just print off another one of those things and let's get it done today."

"Because I deal with families and children, not businesses. George does that, and it will be a lot more complicated."

Frank was silent for a moment, then shrugged. "Can we fudge the numbers?"

"What?"

"The child support numbers with Molly. Can we give them, like, a fake number?"

Back to this. "That's fraud," Angel said.

"And..."

"I'm an officer of the court. I cannot perpetrate a fraud upon the court."

"You are a lawyer, not an officer."

"Yes, but as lawyers admitted to the bar of the State of Iowa, we have an ethical duty to present *truthful* information to the court," Angel said.

"Then how do some lawyers lie?"

"They believe it's the truth."

"Well, then you need to get to believing that I make a lot less money than I do," Frank said, forcing a chuckle, but he wasn't joking.

Angel sighed and ran a hand through her hair. "I won't be able to do that. You know how this works. There will be forensic accountants going through your businesses, valuing them, and combing through your tax returns. Believing an untruth isn't as easy as it sounds."

Frank shrugged. "I'm sure you could manage it."

Was that a compliment or an insult?

"I don't want anyone going through my finances," Frank said.

"Then don't get divorced," Angel said. "Because it will happen."

"I started seeing someone new."

"Did you," Angel said, her gaze shifting to his phone, still upside down on her desk. *Rebecca.*

"Rebecca works out at my gym."

Again, unsurprised.

"I'm worried Molly is going to find out. I was supposed to end it. She's angrier this time than she's ever been."

"Well, can you blame her?" Angel asked.

Frank shrugged. "I don't want her filing first. It will make me look weak. I've got to get ahead of this."

Angel blinked several times. "Do you want my advice?"

"Yes."

"Drop Rebecca and focus on Molly. It'll be cheaper. If your primary complaint is that you're bored with Molly, then find a way to spice things up. Aside from divorce. You did love her once."

Angel couldn't keep her thoughts from straying to Mike. It was hard to believe their marriage had deteriorated in such a catastrophic manner. But it hadn't happened in a vacuum, had it? There were signs. His gym obsession. The steroids. Then Molly. How long had they been using that duplex like a cheap motel?

"I can't do that," Frank said, pulling her out of her thoughts.

"Do what?"

"Fix it. Things have gone too far."

"Is she pregnant?" Angel asked.

"Who?"

"Rebecca."

"God, I hope not. Why? Have you heard something?"

"No," Angel rubbed her temples. "You just said that things have gone too far."

"Yeah. Molly is past her prime. Plastic surgery helps, but it won't rewind time."

"Oh." Mike seemed to find her attractive enough.

"I'll have to come up with something different."

"Okay."

Frank nodded and stood, grabbing the phone and slapping the top of her desk with an open palm. "I need to get out of here. Check with that partner of yours and let me know when I can come and meet with him about the businesses."

A flash of irritation ran through her. "Sure," she said through gritted teeth.

Then he left in much the same way as he had entered. Without permission or apology.

32

MOLLY

Past
February 3

Molly woke up in Nolan's room, fully clothed with a raging headache. Light filtered in from the window, illuminating the tasteful comfort around them. Nolan had decorated the room according to his modern fashion sense, white against black, clean lines, and a large image of Kate Moss with a mustache above the bed.

The sun burned her eyes. She drank too much the night before. The bedside clock read nine-thirty in the morning. The kids and Nolan were still asleep.

Ibuprofen. She needed something for the pounding inside her skull. She rolled out of bed and made her way up the stairs and down the hall to the main bedroom. Frank was sitting on the end of the bed. He looked up as she came in.

"Where were you?" he said.

Molly's heart stopped. Did he know? *No. He couldn't.* He would never be so calm. "Downstairs."

"You slept in the fairy's room."

"Don't call him that." She was too hungover to watch her tone.

Frank scoffed.

"I fell asleep while watching a movie."

"You look terrible," Frank said.

"Thanks." Molly couldn't hide the agitation in her voice.

"You don't usually drink."

"What do you want from me, Frank?"

"What do you want from me?"

"I want you to stop the affairs." It was the most honest answer she could give. Maybe she should have asked for more, but she didn't. She wouldn't ask for love. Frank didn't know the meaning of love.

"You're not leaving me?"

"No."

A smile twitched at the corners of Frank's mouth. It wasn't one of relief, it was more in triumph.

"Not yet," Molly added. Her heart pattered in her chest. She'd never held her ground with him, never spoken to him this way.

"I'll be better."

"Why? What's changed?"

"Angel told me to change."

Molly blinked several times. "She did?"

"Yes."

"When?"

"I just got back from her office. I have that modification thing with Vivian going on. She told me that I have a good thing with you. She said I need to stop dicking around."

"Okay." Molly doubted that Angel simply volunteered the *Molly's a good wife* information. It sounded positive, but she didn't trust it. Angel wasn't the altruistic type. She would make more money with another one of Frank's divorces. Or she knew about her disastrous rendezvous with Mike the night before.

"Give me a hug?" Frank said.

Molly didn't move.

"I said, 'give me a hug.'"

Molly leaned over, placing an arm around his shoulder, a side hug. He turned her and forced a full hug. She didn't fight it. She'd stood up for herself, but old habits died hard. That was why she gave him what he wanted, what he needed in the moment, and ignored her own needs.

His body melted at her touch, molding into her embrace.

The encounter seemed positive, but things weren't always as they seemed. He could be lulling her into a sense of ease, then he'd hit her with something she hadn't expected. Like returning from her daily gym outing to find the kids gone. Taken somewhere he wouldn't disclose. It had happened before. Once about a year ago.

They'd been arguing, and Molly had refused to apologize for commenting on his beer belly. He'd hired a pay-by-the-hour nanny to take the kids to the zoo for the day. He wouldn't tell her where they were, and she didn't find out until afterward that they were safe. She'd been a wreck. The not-knowing was torture.

"Are you going to the gym today?" Frank said.

Molly released him and stood, her heart pounding. What was he going to do? She hoped nothing. But she couldn't stop him. She had to go to the gym. She needed to end this thing with Mike before it really began. The night before had been a reminder that her marriage was imperfect, but there were worse men out there. Frank had never displayed an explosive temper. Molly had been disgusted with him plenty of times, but never frightened.

"I'm going to head that direction as soon as I get changed and ready," Molly said.

"Stay away from Mike Malone."

"I'll try," Molly said, "but you know men."

"Try harder."

Molly bristled. "As hard as you've tried to stay away from Rebecca?"

"Don't argue. Just do it."

In her mind she wondered *why not?* Her meekness hadn't gotten her anywhere.

"He's different," Frank said. "He's dangerous."

"Dangerous? How so?" She'd seen it firsthand, Mike's rage that came from nowhere, but what was Frank's source?

"I met with Angel this morning."

"You said that already."

"She looks terrible."

Molly cocked her head.

"Her neck was all red and she had a cut. It was small, but it looked...intentional."

Molly blinked several times.

"She tried to cover it with makeup, but I've known her for years. Something happened."

"Did she report it?"

Molly was going to end things with Mike. For her marriage, and now for her safety. If Angel reported a domestic assault, it would solve all that for her. Mike would get arrested. He'd be in jail, unable to pursue a relationship with Molly.

"No. She wouldn't even acknowledge it."

"Why not?"

Frank shrugged. "She isn't the type."

"I'll stay away from him," Molly said. *As soon as I can.*

"Okay," Frank said, flopping back on the bed. "Have a good workout. I'm beat. I'm going to catch a nap before heading that direction."

Molly went into the bathroom and downed two Ibuprofen and a full glass of water, willing her headache to disappear.

A workout will help, she told herself. Exercise would burn off the booze. She dressed quickly and hurried for the door. Frank didn't require a lot of sleep. If she wanted a private conversation with Mike, she needed to do it sooner rather than later.

The kids were up eating cereal at the kitchen island when she made it back downstairs. Everyone had slept in. She kissed them on the tops of their heads and put a to-go cup under the coffee maker. When her coffee was ready, she waved goodbye to Nolan and headed to the gym.

The drive felt like forever and no time at all. She was eager to get to the gym, to end it with Mike, but also frightened. She'd never dealt with anyone like him before. Her parents had been drug addicts, violent toward one another, but never toward her. Her foster fathers had shown too much interest, causing her to hide, but they weren't aggressive. Frank was self-centered, but he'd never harmed her outside of taking what he thought she owed him as his spouse. Mike's sort of dangerousness was foreign to her.

She parked, took a deep breath, then went inside. Mike was there. Ready and waiting for her.

"Morning, trainee," Mike said. He flashed a smile baring his teeth.

"Umm, good morning."

"Are you ready to work out?" The remnants of passionate anger mixed with a hangover wafted from his hulking body.

"We need to talk," Molly said. It was best to get the elephant out of the way.

"Do you have Snapchat?"

Molly blinked several times. "What?"

"On your phone. Do you have Snapchat?"

"No," Molly said.

"Download it."

"Umm..."

"Do it now. Download it."

"Why?" Molly asked.

"So, we can talk."

"That's what I wanted to talk to you about. This isn't a good idea." She gestured from him back to her.

"It's an excellent idea. You're going to meet me later today. Same time."

"I don't think—"

"Or I'm going to tell everyone we fucked," Mike said.

"Excuse me?"

"People will believe it. Your reputation will be ruined. Frank's reputation will be ruined."

That was the rub of it all. In a small town like Fort Calhoun, Molly's husband could have as many affairs as he liked. It would be fodder for gossip, but there were no real ramifications to his decisions. But Molly, if she did the same, she was a slut whore that nobody wanted to associate with, and Frank was weak for allowing it. It could hurt Frank's businesses, and her kids' financial security.

"But we didn't," Molly said.

"Who is going to believe you?"

"I..." her voice trailed off.

"Exactly. You'll meet me today at the same time."

"But—"

"You don't want to make me angry. Ask my wife."

That was a threat. One Molly might have been able to use against him if Angel had gone to the cops with the domestic assault. But Angel hadn't.

"You'll be there," he said.

Reluctantly, Molly nodded. She didn't have a choice.

33

TYRONE

Tyrone was waiting outside Angel's office a little before eight o'clock. The elevator dinged, and the doors opened, revealing Angel. She stepped out, looking down at her phone. She hadn't noticed him. She headed straight for the door without looking up, moving with the confidence of someone who had made this trek a million times.

She lowered her phone to shove her keys in the lock. She still hadn't noticed him. As she twisted her wrist, he cleared his throat. She froze.

"Hello, Mrs. Malone."

Angel swung around, holding her keys between her fingers like a weapon.

Tyrone lifted his hands, a gesture of surrender. "I'm just here to talk."

She stared at him, wide eyed as a skittish cat.

"Can we talk?"

"That depends," Angel said.

"On what?"

"Why you want to talk."

"I want to discuss someone I saw leaving your office back in February."

"I can't discuss clients."

"This person was not a client."

"How do you know that?"

"Okay," Tyrone said, crossing his arms. "Fair enough. I don't *know* he wasn't a client, but I strongly suspect that he wasn't."

"Why's that?"

"Because he worked for Frank Sand."

"Lots of people work for Frank Sand."

"His name is Nolan." Was he projecting, or did he see her flinch? "Nolan Weise."

Angel turned back to the door, opened it, and flipped on the lights. "Come on. If we're going to talk, we might as well do it inside."

Tyrone looked to his left and to his right, realizing just how deserted the building was at this time in the morning. He hadn't told anybody he was coming to Angel Malone's office. If something happened to him, nobody would find out for a long time, if ever.

"Don't worry," Angel said, when she saw his hesitation, "I don't bite."

Tyrone hated that phrase. Her ability to bite was not why he was hesitating. Still, he stepped inside. He needed information from Angel, and this was the only way he was going to get it. He had to play the game on her turf. She was a lawyer; she knew better than to accompany him down to the station.

She closed the door behind him and locked it.

"Why are you locking it?" Tyrone said. The lock was a regular deadbolt, one he could easily twist and unlock, but it was still unnerving.

"Because I don't want random clients popping in while we are in my office. You would be surprised how many strays wander in," she nodded toward the closed door. "When our office manager arrives, she'll unlock the door and keep track of them."

"I see." He made a *lead the way* gesture.

She walked past him, leaving a light trail of perfume in her wake. When they reached her office, she walked around her desk and sat behind it, motioning to the two chairs across from it. He sat in the chair closest to the door.

"What brings you to my humble office?" Angel asked when they were both situated.

He would not call the place *humble*. It wasn't ostentatious like Frank Sand's home, but it was tasteful and carefully decorated. A place that didn't scream money, but it said *I'm comfortable.*

"I want to talk about Nolan Weise," Tyrone said.

"What makes you think I know anything about Nolan Weise?"

"Because I saw him leaving your office on February fourteenth. You may have been the last person to speak with him before he disappeared."

"There are a lot of disappearing people in Fort Calhoun."

"Three, to be exact. But all seem to have some connection to you."

"Is that an accusation?" Angel asked.

"It's an observation."

"Fair enough." She leaned back in her chair, threading her fingers together. "Nolan was here. He's never been a client and he didn't visit me looking for legal representation, so our conversation isn't privileged. What do you want to know?"

"Why was he here?"

"He was," she looked up at the ceiling, pausing as though looking for the right word, "alarmed." Her piercing gaze shifted back to Tyrone. "He was fishing for information about Frank. Information I couldn't give. Everything I know of Frank comes from confidential communications, right down to his phone number and address. I couldn't help him."

"What happened next?"

She shrugged. "He left."

Tyrone studied her. He'd been spot on all those months ago when he'd said she had one hell of a poker face. There was no change in her features as she spoke. She could have been discussing the weather rather than a missing man with connections to a murdered woman. He wondered if that was due to a lack of concern or because she'd trained herself to relay information without emotion. It could be a little of both.

"That's it?"

Angel shrugged. It wasn't an admission or a denial. She was holding something back, but that didn't mean it was criminal.

"Have you heard from your husband?"

Still, there was no reaction. Mike Malone was another missing person in Fort Calhoun. Like Tyrone's mother, few people seemed to care about Mike's disappearance. Unlike Tyrone's mom, it sounded like it was entirely due to Mike's personality. The people who seemed to know him best worked out at *Frankly Hot and Heavy,* and they described him as arrogant, self-centered, and hotheaded. Tyrone's one and only interaction with Mike supported that.

"No. I haven't heard from him."

"He hasn't tried to call or email or anything since February?"

"No."

One of the things he found odd about Mike Malone's disappearance went back to the very first time he'd met Angel. Mike had been gone for less than twelve hours and she'd reported it. But when he'd *actually* disappeared within a few weeks of that initial report, she waited a week to report it. Why wait the second time?

"Are there any updates?" Angel's voice cut through Tyrone's thoughts.

"What was that?"

"I said, Are. There. Any. Updates." The words were short and sharp.

"No." It was an honest answer. He had suspicions, but those were only hunches. They both fell into silence for a long moment, then he said, "Do you remember when we first met?"

"Yes."

"You'd called about your husband."

"I remember." She shifted her weight in her chair.

"I was worried about you."

"I know. You told me."

"But I never told you why I was worried."

"Why was that?" Angel leaned forward in her chair. It was a slight movement, but he still caught it.

"When I found him, he said he wanted to kill you."

Something flickered in Angel's eyes, but it was gone as quickly as it had come.

"He was in what I would call a blind rage, saying things that nobody in their right mind would say in front of law enforcement."

Her eyebrows lifted. "Like what?"

"That he wanted to choke you until the life left your eyes."

"Wow," Angel's voice was deadpan. Tyrone suspected that was on purpose. "I can see why you were worried."

"I warned him that his statements were recorded on my body camera. I told him if he did anything to you, his would be the first door I'd knock on."

"Sounds reasonable."

"That must have been enough. He never did assault you. Did he?" He met her gaze, holding it.

Again, something flickered across her features, but it melted back into that blank expression.

"As you can see," she gestured to herself, "I'm alive."

"Yet, he's missing."

This time she had no reaction to his words.

He'd been monitoring all of Mike's social media accounts and his usual haunts. The guy was a gym rat. Records from *Frankly Hot and Heavy* showed that Mike Malone had not missed a single day at that gym for over a year prior to his disappearance. Then *poof*, he was suddenly gone. Coincidence? He thought not.

"Did you know Molly and Mike were having an affair?" He had no idea the question held any truth. He was fishing for information. It was a risk, but sometimes detectives needed to take risks to get to the next step in their investigation.

"Yes. That's why I didn't report Mike as missing right away. I assumed they'd run off together for a tryst and he'd be back. It was embarrassing, so I didn't want to bring more people into it than I had to."

It was possible that Mike and Molly had been on a tryst, but it had ended with Molly dead and Mike on the run. That was still a working theory for Tyrone. It was the primary reason he was so concerned about Mike Malone's disappearance.

"Okay," Tyrone said, rising to his feet. "I've taken enough of your time."

She glanced up at the clock. "Yes, I need to get to work."

"You'll let me know if Mike contacts you?"

"Sure."

He nodded and retreated toward the door. He needed to get to work as well. It was time they tracked down Nolan Weise, dead or alive.

As he made his way out to his patrol vehicle, his phone pinged with a message. He removed it from his back pocket. The screen displayed the same number that had been texting him the day before—the one he believed was Frankie Junior.

You're hiding information, the message read.

Who is this? Tyrone responded.

She's dead and you didn't tell me.

Who? Tyrone knew the answer, but he wanted the person to say it.

Dots appeared on Tyrone's screen, then disappeared, then appeared again. That continued for a few moments, then a message came through. *I didn't do it.*

Tyrone pressed the number on the screen, then clicked the phone button, calling. He was tired of these cryptic text messages. The phone rang and rang, but nobody answered. The person was avoiding the call. They had to be by the phone. They'd sent a text seconds earlier. Just when Tyrone thought he wouldn't get anything from the call, the voicemail picked up.

"Yeah," a familiar voice said, "you've reached my voicemail. Leave a message. Or don't. Whatever." It was Frankie Junior's voice.

Rookie mistake. Now Tyrone knew for sure the cryptic texts were coming from Frankie, not Vivian.

34

MOLLY

Molly regretted plenty of her life decisions, but none more than her choice to get involved with Mike Malone. The past week had been a nightmare. His entry into her life had taken it from bad to worse. He'd stolen her few moments of freedom, times she now knew she'd taken for granted, kidnapping them, and keeping them for himself.

Her phone buzzed on the island in front of her. She jumped but didn't reach for it. She knew who it was. *What would he say, no demand, this time?*

"The little darlings are down," Nolan said, coming down the stairs and into the kitchen. "Matt-attack does not want to nap anymore, and he's a squirrely one, he can..." his voice trailed off when he saw Molly, zoned out and staring at her phone. "Alright," he said, pulling the chair out next to her, "spill."

"Mike."

"What's that asshole doing now?" Molly didn't keep secrets from Nolan. He knew everything that had happened in the last week.

Molly sighed and ran a hand over her face. "Same thing, different day."

They fell into silence. Nolan knew her so well. He understood when she was ready to talk and when she needed a few moments to gather herself. After a good, long, thirty seconds, she was finally ready to face it. The message. She reached out and grabbed her phone, unlocking it. She clicked on the Snapchat icon. Mike had sent a message.

Get here soon, was all it said.

She clicked on the map icon. When Mike made her download Snapchat, he'd acted like it was for communication. He hadn't mentioned the tracking, but when she'd shut that function off, he'd messaged her within moments, telling her to turn it back on. Instead of freedom of choice, she found herself tracked by *two* separate men, both frightening, but in different ways.

She stared at the Snapchat map page, showing Mike's avatar hovering above Nolan's grandmother's duplex.

"Is he still at Nanna's place?" Nolan finally asked.

"Yeah."

Mike had all but moved into Nolan's grandmother's home. The night the officer had appeared was the last night Mike had stayed at his house. Now that he was there, she didn't know how to get him out.

"Why can't he find his own place? He's married to a lawyer."

Molly shrugged. "He says he has nowhere to go. But Angel had wanted him home that very first night. She'd called the cops and asked them to track him down."

"Hmm," Nolan bit his lip. "Unless something changed that night."

Molly chewed her lip. If Frank was right, something *had* changed.

"I'm sorry I brought you into this mess," Molly said. "I should have met Mike somewhere else. I shouldn't have met him at all. And now he's living there." She sighed heavily.

"Don't. Do not go blaming yourself, girlie. I volunteered the place. We didn't know he was a psychopath. We had no way of knowing."

Molly should have tried harder. But she'd been blinded by Frank's philandering and his iron-clad control over her body and her life. She behaved recklessly and it had led to disaster as recklessness often did.

Nolan glanced at the clock. It was nearing two o'clock. "Are you going to see him again today?"

"I don't have a choice." An ever-present sense of doom hung over her head. Molly was walking a tightrope, dangling high in the sky, barely maintaining her balance. Sometimes it seemed easier to jump.

"You should go to the cops. This is basically rape."

Molly shook her head. "I can't. They won't see it that way."

"You aren't consenting."

"I'm also not saying *no*. It's my fault. All of this is my fault." Molly dropped her head into her hands and began to cry. She was more trapped than ever.

"I'm coming with you," Nolan said.

"No." Molly forced herself to stop crying and wiped the tears with the back of her hand. "You need to stay with the kids. I'll find a way out of this. Somehow."

"What about Angel?" Nolan asked. "We should go to her."

"And say what?" Tears rolled down her cheeks, unbidden. "Her husband wants to cheat on her so badly that he forces me to participate. That would not go over well."

"Honey," Nolan's tone took on an edge of exasperation, "this isn't the 1990's. Women are not blaming women anymore."

"Angel would blame me."

"You aren't giving her enough credit. Maybe she would, maybe she wouldn't, but it's worth a try." He gently touched her chin and lifted her head. "It couldn't get any worse, right?"

Molly shook her head.

"Then, let's talk to Angel."

Molly shook her head again. "No. Not yet. I just, I don't know, want to see if I can get him to lose interest in me on his own."

Nolan gave her a skeptical look. "You're dreaming, girlie. Have you seen yourself?"

Molly burst into a fresh set of tears. She had once believed that beauty meant power, privilege, but that was far from the truth. It had only served to cage her. If she ever got out of this mess, if she somehow found a way to live her own life, she'd gain twenty pounds, dye her hair black, and she'd never ever wear another stitch of makeup.

"Hey, hey," Nolan said, wrapping an arm around her bony shoulders, "we'll figure it out. Together."

Molly took a shaky breath and wiped her tears. "You're such a good friend, Nolan."

He nodded.

"I need to get this over with," Molly stood and headed toward the garage, moving like a woman on her way to the gallows. She drove to Nolan's grandmother's duplex and slipped inside. Mike was waiting for her.

"What took you so long?" Mike said the moment she'd come through the door.

"I have kids."

"Frank's out of town." It was a statement, not a question. "I want you to stay the night."

"What about my children?"

"Isn't that what that Nolan guy is for?"

"I don't have anything with me."

"You can sleep naked."

"And my toothbrush?"

"You can use mine."

She cringed at the suggestions, but she managed to quell her derision. There was no choice in the matter. He had nothing to lose by outing their "relationship," she had plenty to lose. Once again, she'd handed all the power to a man, and thanks to Frank, she didn't have all that much to give away.

Their night went as expected. Molly was disgusted with herself, but she participated. Afterward, they went to sleep, his big arm slung around her tiny waist. A visual reminder of his power compared to her frailty. In the morning, she awoke to the sound of Mike's phone ringing. Molly knew it wasn't hers. Hers was still at her house so Frank would think she was at home.

After several rings, Mike answered.

"Who is it?" Molly groaned.

Mike gave her a look that said, *What the hell is wrong with you?*

Molly's hand flew to her mouth, feigning embarrassment, but it hadn't been an accident. She'd presumed the caller was his wife. Over the course of the evening, she had thought over Nolan's words. She still didn't think approaching Angel was a great plan, but if anyone was going to put an end to this thing between Mike and Molly, it would be Angel.

Mike rolled out of bed and went to the next room, the argument quickly turning from heated to shouting.

Molly took that moment to grab her things and head to her car. She'd parked in the garage, as always, but the garage door was wide open. Had she forgotten to close it? *Shit,* she thought. *Anyone could have seen my car here.* Then she saw the note. It was pinned beneath her windshield wiper. She snatched it off her car and read.

"I know what you've been doing. You are a naughty, naughty girl. Call me. We need to chat." It was signed with a flourish *Vivian*, with a number scrawled along the bottom of the page.

"Fucking Vivian," Molly said aloud. Her gaze shifted to the *For Sale* sign posted in front of the duplex next door. Vivian's face grinned at her. There was a mischievous glint in her eyes that Molly hadn't noticed before. If the sign could talk, she imagined Vivian's picture would wink at her and say, "got you."

Molly crumpled the note and threw it into the passenger seat of her car as she got inside. If there was any person who could make her situation worse, it was Vivian. Not because she'd tell Frank, but because she'd use the information to blackmail Molly. Vivian was the type.

She's already taking Frank to court for more child support. What is she going to want from me? If Vivian thought Molly could convince Frank to pay her more money, she was insane. Frank didn't listen to Molly, and Vivian of all people, should know that.

In the span of a few weeks, Molly had become beholden to three people instead of one. Frank, Mike, and now Vivian. It didn't seem like things could get any worse, but of course, they always could.

35

ANGEL

Past
February 10

It wasn't supposed to be this way. Angel had followed every societal standard that was supposed to lead her to happiness, checking them off a mental list. Study hard, check. Ace classes, check. Join honors society, check. Play sports, join clubs, check. "Kept her nose clean and her legs together," as her mother had put it, check.

She'd worked her way through college and through law school. She'd married the person she'd hoped to love after losing her one true love. She'd had babies around thirty. On paper, she *should* be winning. Yet, somehow, after doing everything that society told her was *right*, her life had turned out wrong.

The last week had gone from bad to worse. Mike was like a ghost. A phantom that orbited around her life with the children. He didn't even try with the girls. He'd given up on all three of them, and the girls were noticing. Their moodiness had increased. Angel couldn't blame them; he'd abandoned them. And for what? Molly Sand.

Her work was suffering, too. Caring for the girls as a single parent was eating into the time that she used to reserve for paperwork. Hearings and meetings devoured most of her days, and that left no time for paperwork, drafting motions and responding to filings. That meant she was staying up later to catch up and still falling behind.

That morning, the morning of the tenth, she'd had enough. Her alarm sounded at four in the morning. She flipped it off, stood, and pulled a robe over her shoulders. Then she grabbed her phone and headed down the hall to the guest bedroom, where Mike had been sleeping. But he wasn't there. The bed was still perfectly made. Had he even been sleeping here? She knew he had the night he'd threatened her because she'd seen him there, but she'd assumed he'd been sleeping in the guest room for the past week. But if not here, then where?

A flare of anger shot through her. This last week had been hell for her, trying to keep up with everything. And what was he doing? Playing house with Molly at that damned duplex. That had to be where he was staying. He couldn't be renting a hotel; she'd checked the credit card statements and there was barely any cash in the joint account.

Mike is not going to get away with this, Angel thought, gripping her phone tightly. *He is not going to make a fool of me.* She'd worked too hard for him to ruin her reputation by sleeping with one of her client's wives.

But what should she do? She couldn't send the detective after him again, that would make her seem even more pathetic to law enforcement and infuriate Mike. She couldn't show up at the residence either. If law enforcement learned she'd known the address all along, then they could go after her for filing a false report. Her gaze shifted to her phone. She'd have to call.

She pressed Mike's number. It rang and rang and rang. *At least the phone's on*, Angel thought. When it went to voicemail, she hung up and dialed again. Again, it rang and rang, ending in voicemail. Again, she hung up and redialed. She kept repeating the action until finally, he answered.

"What is it?" Mike said. His voice was groggy with sleep. "Is something wrong with the kids?"

Angel hadn't thought of inventing a problem with the girls, but that was a good one. She should have prepared an excuse. But she hadn't, and his comment had her wrongfooted and unable to respond.

"Who is it?" A woman's voice said from the background. She, too, sounded groggy.

"What the fuck, Mike." Angel had found her words. "Who is that?"

"Is there something wrong with the girls?"

"Who the fuck is with you?"

"Angel."

"*Mike.*"

"Just answer me."

"You fucking answer me first."

She could hear him getting up and moving around. "Angel, I swear to God, if you don't tell me what –"

"You swear what? You'll fucking choke me? You'll slit my throat? You'll teach me a lesson? Which is it, Mike? Or do you plan to do all three?"

He was silent for a long moment, then he said, "You never put the money back in the joint account."

Angel threw her head back and laughed, a maniacal cackle that held no mirth. "You're kidding right? You thought that I would actually give you money after you beat the shit out of me and threatened to kill me?"

He lacked any remorse. Not for his violent outburst, not for the way he was treating his family, and that was when it hit her. He was a psychopath. She was married to a man who lacked empathy. He didn't care about anyone but himself. Not her. Not their girls. Not Molly.

"This is over," Angel said. "You have violated every form of our marital contract."

"See, there's the problem. Marriage *is* a contract to you. You throw my burst of anger back at me, but at least I have passion. Living with you is like living with a robot."

Passion. That was how he had characterized his decision to hold his wife down with a knife to her throat. She knew it had to be something. That he'd justified it in some way. And there it was. In his mind, she'd deserved it because she was not warm enough.

"There can be no love or *passion* when I'm doing everything myself," Angel said.

"Yeah, well, you've made it clear my contribution to the household is my 'job,' yet you stopped paying me for it."

"Our family is not your job," Angel shouted.

"You act like it is."

"You'll never get another dime from me."

"We'll see about that," Mike said. Then he hung up.

He was right. They both knew it. Even with all his bad behavior, it had only been going on for a week. He could switch course now and win everything in a divorce. Alimony, custody, and a boatload of child support. She'd be paying him far more than the dime she'd threatened to withhold.

What was she going to do? She had no idea. Then Frank Sand called.

36

TYRONE

Tyrone took screen shots of the text messages from Frankie Junior and sent them to Jackie before getting into his cruiser. His phone made a *whoosh* sound and then he pocketed it and hopped into his car.

His meeting with Angel Malone hadn't provided much information, but it wasn't a complete waste of time. Tragedy surrounded her, yet she seemed unruffled. Her husband was missing. He was sleeping with Molly Sand. Molly was dead. Her husband could be dead, or he could be a killer. She showed no reaction to any of it. No tears. No anger. Nothing.

He headed the few blocks back to the law enforcement center. He could have walked, but he needed to be prepared in case of an emergency. Jogging back to the station to get to his car was not the police force's idea of preparedness. He parked at the back of the law enforcement building and texted Jackie.

I'm here. Today was the day they'd visit the duplex.

Be there in a sec! Jackie's response was immediate.

He set the phone aside and rested his head back against the headrest, closing his eyes. Jackie was way too excited. But she'd discovered the connection between the duplex and Nolan, so she deserved to be part of it. He just hoped her enthusiasm wouldn't get in the way.

The passenger door opened, and he jerked himself upright at the sound.

"Did I scare you, boss?" Jackie asked.

"No."

Jackie climbed inside and closed the door.

"And don't call me boss. I'm not your boss."

"Close enough," Jackie said, buckling her seatbelt.

It was not close at all. She was misinterpreting knowledge for power. He had plenty of knowledge. Far more than some of the higher-ranking officers in Fort Calhoun, and definitely more than Jake. But he also had very little power. He hadn't been around long enough for the good ol' boys to accept him, if they ever would.

"Are you ready for this?" Tyrone said, fixing Jackie with his most intense gaze. She needed to take it seriously. They weren't on a fieldtrip. They were about to embark on something that could make or break the investigation into Molly's death.

"Oh, yeah. I can't wait."

That wasn't the right answer. "Drop the giddiness."

Jackie straightened her features, but she still wasn't somber enough.

"If we find Nolan, and that's a big *if*, you need to remember that he could be a killer. He could be dangerous to me, to you, to the public. Do you understand?"

"Yes."

"He could also be dead and decomposing inside that duplex. We could be walking in on one very disturbing scene."

Jackie's expression had grown properly solemn. She nodded slowly.

"Good. Let's go." He put the car in gear and headed down Main Street toward the same duplex he'd visited back in February, but on a very different type of investigation.

"Did you get the screenshots I sent you?" Tyrone asked. She hadn't responded or mentioned them.

"Yeah. I saved them in Molly's digital file. Who were they from?"

"Frankie Junior."

"Why do they matter?" Jackie asked. "I mean, on their face, they seem innocent enough. He's upset that you didn't tell him his stepmother was dead."

"I tried to call him, but he didn't answer."

"Okay. He's mad at you, and he's a kid. Avoiding confrontation with a cop doesn't seem that strange."

"It isn't, but it is something to consider. He could be trying to fish for information. If he killed Molly, he's going to want to know if we are on his trail."

"Okay."

"And he said, 'I didn't do it' when I hadn't accused him," Tyrone added.

"Yeah, but he has to know you are looking at him as a suspect. You interviewed him yesterday."

Tyrone stopped at a stop sign and looked at her. "It's no smoking gun, I know, but we can't disregard any potential leads."

Jackie nodded.

They pulled up to the duplex, parking on the street. They got out and approached the door.

"This place could use some sprucing up," Jackie said.

The grass had been cut—a Homeowners Association probably did that —but that was the only sign that anyone had been on this property for a long time. The lantern-style porch light was broken, its glass lying in chunks beneath it. The flowerbeds overflowed with yellow dandelions and nettles. Paint chipped from the exterior, large chunks curling away from the structure.

"That happens with abandoned homes." *Or homes people want you to think are abandoned.*

Tyrone led the way to the front door, Jackie following close behind. Spiderwebs hung from the upper corners of the roof overhang, but there were no cobwebs attached to the door. Someone had recently opened it. That didn't mean a person was living there. Anyone could open the glass storm door, disturbing the spiders' homes. Tyrone did just that as he opened it so he could knock on the wood door within.

"Are you ready?" Tyrone asked.

Jackie nodded. Gone was the giddy girl in the car. She was ready.

He knocked three times, banging his knuckles against the wood. The sound split the silence of the sleepy neighborhood. He stepped back, and they waited. Nothing happened.

"Should we walk around back?" Jackie asked.

"Not yet." Tyrone closed his fist and turned so the bottom of his hand struck the door. *Thump. Thump. Thump.*

A sound followed. A barely audible shuffling. Had it come from inside?

"Did you hear that?" Jackie whispered.

"Yes. Be prepared in case this goes south." He nodded at her taser, then her gun.

Her lips dipped into a scowl. Danger was part of their job, but they weren't often confronted with it. Tyrone rarely drew his firearm.

"*Police!*" Tyrone shouted. "*Fort Calhoun Police Department. Anyone home?*" A nearby bird spooked and took flight, chittering as it disappeared into the distance.

There was another shuffle, this time closer to the door.

"*Open up or I'll kick the door in!*" Tyrone said.

It was an empty threat. They had no search warrant, no reason to enter aside from a hunch that Nolan would be there. The door flew open, but only a crack, marred by a chain. One light blue eye stared out at them.

"Who are you and what do you want?" A voice whispered from behind the door.

"Police Department," Tyrone said, removing his badge from his back pocket and showing it to the person behind the door. Jackie was a patrol cop, so she was in full uniform, which gave Tyrone extra credibility. "Are you Nolan Weise?"

"Yes."

The door slammed shut. Tyrone and Jackie exchanged a look. Then the door flew back open, this time unmolested by the chain. A skinny white man stood behind it. He was in his mid to late twenties, dressed in a pair of fitted jeans and a t-shirt with a rainbow and *Pride Proud* written below it. His brown hair was longer in front and brushed off to the side.

"Get off the street," Nolan said, his head swiveling while he motioned for them to enter. "Someone might have seen you."

Tyrone entered first, Jackie followed. Nolan closed the door behind them, locking it and sliding the chain into place. *Click. Swish.* He moved in one fluid motion, then slowly turned to face them. His eyes narrowed, his hands on his hips.

"You found me." It was an accusation.

"It wasn't easy," Tyrone said.

"Few people know about this place."

I did. But did Nolan know that?

Nolan led them deeper into the home. A sound came from upstairs, the low *creak* of floorboards. Tyrone froze. Jackie did the same. They both looked toward the ceiling, trying to gauge where the sound had originated.

"Are you here alone?" Tyrone asked, his gaze still locked on the ceiling.

"Yes."

"Who made that noise upstairs?" Tyrone asked.

Nolan shrugged. "It's an old building."

Tyrone and Jackie's gazes met. She didn't believe Nolan either. He wanted to send Jackie to clear the residence, to make sure nobody could jump out at them, but they were not there for a search warrant or an arrest warrant. There was no legal cause to perform a protective sweep.

They continued following Nolan. Most of the lights were off, but the windows provided enough light to see. Tyrone wondered what Nolan did at night. Did he sit in the dark?

"How long have you been staying here?" A better word would be *hiding* but "staying" sounded less like an accusation.

"Since Molly disappeared on the fourteenth."

They followed Nolan past an open living area, and to the kitchen at the back of the duplex. Packages of junk food covered the counters. Pop Tarts and Doritos. Hostess cakes sat next to the largest package of Sour Patch Kids candy that Tyrone had ever seen.

"Not on a health kick, I see."

Nolan's gaze settled on the snacks. "Yeah, well, I've got to find joy somewhere. I lost my bestie and my two darling children. I raised them, you know. Me and Molly. Frank is a terrible father. How are the kids? Have you seen them?"

Tyrone nodded. "They seem fine. Rebecca is the new au pair."

"Rebecca? That bitch. She's only there because she's banging Frank. She doesn't care about the kids. My poor, poor babies."

"They're surviving," Tyrone said with a shrug. They didn't seem happy, but he saw no overt signs of abuse.

"Why are you here?" Jackie asked. It was a hard-edged question that cut through the room.

The question wasn't inappropriate, but Tyrone still gave her a look. She was supposed to stay quiet. The wrong question or even the right question worded in the wrong way could cause a witness or suspect to shut down. Jackie was too inexperienced, and the case was too important to risk Jackie posing questions of her own.

She recognized her misstep and snapped her mouth shut.

"I'm scared," Nolan said. He said it so simply, so openly that it seemed completely genuine. Yet, it also sounded a little rehearsed. Like Nolan had known that they would come knocking, and he'd spent every night leading up to it looking in the mirror and repeating those two words *I'm scared*.

"Does anyone know you are here?" Tyrone asked.

Nolan shook his head, moving it from side to side in an exaggerated manner.

"I talked to your exes," Jackie said.

Nolan's eyes widened, but he said nothing.

Tyrone would have given Jackie another warning look, but Nolan's expression had him intrigued. What was it about his exes that had him suddenly fidgeting?

Jackie looked to Tyrone, a question in her eyes. *Should I continue?*

Tyrone nodded.

"Why didn't you tell Naomi that you are here," Jackie said, gesturing around her, "and that you are safe? She said you talked daily before you disappeared. She's really worried."

Nolan issued a heavy sigh and his shoulders relaxed. "It's simple. I don't trust anyone."

Tyrone studied the man in front of him. Nothing about his story made sense. There was no reason for him to hide like this. If Frank was truly a threat to him, then he could have reported the threat to law enforcement. Hiding for months on end was dramatic at best, suspicious at worst.

"The place belongs to my grandmother," Nolan said. "She's in the nursing home here in town."

Nolan was at least telling the truth about *something*, but this fact was easily verifiable, and Nolan knew that. If they could find him, they could certainly find his grandmother.

"She's been in that nursing home for over a year, and this place has sat empty," Nolan said.

"Not entirely empty," Tyrone said.

Nolan raised an eyebrow.

Tyrone fixed him with a hard look. "I responded to a call here. Back in February. That was before Molly Sand and Mike Malone disappeared. I was investigating an unrelated call and I found Mike Malone here," he pointed to the ground, "in this duplex."

"Yes," Nolan said with a nod. "Molly told me about that."

"What else did Molly tell you?" Tyrone said.

Nolan issued a heavy sigh. "Don't judge Molly. Her marriage was not all sunshine and rainbows." He gestured to the rainbow on his shirt. "Frank was gone all the time, and he was always having affairs. He'd pick women who worked out at the gym. Molly went to that gym. Of course, she noticed. Even if she didn't notice herself, someone would tell her. People loved to gossip. Especially about Molly."

"Tell me something I don't know." Tyrone removed a small notepad from his pocket and a pen. His body camera would catch the conversation word for word, but it was best to have a quick reference as well.

"Molly and Mike were," Nolan paused, chewing on his lip, "involved," he finally said. "That's all I know."

Tyrone doubted that.

"What about Mike's wife? Did Molly care about her feelings on the matter?" Tyrone asked.

"Not really. Angel represented Frank. Molly knew that. Everyone knows that. Everyone also knows that Angel is willing to get Frank out of anything. Vivian got screwed in their divorce. She should have gotten so much more than she did. Frank took her to the cleaners, all with Angel's help. She'd been a new attorney back then, but her ruthlessness was obvious. Now she's known for it. Nobody goes to Angel Malone unless they want war."

"Okay." Tyrone didn't know what to say to that, so he focused the conversation back on the two lovers. "Molly and Mike would stay here sometimes, is that right?"

Nolan nodded. "Molly usually didn't stay the night. They'd come here for a couple hours to do," he cleared his throat, "you know. And then they separated. Molly would return home and Mike stayed here."

"I see."

"Don't judge Molly."

"You've already said that," Tyrone added. "And I don't judge dead people, especially if they were murdered."

Nolan nodded, tears springing to his eyes.

"If Mike Malone was staying here, where is he now?"

"That's why I originally came here." He gestured around him. "I was looking for Mike and Molly."

"I suppose you didn't find them."

"Nobody was here."

Tyrone looked at the filth surrounding them. The house was disgusting. If any evidence existed, it was long gone now. Still, it didn't hurt to ask. "Did you notice anything in disarray? Any blood? Anything?"

Nolan shook his head. "No blood. Some of the living room furniture had been knocked over, but before February, I hadn't been here for over a year. I don't remember how I left it. And Mike had basically been living here."

"Do you know what happened to Molly?"

Nolan shook his head. "I thought you'd be able to tell me."

"Then why are you hiding?" It was time for Tyrone to lean a little harder on Nolan.

"What do you mean?" Nolan shifted his weight.

"You were the last person to see Molly alive. You have information that would have been nice to know back in February. None of it was reported."

"What would you have done with that information? If I told you that Mike and Molly were meeting here regularly and they both disappeared after meeting up, would that have changed the police's theory of two lovers running off together?"

"No. I suppose it wouldn't," Tyrone said. "Who do you think killed Molly?"

"That's easy."

"Oh?" Tyrone raised an eyebrow.

"It has to be Frank, Frankie Jr., Rebecca, Vivian, or Mike Malone."

"What about Angel Malone? Could it be her?"

"Yes, but I get the impression that she doesn't care all that much about her husband. She wouldn't kill for him. Nobody would."

"What does that mean, 'nobody would,'" Tyrone said.

"You've met Mike. He sucks. Molly was only spending time with him because he blackmailed her into it. If you want my opinion, he's a rapist. He was forcing Molly to do it."

"Okay," Tyrone said. "If that's the truth, then Molly was kidnapped. Back in February. Why wouldn't you report it?"

"Molly swore me to secrecy. I kept her secrets."

"Even if it was to her detriment."

Nolan narrowed his eyes. "I'm not on trial here."

Tyrone nodded, then paused. He needed to lift up on the gas. He was pressing too hard. Nolan was on the verge of ending the interview and kicking them out. "Did Frank know about the sexual assaults?"

Nolan shrugged. "If he did, he would have blamed Molly. She was an object to Frank. He thought he owned her. He could do whatever he wanted and whoever he wanted, but Molly was supposed to stay at home, silent and submissive, the perfect housewife."

"You met with Angel Malone the same day Molly disappeared," Tyrone said. He let the statement hang in the room, heavy and dense, then he added, "Why?"

"I wanted her help."

"I thought you said that she would do anything for Frank."

"Her husband was part of this. If Frank killed Molly, he was probably after her husband as well."

"I see."

"Angel knew about the affair. She pretended she didn't, but she knew. She's not dumb. I went to her for help. I thought she'd have some sympathy, but she didn't. She was cold."

"Why would Angel have sympathy for her spouse's mistress?" Tyrone asked.

"Because she didn't care about Mike."

"How do you know that?" That logic was contradictory. If Angel didn't care about Mike, she was even less likely to get involved.

"I just know."

"Okay," Tyrone said. Angel was unemotional, but unemotional was not the same as uncaring. "Tell me about the last time you saw Molly." Tyrone said.

"Valentine's Day. She left the house for a little while."

"What was she doing?"

"She was coming to end things with Mike."

"Molly ended it with Mike on the same day she disappeared?"

"Yes. And he probably didn't take it well," Nolan said.

That would explain why Molly had been missing so long. Mike grew angry and kidnapped her. He held her somewhere, trying to convince her that he was the one for her. When she didn't comply, he killed her and tried to get rid of the body. But where would he have kept her?

Tyrone would have to check with Angel. He wondered if their finances would show a large purchase around that time. An RV out in the country or a rural storage unit would be the perfect place to keep a hostage.

"Why were Frankie Junior and Vivian on your list of potential suspects?" Tyrone asked.

"Frankie Junior is infatuated with Molly. I told her, I warned her, but she wouldn't believe it."

"Warned her about what?"

"I caught the kid going through Molly's things."

"Okay."

"He was sniffing her used underwear from the laundry hamper."

That was gross, but it didn't mean he was a murderer.

"He would steal things from her. Like a lipstick or perfume. Things that were distinctly Molly. She was always looking for lost items. She thought she was so forgetful. I told her it was Frankie Junior, but she wouldn't or couldn't see it. She wanted to believe he was a good kid."

"What about Vivian? Why would she want to kill Molly?"

"She was fixated with Molly, but in a different way. She hated her. She hated Frank, too. She stalked her. She'd leave nasty notes on her car."

"How did you know the notes were from Vivian?"

Nolan chuckled, but it held no mirth. "She'd sign her name right there on the note. She wanted Molly to know that she was following her."

"Why didn't Molly bring any of the notes to the cops?"

"Because she thought it was a family issue. She also didn't want to get Frankie Junior's mom in trouble. The kid had enough problems."

"Are the notes around anymore?"

"No. Molly threw them out. She didn't want Frank to know about it. Despite Vivian's treatment of her, Molly didn't want Frank to go after Vivian."

"Why not?"

"Those two are like vipers. It's easy to see why they originally got together. They are the same person. Narcissistic and spiteful. A war would have lots of casualties. Not Vivian or Frank themselves. They were too careful, but Molly's kids, they would definitely get caught in the crossfire. That's who Molly was protecting, not Vivian."

"Well," Tyrone said, flipping his notebook shut. "I think that's all the questions we have for today."

"Are you going to tell anyone I am here?"

"No. But you better not disappear again." Tyrone looked pointedly at the counter. Next to the Sour Patch Kids was a box of black hair dye. "That means changing your appearance and going on the run."

"I won't," Nolan said, clasping his hands together.

"You'd better not," Tyrone said.

Tyrone and Jackie left the residence. Once again, they had more information, but no solid leads. Everyone involved in this mess had reasons to want Molly dead. Everyone had reasons to lie. It seemed like the more information Tyrone scraped together, the muddier everything got.

He needed a break. A solid lead. Something that would make one person on his long list of suspects jump out as a front runner. He had lots of motives and lots of suspects, which also meant that he had nothing.

37

ANGEL

Past
February 10

"This modification thing," Frank said, "can we get it resolved?"

"Why?" Angel had barely brought the phone to her ear. Frank's lack of small talk alarmed her. He was a good ol' boy, a businessman, the type of person who started phone conversations with meaningless chatter. It wasn't his style to dive right in.

"Because."

"I don't get it. You fight Vivian on everything."

Angel cast her gaze around the room, looking for a pen and notepad. She was still at home, in her bedroom.

"She fired her attorney," Frank said.

"Why?" Angel stepped into her closet, considering her clothing. She selected a blue skirt suit with a white blouse and switched the phone to speaker as she dressed.

"I don't know. She doesn't tell me anything unless it benefits her."

"How did you find out about the lawyer?"

"People talk," Frank said.

Vivian's release of her attorney would mean that Angel could contact her directly. Represented parties had to have attorneys present always, but unrepresented parties were different. Angel usually hated dealing with *pro se* parties. They were emotional and she couldn't answer any of their questions. It usually prolonged settlement, but Vivian would be different. She was a businesswoman; she was cunning. She would make choices that benefited her, and her alone. Angel understood her motivations, which made negotiations possible.

"Alright, what do you want to offer?" Angel said.

"I don't care. Offer her whatever she wants. It's only until Frankie Junior is eighteen in a couple months, right?"

"Yeah," Angel said. "Honestly, if you fought it, you could draw it out, but you'd end up paying me the same amount you'd pay Vivian. It will end up as a wash for you either way."

"Nothing like having two women that aren't banging you in your pocket, am I right?"

Angel was in front of the mirror, applying makeup. She studied her own expression and was happy to see that nothing changed, despite his offensive comment. Years of courtroom training, countless hours of reminding herself to stifle her reactions, had paid off. She truly did have a fantastic poker face.

"I'll give Vivian a call. Is her number still the same?" Angel asked.

"Same as it's always been."

"Okay," Angel said.

"Talk to you soon. I hope with good news. You'll try to keep the amount down, right?"

"Yes," Angel said. "That's my job."

The call disconnected. Angel finished her makeup and headed down the hallway toward the kitchen, peeking in on her girls. They were still sound asleep. She would let them sleep in today. At least until she finished talking to Vivian. She closed the door and continued toward her laptop. It was in its usual spot on the kitchen island. Vivian's number was listed on the petition for modification. Before she made it to her computer, her cell phone started buzzing. It was an unknown number.

"This is Angel Malone," she said, bringing the phone to her ear.

"Angel," a silky voice said, "Vivian. Good morning."

"I was just about to call you."

"I'm sure Frank told you about my attorney situation," Vivian said. "He's so predictable."

"Men always are."

Vivian laughed, a deep chuckle that held mirth, but in a dark way. "But women aren't."

"No. We aren't."

"That's why I fired my attorney," Vivian said. "I don't give a fig about settling this modification thing anymore. I've got something I want to tell you."

"Okay," Angel said. This conversation was not going in the direction she had expected.

"Did you know that Molly Sand and your husband have a thing going?"

Angel didn't know how to answer the question. She didn't want to admit it, but she didn't want to shut the conversation down either. She wanted to know what Vivian knew. "No comment."

Another dark chuckle. "Way to dodge the question. You're too funny. There's more to the story, though."

"Okay."

"Molly doesn't know this, but Nolan and I are friends. We work out at Frank's gym, and we got to talking. He called me early this morning in a tizzy, worried about Molly, you know. He said that your husband has been forcing her to have a relationship with him. She claims he's basically black-mailing her."

"I wouldn't put anything past my husband these days."

"You see, that's exactly why I wanted to talk to you. I wouldn't put anything past my ex-husband either. So, I thought there was a way we might be able to help one another out. I pat your back, you pat mine."

Angel had no idea what that meant, but she knew she was about to find out.

38

TYRONE

Present
June 16

Tyrone and Jackie left the duplex and walked across the street to Tyrone's unmarked cruiser in silence. They got inside and sat for a moment, still in silence.

"What now?" Jackie said. She sounded as defeated as he felt.

"We keep going," Tyrone said with a sigh. "That's all we can do." He turned the key in the ignition and put the vehicle in gear. He started to lift off the brake pedal when Jackie's voice rang out.

"*Wait!*"

Tyrone slammed his foot back down on the brakes. "What? What's wrong?" His head swiveled in search of unseen danger.

"I know that person," Jackie said, pointing at a car that was pulling into the duplex driveway.

"And..."

"It's Naomi White."

"I still don't follow."

"Let's see where she goes. She's one of Nolan's exes. She claimed she didn't know where he was, and she was worried about him."

Tyrone's gaze followed the woman as she got out of her vehicle. They both sank down in their seats as Naomi looked in all directions, then she hurried to Nolan's front door. She had a large bag with *Home Health* written on the side slung over one shoulder and two grocery style bags in one hand.

"Looks like she lied to you," Tyrone said.

"Looks like it."

It was no smoking gun, but it gave them another angle to approach. Naomi could have been protecting Nolan or she could have been covering for him. The difference between the two words sounded like semantics, but it could easily lead to the difference between guilt or innocence.

What is your game, Nolan? Tyrone thought as he put the vehicle in gear. He tapped the gas and took off. He didn't want to be there when Nolan opened the door. If Nolan knew they'd seen Naomi, he might use that box of black hair dye, change his appearance, and go on the run. Right now, he had no reason to believe he was a person of interest. He had no reason to think any of his lies were unraveling. Tyrone needed to know his location.

39

ANGEL

Past
February 12

Frank and Vivian's modification case settled. Most cases, especially those involving Frank, didn't resolve so easily or quickly, but Frank was motivated, and Angel had given him a little shove in the right direction. The increase in child support would only last for a few months. Then Frankie Junior would turn eighteen, and Frank's support obligation would terminate.

The problem was that Angel would have to draft the settlement stipulation. It needed to be done now, preferably yesterday, but Angel's schedule with the girls made that problematic. She drove to and from daycare, got groceries, made dinner, constantly checked Lily's blood sugar and when she wasn't checking it, she was worrying about checking it. That left little time in the evenings for work.

That was how she found herself awake at two o'clock in the morning, sitting in the dark in her daughters' room behind a locked door. She really needed to change the exterior locks. Mike hadn't been home, but he could return at any time. She was not going to leave her little girls to his mercy, especially after he'd called them *bitches like her*.

She looked down at her laptop. It was balanced on her legs and her notes were sitting next to her, illuminated by her cell phone light. This was not a long-term solution, but her situation would not last forever. It was temporary. She had a solution.

Finish the stipulation, Angel told herself.

She turned back to the computer, focusing on the document captioned *In Re the Marriage of Frank Sand, Petitioner, and Vivian Sand, Respondent.* Frank was still technically the "Petitioner" because he was the one who filed for divorce all those years ago. Even though it was Vivian who had asked for the modification, the caption remained the same, naming her the "Respondent."

Angel's gaze shifted to her notes. Frank had agreed to pay an extra five thousand dollars per month until Frankie turned eighteen on June second. The agreement included the month of February even though they were close to halfway through it, and June. It was a lot of money, twenty-five thousand extra dollars over the next several months. That was on top of the current support obligation. But Frank had agreed to it and Angel had encouraged that agreement because of the informal agreement that would not be included in the written document. A promise Vivian was all too willing to make.

Angel continued plugging away at the stipulation, and finally finished at three in the morning. She set an alarm for five and laid down in Lily's twin-sized bed. Lily had vacated it sometime during the night to squeeze into bed with her sister. Angel closed her eyes and drifted off to sleep.

It felt like seconds later when her alarm sounded. Angel shot up and grabbed her phone from the floor beside her, grappling to silence it before the girls woke up. They both stirred, Angel's heart pounded, but they settled back into sleep, nestled in close to one another. Angel got up and started the morning routine of showering, getting ready, getting the girls ready, driving to school, then driving to work.

It was always a relief when she stepped through the front door of her office. This morning was no different. The atmosphere completely changed from total chaos as a single mother to calm, quiet, and orderly. She was back in her element.

This is only temporary, Angel reminded herself. Once everything was settled, she could hire someone to help in the evenings. Until then, she needed to grit her teeth and move forward.

"Look who it is," a voice caught her attention.

Angel turned and saw an elderly man sitting in the waiting room. "Good morning, Old Pete," Angel said. It was always strange calling an old man *old* to his face, but he insisted on it. "You're a sight for sore eyes."

"You too, my girl," he grunted as he rose to his feet. He shuffled over to her and pulled her in for a hug.

Old Pete was one of the few people that Angel would allow to hug her. He'd been a client of George's since Angel first started practicing law. He and George became close friends over the years, causing Old Pete to stop in often. He had children her age. Over time, he started treating her like one of his children, pestering her to take care of herself and inviting her over for Sunday night dinners. She rarely went, but it was nice to receive an invitation.

"Is George making you wait?" Angel said, stepping back. "Shame on him."

"Oh, I'm early. You know me. I came straight after feeding the pigs."

"Well, you don't smell like you've been feeding pigs." She'd been to Old Pete's farm several times. He'd shown her all the animal pens, including the pigs.

"Oh, I don't spend a lot of time with them. They'll eat me alive."

Angel gave him a sidelong look. "Pigs don't eat people."

"They sure do. They'll eat everything. Bones. Clothes. Blood. Brains."

"Gross."

Old Pete shrugged. "They can go feral lickity-split. Just like that," he snapped. "I'm telling you, you've got to keep your eyes on them at all times."

"I'll keep that in mind," Angel said, patting him on the shoulder. "I ought to get back to my office, but it was nice seeing you, Old Pete."

"You too, sweetheart."

Sweetheart. That simple word melted her heart. Nobody ever called her sweet. "I hope George doesn't leave you waiting too long."

"I've got time. All I've got is time anymore."

She flashed him one last smile, then headed back to her office, flipping the lights on, and reviving her computer.

Vivian and Frank arrived at eight o'clock sharp. They came strolling into Angel's office without knocking or waiting for Angel's office manager to announce their presence, per usual for Frank.

"My Angel," Frank said, holding his arms out, a wide grin split fully across his face. "You're ready for us to sign, right? You've got to be ready for us to sign." He winked at her.

Angel's gazed shifted to Vivian. If she saw the gesture, she ignored it. "Everything is ready," Angel said.

Vivian met Angel's gaze and grinned, but she didn't speak.

"Great. Great," Frank said.

Angel motioned toward the two chairs across from her desk. "Have a seat."

Frank was unusually gentlemanly, waiting for Vivian to get situated first, then he lowered himself into his own chair.

Angel slid the stipulation across the table, placing it in front of Vivian first. Vivian grabbed it and began to read. Vivian's gaze shifted from left to right, taking in the contents of the stipulation. She was a real estate agent, a successful one at that, so contracts and legalese were not new to her.

Frank shifted his weight. He was growing impatient, but somehow, he kept his mouth shut. It must have taken a herculean effort. Vivian finished reading, then placed the document back down on the desk. She held out a hand, palm up, reaching toward Angel.

Angel looked at her hand, confused.

"Pen," Vivian said.

"Right," Angel placed a pen in Vivian's hand.

Vivian signed with a flourish, then slid the document over to Frank, handing him the pen. Frank didn't read anything and signed his name, sliding the document back to Angel.

"Thank you," Angel said, signing the document herself. "I'll get it filed. I expect the judge to issue an order adopting it sometime this afternoon or tomorrow morning. Then it will be official."

"So, we are done then?" Frank said, rising to his feet.

Vivian followed suit.

"Yes," Angel said. "I'll email a signed copy to you when it comes through the electronic filing system."

Vivian and Frank left together. But before they stepped out the door, Vivian turned and cast Angel one last look. A smile flashed across her lips, and she winked.

Angel nodded.

Vivian turned and joined her ex-husband at the end of the hallway.

During their last phone call, Vivian had revealed a plan so intricate that even Angel couldn't have come up with it herself. That was how Angel had known it would work. Signing the modification was a tiny piece of that plan.

Things were running smoothly, at least so far. The next few steps would be far more difficult to pull off.

40

TYRONE

Molly's murder was starting to catch national interest. Podcasts were popping up. Bloggers and armchair sleuths clogged the police station phone lines. While it seemed helpful, it wasn't. None of the information so far had led to evidence, but Tyrone still had to follow up on everything.

The Fort Calhoun Police Department designated a line to keep up with the torrent of incoming calls from tipsters. The department even hired a new person to handle the influx of calls. Yet, there were no new additions to Tyrone's investigation team, despite his constant request for assistance. He didn't know if that was because Jake had warned the other officers away with his tales of jobs as janitors or if the Chief just wouldn't do it. Either way, Jackie was all he was going to get. It was woefully inadequate.

Everything hung on this case. If Tyrone got it right, if he solved it with so few resources, he could return to Chicago, point to it, and say, *look what I can do*. They'd have to give him a detective position. If he didn't solve Molly's murder, he might never get out of Fort Calhoun. The very idea sent a burst of anxiety through him. He couldn't wait to get back to the busy streets of his hometown. Crickets and quiet towns were not for him.

"What's on the agenda today?" Jackie said, greeting Tyrone as he stepped into his office, red-eyed and exhausted.

"You tell me." The days were bleeding together. Tyrone felt like a robot in a factory assembly line, repeating the same action, building something, but never seeing the finished product.

"Harper wants to talk to you. She called earlier and said you should call her when you got in," Jackie said.

"Why didn't you lead with that?" Tyron said, irritated.

"Sorry. I didn't realize it was that important. She didn't say it was important."

Tyrone sighed. Jackie had a lot to learn. It may not be important, but the prosecutor thought it was, and that's all that mattered. He grabbed his phone and pressed Harper's name. It rang once, then she picked up.

"Hey, Tyrone. We're in the conference room," Harper said.

"The conference room here? At the police station?"

"Yes."

Tyrone's gaze shifted to Jackie.

She shrugged and mouthed *I'm sorry. I didn't know.*

"I'm headed there now." He hung up and dashed down the hall toward the conference room.

"Do you want me to come?" Jackie asked, following behind him.

"No. You keep following up with tips," he called over his shoulder.

"Okay."

She sounded crestfallen, but it made no sense for them both to waste their time in the meeting. It wasn't a punishment, it was practical. He hurried into the conference room, finding the Chief of Police and Harper both seated at the table.

"There you are," Harper said. She did not even attempt to smile.

"The brain needs sleep to function."

"True." Harper verbally agreed, but her gaze was critical and assessing. "I have to make a statement today."

"A statement?" Tyrone said, dropping into the seat across from Harper and the Chief of Police.

"A public statement. It is scheduled for four o'clock today. I can't hold it off any longer. The public needs to know that they are not in danger. They need reassurance."

"Can you honestly say that?" Tyrone said.

They did not have a primary suspect. It could be someone close to Molly, but they had nothing solid to directly connect any one person. That meant that there was still a possibility it could be a random killer.

"That's not my fault, is it?" Harper said. "You have been given days to find a solution. The public needs reassurance. I have to give it to them."

"You can't put it off?"

"I can't."

It was a political thing. Politics shouldn't play a role in investigations, but they did. There was no point pushing against it. Harper was going to do what she was going to do. That included lying to the public.

"Thank you for the information," Tyrone said, rising to his feet. "I have an investigation to get back to."

"Good. You've got all day to make my words accurate," Harper said, forcing a smile that looked more like a grimace.

Tyrone left the meeting more dejected than ever. They had no solid leads and little evidence from the scene, thanks to those filthy pigs. Forensics was painstakingly slow, but that was nothing new. It was the same way in Chicago. Testing took time.

He headed down the hallway toward his office, his mind going over what little evidence they had. They knew the blood was Molly's, they suspected the hair was hers as well, but that was all they knew. They'd pulled several fingerprints off Molly's purse. Some were attributed to Molly, but a few were unidentified. They didn't match anything in the database. That only meant the killer wasn't a felon or someone fingerprinted for their job, like law enforcement.

Jackie was waiting for him in his office. She bounced from one foot to another. A wide grin brightened her features.

"What is it?" Tyrone said, his heart leaping. Her excitement was contagious.

"Frankie called."

"Frankie Junior?"

"Yes. He called the tip line."

Finally, Tyrone thought, *a tip that's worth serious consideration.* "What did he say?"

"He told me to look at the divorce docket."

"What?" All Tyrone's enthusiasm evaporated. Divorce filings were public record. Anyone could access them. The electronic filing system made it even easier. All someone had to do was create an account and start searching. It wasn't a place a killer would hide information. "How is that helpful?"

"I thought the same thing," Jackie said, her smile still firmly in place, "but I followed up on it anyway. Just like you said. You told me to check any and all leads, no matter how ridiculous."

He had said that, but he hadn't expected a reference to legal documents available to the public. They were boring and filled with legal jargon. They had all been approved by attorneys and at least one judge. If there was any evidentiary value in them, one of the legal professionals would have caught it. Wouldn't they?

"I found Frank and Vivian Sand's original divorce file."

"Okay." He crossed his arms. He had no idea where this was going, but Jackie had better get there fast. He was losing patience.

"Here," she motioned toward the computer, "it would help to see it."

Tyrone crouched down and stared at the screen.

"See there," Jackie pointed to a filing near the top of the screen. "That's a new stipulation for modification of child custody. It was filed on February thirteenth."

"Okay." It was the day before Molly disappeared, but it meant nothing alone.

"Frankie Junior was almost eighteen at the time. That's what he said bothered him so much about it."

It was an odd time for a modification, but it still didn't mean anything. What was Frankie Junior's game anyway? Why would he call to report his parents? He could be trying to divert interest from himself. Frankie had expressed dislike for his parents, but to report them to law enforcement, that was something more than regular family drama.

Jackie clicked on a link and a document filled the screen. The caption listed Vivian and Frank Sand's names, naming Frank as the Petitioner and

Vivian as the Respondent, and said *Stipulation for Modification of Custody and Support.* Jackie scrolled down, stopping at the third paragraph. Tyrone started reading.

The parties stipulate and agree that the Petitioner's support obligation should be increased from $3,500 per month to $8,500 per month starting this month, the month of February, and continuing through and including the month in which the minor child, F.S., reaches the age of majority.

Tyrone whistled. "That more than doubles Frank Sand's child support obligation."

"Yes," Jackie said.

Tyrone stared at the document, his excitement growing. "The day before Molly Sand disappeared."

"Yes."

"Vivian hated Molly," Tyrone said.

Again, she nodded.

"And Frank was having an affair with Rebecca."

Jackie motioned for him to keep going.

"This could be a payoff."

"Exactly," Jackie said beaming. "Frank wanted to get rid of Molly. Vivian was all too happy to oblige. For a price, of course."

"A twenty-five-thousand-dollar price tag." Frankie Sand turned eighteen in June. That meant five months of five-thousand-dollar payments.

It was genius. Tyrone and Jackie had already subpoenaed everyone's bank records to see if there was a possibility of a murder-for-hire scheme. It, too, had been a dead end. But Frank and Vivian were too smart for that. They were highly intelligent people, ruthless too. They'd known that the police would never think to look at a public document as a piece of evidence. But their son, apparently, was just as cunning.

"I think it's time we pay Vivian Sand another visit," Tyrone said.

They finally had a frontrunner.

41

MOLLY

Valentine's day was Molly's breaking point. By ten o'clock in the morning, Mike had already sent ten Snaps. Five were messages begging for her to come to the townhome. The other five were dick pics. Frank, for all his drawbacks, had never sent her pictures like that.

When she received the fifth picture, she looked at it, recoiled, then slammed her phone face down on the table.

"What now?" Nolan asked, lifting an eyebrow.

Nolan and Molly were at the kitchen island. The kids were in the living room watching television.

"Mike. He keeps sending those, those pictures," Molly said.

Nolan wrinkled his nose. "Distasteful."

"Disgusting."

"Uncivilized," Nolan said.

"Cringy." If the situation wasn't so dire, Molly would have laughed.

"Some people like them," Nolan said, picking at his nails. "I'll never know why."

"Maybe Rebecca knows."

"Maybe Rebecca and Mike belong together. Should we introduce them?" Nolan asked.

"I'll be sure and ask when I see Mike in a little while."

Nolan looked up. "You're going to see him?" He paused. "On Valentines' Day?"

Molly nodded.

"What if Frank comes home early?"

"It's a risk I have to take."

It was a risk, but not a major one. Romance was not Frank's strong suit. If he caught her, it would be because the florist delivered flowers when she wasn't there to sign for them. Flowers came every year. Mostly because Frank's personal assistant handled gifts for major holidays, birthdays, and occasions. Frank rarely even knew what Molly was getting before she did.

"Why don't you wait until tomorrow or the next day?" Nolan asked.

"Mike won't allow it. He'll message me and message me. With my luck, Frank will come home early, see my phone buzzing with messages, and then I'll really be in trouble."

"I thought you were going to file for divorce."

"I never said I was *going* to."

"You seemed interested in the idea."

"Yeah," Molly said with a sigh. "I am interested, and it is comforting to know that I would get *something* if Frank files, but I have to think of the kids. He isn't a great father, but he doesn't physically harm them."

"He sucks, but he could be worse. He could be a criminal," Nolan said. "You bagged yourself a winner, there."

"At least I know where the kids are. If I divorce Frank, he'll have them at least every other weekend—if not more—and I'll have no way to check on them."

"You have a point."

"So, I'd like to make it work if I can." If Mike had taught her anything, it was that the grass wasn't always greener on the other side. Frank was terrible, but Mike was worse.

"What about school?"

"I'll find a way to make it work. Maybe there is a way to enroll without Frank knowing."

"Are you hearing yourself?"

Molly sighed. "I get it. I just…I don't know. I don't have the energy. That's why I'm going to go over to your grandmother's duplex today. It's time I end this thing."

"Do you want me to come with you?"

"No. You need to stay with the kids."

"We could bring the kids."

"It isn't safe," Molly said.

"That's why you shouldn't go by yourself."

"I got myself into this mess, Nolan. I'll get myself out of it."

"Fine," he crossed his arms, "but I don't like it."

She didn't like it either, but the alternative was to place her children in danger, and she was not going to do that. She sat there for another long moment, sharing a knowing look with her best friend, then she squeezed his hand and stood. She couldn't linger. She needed to deal with the problem. Rip off the Band-Aid. Expose the wound to the elements so it could start to heal.

"You're leaving now?" Nolan asked.

"Now or never."

Molly said her goodbyes to the kids, kissing them both on the top of the head and giving them long hugs. She smelled their hair and pulled their little bodies in close to her. Then she made her way toward the door.

"Are you bringing your phone?"

"Yes."

This time, she would. If there was danger it would come from Mike. She was ending their relationship. Frank tracking her iPhone was the lesser of two evils. Besides, she didn't plan to be there long. She'd tell Mike it was over, then pop over to the gym for a surprise visit or something. It was Valentine's Day. She could use it as an excuse to see her husband at work.

"Okay. Call for help if things go sideways."

"I will," Molly said.

"Promise?"

"Promise."

As Molly was leaving, Nolan picked up his phone to make a call. He held the phone pressed to his ear, waving at her as she made her way to the door, his gaze full of something she couldn't place. Was it anxiety? Was it agitation? She didn't stop to ask. If she did, she might lose her nerve.

When Molly stepped into the garage and closed the door to the house, it was for the last time.

42

TYRONE

Present
June 18

Tyrone and Jackie had planned to visit Vivian Sand for a second interview, but that didn't happen. As always, the second Tyrone had a lead, something took the wind out of his sails. This time it came as a phone call.

"Harper," Tyrone said, eager for her to know that he was finally getting somewhere.

"You need to get out here," Harper said.

"Out where?"

"Do you know Legends State Park?"

It was a park on the outskirts of town, not far from Old Pete's farm, where Molly had been killed.

"I know it."

"A hiker found Mike Malone," Harper said.

"He's been hiding out?"

"No. He's dead."

Tyrone placed his fingers to the bridge of his nose and released a heavy breath. This was not good news. "Give me your coordinates."

She did and he hung up, rushing down the hall.

Jackie kept pace. "What's going on?"

He filled her in as they walked. They jumped in Tyrone's cruiser and headed out to the scene, using lights and sirens. They made it in less than ten minutes. The Chief of police was present. So was Harper and a whole set of patrol officers, including Jake who had set up barriers and was holding a perimeter.

"Here for another bite at the janitorial apple," Jake said, baring his teeth in a mirthless smile.

Tyrone ignored him and walked up to the huddle that included the Chief, the prosecutor, and other senior officers. They stopped talking and nodded to Tyrone, ignoring Jackie.

"Thanks for coming," the Chief said.

"Sure." Tyrone had little choice.

"I'm assigning Detective Weekly and Officer McKee to oversee Malone's murder case," the Chief continued, "but I wanted you here due to the potential tie between your victim and Mr. Malone."

Jake sidled up to the group, clapping the only other detective on the force on the shoulder. A man called Markus Weekly. "Chief put the big guns on this one," Jake said with a smile. "We'll probably solve both cases within a day. You're welcome in advance."

Tyrone didn't respond. It was not lost on Tyrone that the chief had assigned a detective and a seasoned officer—wannabe detective—to Mike Malone's case but given Tyrone a newbie cop to assist him.

"The medical examiner is here." Chief said, also ignoring Jake's antics. "You might want to speak with her."

Tyrone nodded and stepped away from the group, thankful to put some distance between himself and Jake's sneer. He approached a small woman standing off to the side, holding a clipboard and staring down at a large object on the ground. Her face was cut by laugh lines, but she wasn't smiling now.

"Are you the medical examiner?"

"That's me. Get it M.E.?" She said, flashing a quick smile.

Tyrone almost laughed at the absurdity of a joke in such somber surroundings. But then again, in their professions, you had to find humor wherever you could.

"Tyrone Gully," Tyrone said, extending his hand.

"Tiffany Lee," she shook his hand, her grip firm.

"What are we dealing with?" Tyrone asked, cutting to the chase.

Tiffany whistled. "It's a doozy."

"How so?"

"He's frozen."

"What?" Tyrone said. He wiped a bead of sweat from his brow. It was close to one hundred degrees that day. "I don't think I heard you correctly."

"I've got to run some more tests, but I'm pretty sure the cause of death is asphyxiation. I won't know for sure until I cut him open for a full examination."

Tyrone looked at the body. A plastic bag lay beside it along with what looked like a cell phone charging cord.

"The bag was over his head when the hiker found him. The wire was securing it in place."

"Who removed them?"

"The first officer on scene," Tiffany said with a cluck of her tongue. She looked down at a notepad. "An Officer McKee. Know him?"

"Unfortunately."

"That idiot said he wanted to provide CPR. You'd think he'd notice the body temperature, but I guess not."

"Tell me about the body temperature."

Tyrone couldn't quite wrap his head around it.

"I won't be able to get a good determination on the date or time of death," Tiffany said.

"You won't?"

"Of course not." Tiffany gestured to the body laid out only a few yards away. "He's frozen. Like any other meat in a freezer, that slows decomposition. The elements aren't the reason he's in this condition either. Obviously. It's hotter than the molten middle of a hot pocket out here. It's been that way all week."

"How is that possible?"

Tiffany shrugged. "The same way anyone freezes meat. A freezer. That would be my best guess."

Tyrone's gaze shifted back to the body. Mike Malone's hulking frame lay sprawled across the ground, his arms splayed out like he'd been crucified on a supine cross. "But he's intact."

A body would have to be dismembered to fit into a freezer. That was what Jeffery Dahmer had done, although he might have kept body parts in the refrigerator, not the freezer. Tyrone couldn't remember.

"It must have been a very large freezer." Tiffany said.

A very large freezer indeed. Restaurants had freezers. Mike and Vivian Sand owned restaurants. It brought Tyrone and Jackie right back to where they'd left off, Vivian. But this time there was a second body.

43

MOLLY

The drive to the duplex was intense. The silence had a weight that pressed down upon Molly as her mind raced. How would she end things with Mike? *We need to talk? This isn't working?* She wanted to convey her point, but she couldn't trigger his temper. *It's not you it's me?* Molly groaned. None of the cliché statements would work. He would never allow her to break up and leave.

"What are you going to do?" she asked herself, her words slicing through the quiet. "Let him do this for the rest of your life?"

She shook her head. She couldn't allow it. She wouldn't. She thought her life was bad before, and it was, but her entanglement with Mike was pure torture. Her anxiety increased when she passed the *Welcome to Fort Calhoun* sign. She had entered the city limits. As she continued down the sleepy streets, her mind continued to whir, and her solutions remained none. At this rate, she'd end up walking in there and saying, "I don't want you. Glad that's over. Okay, bye." Mike would probably kill her before he let her leave like that.

But there was no more time to plan. Not that time would have provided an answer that didn't exist. She pulled into the driveway of the duplex. Mike's car was parked out front. She scoffed at his ridiculous silver Lexus with a *MUSCLE* vanity plate.

She reached up toward the garage door opener hanging from her visor, but she didn't hit it. A movement in the duplex next door caught Molly's attention. The front door swung open, and a figure came charging out, headed straight for Molly's car. For a moment, Molly thought she was seeing things. Then her heart skipped a beat and began pounding in her chest.

It was Vivian.

"Oh, no," Molly said, just as the passenger door swung open and Vivian jumped inside.

"Surprise," Vivian said. The corners of her mouth tipped up into a smile, but it was not one of mirth. It mocked her.

What did Vivian want now?

44

TYRONE

Now
June 18

Nobody wants a law enforcement officer knocking on their door. Two was worse. They never brought good news. They came with search warrants, news of unexpected deaths and serious accidents, reports a family member was a victim of crimes. They had questions that stretched into interviews, and sometimes turned into interrogations. When Tyrone knocked on Vivian's door for the second time, Jackie was with him. Vivian greeted them with little warmth when she opened the door.

"Hello, Ms. Sand," Tyrone said.

"Good day," Vivian said. Her gaze flicked from Tyrone to Jackie, before settling back on Tyrone. "What can I do for you?" There was no hint of flirtation, a stark difference from the first time they'd met.

Once again, Vivian Sand was dressed impeccably. Her top was bright, canary yellow and silk, tucked into high-waisted white pants. She was toothpick skinny, and her hair was unnaturally thick, making it appear far fuller and wider than her waist. A lot like a life-sized Barbie.

"We need to talk," Tyrone said. "Are you willing to speak with us?"

Vivian patted her hair, a nervous gesture. "Of course, come in." She opened the storm door and stepped aside, gesturing for them to enter. She led them to a formal living room with all white furniture, motioning for them to have a seat.

"Oh, no," Tyrone said. "I can't sit there." He'd been at a murder scene that morning. He was not clean enough to sit on stark white furniture.

"Suit yourself," Vivian said, clasping her hands together. She turned the full force of her gaze on him.

Silence descended. She stared at him. He returned her gaze. Nobody spoke. After a long moment, he spoke.

"You know Molly's dead."

"Yes. But what does that have to do with me?"

Tyrone ignored the question. "We found Mike Malone today."

"Mike Malone?" Vivian attempted to furrow her brow, but the Botox wouldn't allow it.

"Yes. Molly Sand's lover."

Vivian scowled at the word *lover*. "I doubt love was involved, detective."

"Did Frank know about the affair?"

"If he didn't, he had his head in the sand."

"What do you mean by that?"

Vivian tapped a heel against waxed wood flooring. *Tap. Tap. Tap.* "He either knew or he intentionally ignored it."

"Is that something he would do with his spouses, intentionally ignore cheating?"

Vivian bristled. "No. Frank is a jealous and controlling man."

"I see. Would your son say the same thing about his father?"

"Leave my son out of this. He's a kid."

"He's an adult." *And he's the one who ratted you out.*

"Eighteen-year-olds are not adults."

"Legally, they are. But I agree, emotionally, they can be a bit childish. Especially boys. You see, I've heard some interesting things about your son."

Vivian crossed her skinny arms. Tyrone could tell she wanted the interview to end, but she wasn't quite ready to lawyer up. She thought she was too smart, that she could weasel her way out of anything with words.

Except that wasn't true. Words often led to trouble. The more a suspect talked, the more trouble followed.

"I heard your son was obsessed with Molly Sand."

"Obsessed is a strong word."

"That he'd steal her perfume and wear it."

"That's not true."

Tyrone lifted his eyebrows. "How do you know? You weren't present at Frank and Molly's home, were you?"

"Of course not. I don't go there. Frank is my ex-husband for a reason."

"You don't get along?"

"No," Vivian said. "I go to Frank's gym because they have the best Pilates instructor in town. That's the only reason. The workout classes are the reason most women go there."

"Why?"

"It is a gym created by a man for men."

"Okay."

"I don't believe that about my son. He's a good kid. He might have been attracted to her. Look at her," she gestured to her television hanging above the fireplace. It was on mute, but the station must have been doing a segment on Molly, because a picture of her smiling face looked out at them. "She was twenty-eight. Only ten years older than my son. They were far closer in age than Frank and Molly."

"Where were you when Molly disappeared on February fourteenth?"

Vivian picked at her polished nail, her hand shaking. "I have no idea. That was a long time ago."

"Did you sell the duplex next to...," he looked down at his notes and recited the address to Nolan's grandmother's duplex.

"Maybe. I sell a lot of real estate in town."

"That duplex went on the market in January and sold in mid-March." Jackie had found the information days ago. Tyrone wasn't sure if it meant anything, but it wouldn't hurt to ask.

"I'm not sure where you are going with this line of questioning, but I don't like it."

"Don't worry about where my questioning is going. Just answer honestly. That's the best way to get things off your chest and the past behind you."

"Fine," Vivian crossed her arms. "I believe I did sell it, and I'd have to look back at land records to know when, exactly, it sold, but March could be right. The real estate market slows in the winter and picks back up in the spring."

"You didn't see Molly and Mike Malone sneaking off to that neighboring duplex?"

She attempted to furrow her brow, but again, the Botox didn't allow it. "No. I didn't."

He didn't believe her. This was a small town and the three of them attended the same gym. He doubted that Vivian wouldn't recognize Mike and Molly's cars.

"I know what you are insinuating, and it makes absolutely no sense." Vivian's tone was stern.

He made a *go on* gesture. It was always interesting when a suspect tried to piece things together for him. It gave insight into their thought patterns.

"You think that I had something to do with Mike and Molly's deaths, and that makes no sense. Sure, I didn't like Molly, but I don't like lots of people. I hear rumors about who is sleeping with who, but that gym is a cesspool of affairs. I do not keep up with all the nonsense. Most of all, I have absolutely no motive to be involved. I could have told Frank about Molly's affair, sure, but I kept that information to myself. Between Molly and Frank, I don't know which one I prefer. I know my son prefers Molly."

"And that doesn't make you jealous?"

"My son better not look at me the same way he looks at Molly."

"Right," Tyrone said. "You have addressed jealousy and revenge as motives."

"Obviously."

"But what about money?"

"I don't need money," she gestured to her spacious home. "Like I said, I sell a lot of real estate."

"And you get child support."

"I did. As you pointed out earlier, Frankie Junior is technically an adult.

He turned eighteen on the second. I won't receive anything from Frank anymore."

Tyrone always carried a folder containing a legal pad, and a pen. Before leaving for this interview, he'd added a document to that folder. A printed copy of Vivian and Frank's stipulation of modification, signed and filed on February thirteenth. He produced it and handed it to Vivian.

"Do you recognize this document?"

The color drained from Vivian's face. "Where did you get this?"

"It's public record, Vivian. Anyone can get it."

"But why?" Her gaze flickered up from the document to Tyrone's face.

"Never mind why. Do you recognize it?" He needed to cut off the argument that it was forged before Vivian thought of it.

"Yes. We signed it in February. We met at his lawyer's office to do it."

"That's a mighty big change in support right before your child turned eighteen."

"Yes, well, I thought it was a long shot when I filed for the modification. I assumed Frank would handle it one of two ways, throw money at it to get it over with or postpone until Frankie Junior turned eighteen and the issue was moot. Obviously, I hoped he'd choose the first option, and he did."

"Why? Why did he choose it?"

"I don't know."

"He's never been willing to give in on anything in the past, has he?"

Tyrone had gone through that entire divorce file. In the electronic filing system, each document was stacked on top of the other with the oldest documents at the very end. Tyrone had to scroll and scroll and scroll to get back to the start. The case had lots of filings, which meant lots of motions and lots of arguing. These two were not the type to settle easily. Their original divorce had gone to trial. That wasn't common, and it was very expensive.

"No. He's not usually agreeable."

"So, what was different this time?"

Vivian sighed and pulled her hair over one shoulder. She began twisting a lock of it through her fingers. "I made a promise," she finally said.

"A promise," Tyrone repeated.

"Yes. It was an odd promise, and it obviously isn't in the paperwork." She handed the stipulation documents back to Tyrone.

"Frank told me he wouldn't fight if I stayed away from Old Main."

Old Main was one of Frank and Vivian's restaurants. One of the many that they both got in the divorce. She was a partial owner, so she had every right to be present. It was right next door to Frank's gym.

"I don't understand," Tyrone said.

"I don't know details either. Frank just told me that he wouldn't fight my request for modification if I stayed away from Old Main until he told me otherwise."

"Are you allowed to go back there now?"

"Yes. He told me just yesterday that I can return to the restaurant."

"When were you supposed to stop going?"

"The same day we signed the stipulation. February thirteenth."

That was the day before Molly Sand disappeared. The exact date of Mike's disappearance was trickier, but Tyrone had subpoenaed the gym scan card records and the morning of February fourteenth was the last day that Mike had scanned his card to enter *Frankly Hot and Heavy*.

"Is there a freezer at the restaurant?"

Vivian frowned. "There are freezers at every restaurant."

"I mean a large freezer."

"How large?"

"One big enough to hold two bodies."

Vivian gasped and placed a hand over her mouth. "You have got to be kidding."

"No, I'm not kidding. Answer the question." He was ninety-eight percent sure of the answer, but he needed certainty. Absolute certainty.

"Yes. Old Main has the largest freezer. We usually store some of the extra meat needed for the other restaurants there. It could fit two people easily. It could fit five."

"Thank you," Tyrone said, nodding toward Vivian. "That's all the questions for now." He motioned for Jackie to stand and started heading toward the door.

"What are you going to do?"

"I'd ask that you keep the contents of this conversation between us for now," Tyrone said, giving Vivian a hard look. "Warning Frank would not bode well for you."

Vivian nodded, her eyes wide, an almost exaggerated deer-in-head-lights expression.

Tyrone and Jackie left the residence, headed back to the office to type up a search warrant. It was going to take a while to get everything in order. The traditional eight to five workday was over. The County Attorney's Office would be closed, and all the judges would be home for the evening. He'd have to track Harper down to review and sign off on the search warrant and then find a magistrate to issue it. Nobody would be easy to find. But he was going to get it done, and tonight.

Frank Sand would not be happy to see Tyrone. Nobody liked when a group of law enforcement officers showed up at their doorstep. They liked it even less when they appeared at their place of business. Especially when they had a search warrant in hand.

45

MOLLY

"What do you want Vivian?" Molly said, trying to keep her voice even. She was on the verge of tears. Not tears of sadness, but of frustration.

"You didn't call me."

Molly blinked several times. "What?"

"I left you a note. I told you to call me. You didn't."

"Yeah, well, my world doesn't revolve around you."

"Pity, darling," Vivian said, clucking her tongue. "If it did, you'd be a hell of a lot happier than you are now."

"What do you know about happiness?"

"Admittedly, not a lot. But I know more than you," Vivian said.

Vivian had something in her hand. She held it up and Molly could see it was a garage door opener identical in size and style to the one that hung from her visor. Vivian clicked the button and the neighboring garage door trundled open.

Vivian nodded to the empty garage. "Pull in. We need to chat."

Molly's gaze shifted from the open garage to Nolan's grandmother's duplex. Mike was sitting inside, waiting for her. She was ready to break it off with him, she'd geared herself up for it. If Vivian diverted her now, she would lose her nerve.

"I have something I have to do first," Molly said.

"I'm sorry," Vivian said, producing a gun, "you seem to think I'm giving you a choice."

Molly's breath hitched; her gaze focused on the object in Vivian's hands. It was small with a black barrel and pink grip. "Why do you have that?"

"Protection."

From what? Molly thought. Vivian certainly wasn't using it for protection in that moment. Molly was no threat to her.

"It's unfortunate I had to use this," Vivian nodded at the gun. "I really didn't want to, Molly, but here we are. Now, pull into the garage before anyone sees you out here idling. It's for your own good."

Molly did as she was told. She moved forward and pulled the car into the garage. Vivian pressed the button to the garage door, and it started closing the moment Molly's car was fully in the garage.

"Turn the engine off," Vivian said.

"What are you going to do to me?" Molly's voice shook. Even her body was betraying her. If she was going to die, she wanted to at least sound brave.

"Well, if you don't turn that engine off, we're all going to die of carbon monoxide poisoning. So..." Vivian nodded to the ignition button. "Turn it off."

"Are you going to kill me?" If she was going to die, she might as well take Vivian with her.

"God, you're a moron," Vivian said, rolling her eyes. She released the magazine and displayed it to Molly. "Empty. I was never going to shoot you. I just needed you to get going."

"Oh," Molly shut the engine off. She was scared, but now she was confused. What the hell was happening?

Vivian grabbed the keys so Molly couldn't restart the car just as the door into the duplex creaked open. The lighting in the garage was dim, illuminated by one bare bulb triggered with the operation of the door. The house lighting was bright, shining all around the person silhouetted in the doorframe. Angel Malone.

Fear enveloped Molly. Vivian wasn't going to kill her. She wouldn't have to. Angel was there to do the job.

46

TYRONE

Search warrants were not easy to organize. So many officers uttered the phrase, *I'll just go get a search warrant,* when someone didn't consent to a search, but that statement wasn't true to the effort it required. It wasn't simple. The word *just* did not belong in the same sentence as *search warrant.* Ever.

First, Tyrone had to draft an Affidavit explaining all his evidence and how the evidence tied to the location where he believed the evidence existed. The information had to be current, or it would become stale. That meant it had to come into existence within hours, and potentially days, but certainly not weeks ago. The witnesses who provided the evidence had to be reliable. Everything had to be typed out clearly and concisely, in a way that a magistrate could read it and sign off with no questions outside the four corners of the document.

In this case, Tyrone had to list Vivian Sand as a witness and explain her background, history, and knowledge of Frank Sand's business. He had to describe her as reliable and explain the statements she'd made about Frank paying her to stay away from the Old Main restaurant, starting the day before Molly Sand disappeared and around the time that Mike Malone disappeared.

He described the size of the freezer inside Old Main restaurant and the condition of Mike Malone's body. *Frozen in summer*. He described the affair between Mike and Molly and the fact that Frank had likely known of its existence. He explained that Old Main was next to the gym where Molly and Mike frequented, an establishment also owned and operated by Frank Sand.

He condensed everything he knew about the case into a few pages, signed his name to the bottom, scanned it and emailed it to Harper for her to review and sign. He'd already warned her that it was coming, so he sat there for the next several minutes, staring at the computer, refreshing his email to see if she'd responded. Ten minutes later, his inbox had a new arrival. An email with the search warrant as an attachment, containing the Assistant County Attorney's signature. The subject line on the email was *Go get him.* Tyrone intended to do just that. But first, a signature from the magistrate.

The magistrate could not sign electronically, she had to sign in person. That meant Tyrone had to track her down. She could be anywhere. It was after hours. He started by calling her cell phone. She didn't answer. He sent her a text message.

I have a search warrant. Are you available to sign? He sent the text and stared at the screen, waiting for the tiny bubbles to appear, indicating that she was typing a response. A few minutes passed and he was about to call again, but then the bubbles popped up. They danced along the screen, then disappeared. He groaned. Then the bubbles reappeared, jumping up and down as she typed.

I'm at home. Come by. Was the magistrate's return text.

Tyrone hurried down the hall, grabbing Jackie. She was in the break room guzzling coffee— desperate attempt to stay awake to see the excitement through.

"What's happening?" Jackie said, running to keep up with his quick strides.

"Search warrant. The magistrate is available to sign."

They jumped into the car, drove the five miles to the magistrate's house.

He handed her the search warrant. She told him to raise his right hand, and she swore him in. He told her the documents were true and accurate, and she signed.

The next step was forming a team, also not an easy task. They needed multiple law enforcement officers for the search and for security of the scene. Nobody knew what employees would be on site when they arrived. All those people would need to be corralled, contained, and interviewed. This would all have to be done before Frank Sand or his attorney caught wind of it and started meddling. It was going to be a large operation.

First, he called the police department, gathered everyone they could provide. Thankfully, Jake worked days and couldn't be reached. Tyrone didn't have the energy to execute the search warrant while worrying about how Jake might twist things to take credit for all Tyrone's work.

Then he contacted the Sheriff's Department. They had three or four bodies to throw at the search warrant. Then he turned to the state troopers. Everyone there wanted to help—all they ever got to do was investigate drugs and car crashes. He had to tell half of them *no, that's too many*. In the end he had seven good guys, and two truly fantastic female officers, one of which was Jackie, and they were ready to go.

It was minutes before eleven o'clock, closing time at Old Main, when all the officers, deputies, and troopers were in position around the restaurant. They waited until the old bell above the nearby church started chiming the hour, then they moved in unison with Tyrone leading the way. One third of the group approached from the back, another third approached from the front, the remainder were positioned outside side doors and patio doors to ensure nobody tried to make a run for it.

Tyrone was in the group coming from the back. The restaurant was one of the nicer in town, but the back side did not reflect that. It was dirty, smelled of raw sewage and sunbaked garbage, and the door was small and uninviting. A person stepped out holding a bag of garbage while whistling a tune. It was a young man, possibly eighteen or nineteen. He froze when he saw the group of law enforcement, his eyes wide.

"Do you work here?" Tyrone said. He had the search warrant in hand, ready to serve any adult rightfully present.

"Umm, yes."

"What's your name?"

"Riley." His gaze shifted back and forth, jumping from one officer to the next. "What's going on?"

The kid seemed panicked. He probably thought something horrible had happened. Which, it had, but it didn't involve this kid. At least Tyrone didn't think it did.

"Is your boss here?"

"Umm, no." Riley visibly relaxed. "Do you want me to call him?"

"That won't be necessary. Are you eighteen?"

"I'm twenty." The kid said. He tossed the garbage in a dumpster and crossed his arms.

Eighteen was a fine guess. It was impossible to tell the age of some of these teenage boys. They were all skinny. All tall. All had acne until they were in their mid to late twenties.

"We have a search warrant," he handed a copy of the search warrant to Riley. "Is anyone else here?"

"Umm, yeah. There is one other employee locking things down up front."

"Anyone else?"

"No"

Tyrone nodded. That was good. If they only had to supervise two employees, that left far more officers available to search. He radioed to the group out front. They'd met the employee up there and detained the person.

"You can stay out here," he motioned for one of the troopers to join Riley. The trooper was a middle-aged guy. A big man with a buzzed military-style haircut. Tyrone didn't know him personally, but he'd heard he was one of the better investigators within the local state trooper system. He'd busted a lot of narcotics running in and out of the state through the highways. "The trooper here might have a few questions for you."

The remainder of the group headed inside. It didn't take long to find the freezer. It was huge, like a small room. Vivian had not exaggerated its size. Five full-sized people could easily fit inside.

"Protective gear," Tyrone said, as he snapped on his gloves and pulled booties over his feet. The other deputies and officers did the same.

If they found anything, it was imperative that they preserve the crime scene. Angel Malone understood chain of custody and evidence all too well. If they messed anything up, she could easily swoop in and start causing problems. Tyrone did not intend to give her that opportunity.

"Everyone ready?" Tyrone asked.

When he received affirmative responses, he placed his hand on the freezer door handle and pulled it open with a *whoosh*. A blast of cold air rushed out, catching in his lungs, and causing him to cough. A deputy held the door open while Tyrone and Jackie stepped inside. After the briefest of pauses, they both began to search.

The first thing Tyrone noticed was that the freezer held no food. There were no meats or vegetables anywhere. Not on any of the shelves or pushed back in corners. Yet the place was not clean by any stretch of the imagination. There were empty bags that had once held food strewn about. It had to be a code violation, right? Maybe not if the food was all gone. He was no restaurant inspector.

Tyrone took pictures of everything in the room, each empty bag, capturing the sheer number of them. There were piles upon piles of the discarded bags, each large enough to step inside and use for a sack in a sack race. None of them were sheer. They might have covered the bodies, hiding them from anyone who would peer into the small window built into the door.

"Look at this," Jackie said. She was in the back corner, pointing to something on the ground.

Tyrone came back and joined her, crouching down next to the object.

"Is that what I think it is?"

"Yes, I think it is." Tyrone took a close-up picture, then he stood and took several steps back, taking a wider shot to show where within the vast freezer the item had been found.

The item was a wallet, brown leather. A man's wallet. That didn't necessarily mean anything yet. An employee could have been in here for one reason or another and accidentally dropped their wallet. Tyrone needed to see what was inside. He removed an evidence bag from his back pocket, prepared to bag it once he inspected the inside. Then he opened it, and everything changed.

There, staring back at him, was Mike Malone's face, Angel Malone's dead husband. It was his driver's license photo. There were also a few credit cards bearing Mike's name and a health club membership card to the gym next door.

"Bingo," Tyrone said, placing the wallet into an evidence bag.

He brought the bag to the deputy in the doorway, telling him to note on the property inventory where in the freezer it had been found, then he returned to the search. They'd found proof of Mike's presence, but they needed to tie Molly to the place.

Tyrone continued looking in the area, and he found several long, light-brown, almost blonde hairs. They appeared to be the same shade and length as Molly's hair, but there was no way to be certain of that. At least not until forensics could examine the color and test the roots for DNA. The hairs were photographed, bagged, and tagged, then handed to the deputy to document their location on the property inventory sheet.

Tyrone and Jackie finished searching the freezer, but they didn't find anything more. He called Harper to fill her in, and she decided she'd call the Iowa Division of Criminal Investigations and ask them to send a forensic evidence team down. They needed to comb the place for skin cells and other microscopic evidence. Tyrone agreed and ended the call.

The day had started off hectic. They'd had no solid leads, no firm line of evidence to follow. But the search warrant had changed all that. Now the investigation could kick into high gear. There were lots of new witnesses to interview. He would have to talk to every employee at both businesses. There was no use wasting time. They were closing in on a suspect.

47

ANGEL

Past
February 14

Abject terror. That was the look on Molly's face. The way Molly's face contorted when she saw Angel standing in the doorway.

Good.

Vivian stepped out of the passenger side of the vehicle. "Get out of the car, Molly."

Molly shook her head.

"Just do it," Vivian said.

"No," Molly said.

"What are you going to do?" Angel said. "You can't drive away."

Vivian held up Molly's keys.

"And we aren't going to let you walk away," Angel continued. "So, you might as well come inside."

Molly sat still for another long moment, then she opened the door and stepped out of the car.

A positive development. Angel and Vivian did not want to drag her out of the vehicle kicking and screaming. They could do it, but the less violence, the better.

"Now, come inside." Angel was careful to keep her features even.

Molly trudged toward the door, Vivian following close behind, like a hangman following her quarry to the gallows. Angel stepped back as they came through the door.

"Have a seat." Angel gestured to the Formica kitchen table. It was connected to the counter, a permanent peninsula jutting out.

Molly did as directed, her eyes downcast, her frown deep. She'd be in tears in moments. Angel hoped it wouldn't come to that. Crying was for children. Adults, especially women, needed to buck up and fight. But Molly, she was more defeated than Angel had expected. There was no fight left in her.

"This kitchen should be a mirror of the one you are used to."

Molly nodded, keeping her head down.

"The one my husband is probably sitting at now."

Molly nodded again.

"Your husband is there, too."

Molly stilled, her entire body tense.

"He brought a gun, of course."

"His is probably loaded, though," Vivian called from the other side of the kitchen. She stood leaning against the counter, close enough to intervene if needed, but far enough to indicate Angel was running this show. "Frank is nothing but prepared when it comes to victimizing others. You know that." Vivian paused. "I do, too."

"I don't understand," Molly said, shaking her head.

"You will," Angel said, leaning down so she could catch Molly's frightened gaze. "Very soon, you will."

48

TYRONE

When the forensic team arrived at Frank's Restaurant, Tyrone stepped outside to give them some breathing room. He also wanted to interview the kid, Riley. The twenty-year-old that worked for Frank. The kid had been scared when law enforcement had first arrived. After a full hour of detention, he would be terrified. It was a perfect time to get information from him.

The outside air was muggy. Even though it was night, the heat from the day hadn't fully dissipated, and moisture clung to Tyrone's skin. Summers in Iowa could feel almost tropical. Hot and sticky, but without the benefit of an ocean breeze. Tyrone scanned the scene. Riley sat on the curb. A trooper and a deputy stood nearby, chatting. They paid little attention to Riley, who looked more like a child than ever.

"Hello, Riley." Tyrone said, making his way to the kid's side in a few long strides.

Riley rose to his feet and dusted his pants off. "What's going on? Did I do something wrong?"

There was no way Tyrone could answer that question in a way that would appease the kid. He didn't know. Riley may be uninvolved. He may be innocent. He could also be as culpable as Frank. Or potentially more culpable. There were just too many unknowns at this point.

"How long have you worked for Frank?" The trooper had already read Riley his Miranda Rights, so Tyrone didn't bother going back through them.

"I've been working here for close to a year now."

"What do you think of your boss?"

"Which one?"

"There's more than one?"

"Yeah. Frank and Vivian."

Tyrone hadn't thought of Vivian as this kid's boss, but he supposed that was accurate. Vivian was a fifty-percent owner of the restaurant. Frank couldn't do anything without her acquiescence or her permission. That was why he'd had to pay her to stay away, assuming Vivian had been honest about all that.

"How do you feel about Vivian?"

"She's a little," he paused, looking up at the sky, "much."

"What do you mean by that?"

He shrugged. "She's all up in everyone's business. Frank cares about the money side of the restaurant, Vivian cares about the social side. She watches too much crappy TV."

Tyrone cocked his head. "I don't follow."

"Vanderpump Rules. Have you seen the show?"

"No."

Riley sighed. "It's a reality TV show. Lisa Vanderpump and her husband own these restaurants in California. Their employees are always doing crazy stuff. They made a whole TV series out of it. It's very popular. You should check it out."

"I might," Tyrone said, although he planned to do the exact opposite.

"Anyway, Lisa Vanderpump gets involved in her employees' lives. She knows who they are dating, what they are up to at night. That kind of stuff. That's what I mean when I say Vivian is a little *much*. She wants to know everyone's business."

"I see."

"It's been nice that she's been gone."

"Gone?" Tyrone had heard this from Vivian, but corroboration from an employee would go miles in adding credibility to Vivian's version of the child support payoff story.

"Yeah. She used to be here every day nosing around. I haven't seen her for a while."

"How long is a while?"

The kid bit his lip, looked up at the sky. "February sometime. Things got really tense when Vivian filed that child support thing. That was probably sometime in maybe late January. I just remember Frank coming into work ranting about her always wanting more. He'd tell us to ignore Vivian, but she was our boss, too, and she wanted our attention. Nobody knew what to do."

"Okay."

"Then it all stopped around the middle of February. Vivian stopped coming and Frank settled down."

"Do you know why he settled down?"

"No. And I didn't ask. Frank said that Vivian had agreed not to come around for a while. We were supposed to call him if she showed up."

"Did Vivian ever show up?"

"No. Not here. She goes to the gym, but Frank didn't care about that. I guess because she was paying money."

"What about Frank?" Tyrone asked. "How do you feel about him as a boss?"

"You know he owns half this town. Vivian owns Old Main with him, but he's opened lots of businesses since their divorce. I also work at Frankly Hot and Heavy."

"You didn't answer my question," Tyrone said.

"That's because I don't want to."

"You don't like your boss?"

"You said it, not me," Riley said.

"You work two jobs?"

Riley shrugged. "Gotta pay the rent somehow."

This was a fortunate turn of events. Tyrone hadn't expected that there would be overlap in employees between the two businesses.

The kid pulled out a pack of Marlboro cigarettes and a lighter. "Mind if I smoke?"

"Have at it."

Tyrone didn't smoke. He didn't even like being around cigarettes, but they were outside, and it gave the kid a sense of freedom. Some control over his movements and choices. That would keep him talking.

"Thanks." Riley flicked the lighter and held it beneath the end of the cigarette as he sucked in deeply. He released a puff of smoke and sighed.

"Tell me about the freezer."

"The freezer?" Riley looked confused.

"Yeah. The freezer in Old Main. Why isn't there any food in it?"

"It's broken."

"How so?" It felt plenty cold when Tyrone had been inside it.

"The latch on the door is broken," Riley said. "You could get locked inside."

"How do you know that? Did someone get locked in?"

"No." He took another puff. "Frank told me. He told all the employees. We weren't to go near there. It was a 'hazard.'" He made air quotes around the word *hazard*.

"Did you listen?"

"Yeah."

"What about the rest of the employees?"

"I think so. Nobody wants to die in a freezer. Can you imagine?"

Tyrone didn't want to imagine.

"Frank was the only person that went near there," Riley said.

"Frank still went inside?"

Riley shrugged. "I assume so."

"How long has the freezer door been broken?"

"Since shortly after Vivian stopped coming. Maybe even the same day."

"Did Frank say why he didn't get it fixed?" Frank was running a restaurant. Freezers were an important part of that business. It didn't make sense for him to put repairs off for months. Unless, of course, it wasn't broken at all and there was a separate reason to keep employees out.

"No. And I didn't ask. Someone did one time and Frank lost his shit. Nobody asked again after that."

"That's strange."

"Frank is a strange man."

"Do you think his businesses were in trouble? I mean, so much so that he couldn't afford to fix the freezer door?" Tyrone asked.

"I doubt it. There are always lots of customers at both the restaurant and the gym."

"Speaking of the gym, did you know Frank's wife, Molly?"

"Everyone knew Molly. She was a cool chick. Frank didn't deserve her."

"Have you ever met Mike Malone?"

"Yeah. He was in the gym, like, every day. He's one of those muscle guys. He was always in shape, at least as long as I have been working there, but he had gotten huge by the last time I saw him. He's taking roids. Nobody gets that big that fast."

"Steroids?"

"Yeah."

"When was the last time you saw Mike Malone?"

"Oh, it had to be around the same time I last saw Molly. That would be the middle of February." He took another puff of his cigarette. Then he blew it out and his eyes lit up, like he had just noticed something. "Do you think there is a connection?"

"A connection?" Tyrone had to play dumb here. He was questioning the kid, not the other way around.

"Yeah. Between Mike and Molly's disappearance and the 'broken' freezer." He used air quotes around the word "broken."

"Why do you say it like that? Do you think the freezer was fine?"

Riley shrugged. "Frank isn't the most honest guy."

"Do you know Angel Malone?"

Riley shook his head. "I've heard of her. She's a lawyer, but she doesn't work out. If she does, she doesn't do it at Frankly Hot and Heavy."

"Have you ever seen Mike, Molly, and Frank all together?"

"No. I've seen Molly with Frank and Molly with Mike, but never all three together. Frank did not like Molly talking to Mike, though. I can tell you that. He told me to save all the security camera footage from the gym so he could see what they were 'up to.'"

"Do you still have the recordings?"

"I don't, but Frank probably does."

Tyrone made a mental note to get another search warrant for the computer and video surveillance systems at the gym.

"I don't know why Molly talked to Mike Malone. He was a dick."

"You're not a fan?"

"I'm not," Riley said, "but I'm not the only one. Nobody liked him. Molly was the only person who could stand spending any time around him."

"What happened to Mike? Why did he stop coming to the gym?"

Riley shrugged. "Don't know. Don't care. I assumed he started going to a different gym. Apparently, he was dead."

Tyrone asked a few more questions, but the kid didn't have anything else significant to add. Which was fine, he'd provided quite a lot of information already. The question was what it all meant. The freezer information was damning, but it didn't prove that Frank *killed* Mike. Only that he'd stored the body there. The most they could charge was accessory to murder.

Tyrone needed to speak to Frank again, but he knew Angel would not allow it. How could he get access to the client without notifying the attorney? He was going to need some guidance from the County Attorney. His next stop would be Harper Jenkins' office.

49

ANGEL

Past
February 14

Molly had more questions, but she was too afraid to ask them. Angel could see it in the way she worked her jaw, in the pleading in her eyes. Frank had trained her, beaten her into submission. Mike had tried to do the same to Angel, but he had failed. It made sense he was ready and willing to swoop in on all Frank's hard work and reap the benefits.

They fell into an uncomfortable silence, Molly's eyes darting like a cornered dog, Angel waiting for a signal. It came within moments. The sound of the neighboring duplex door opening split the silence.

Molly tensed, her gaze pinballing between Angel and Vivian. Nobody spoke. Vivian and Angel moved, almost as one. Vivian claimed Angel's spot at the head of the table as Angel headed to the front door. She stepped outside into the frigid Iowa winter, shivering as she made her way from one duplex to the next. As she walked, she passed their third accomplice. Nolan. They nodded to one another as he hurried to join Vivian.

Angel stepped into Nolan's grandmother's garage, passing by Nolan's still warm car. When she made it to the doorway, she reached up and struck the garage door button, causing the door to slowly close, bringing darkness along with it.

Once the garage door was shut, she opened the door into the kitchen. As expected, her husband was staring down the barrel of a gun.

"Good afternoon, Mike," Angel said, her tone cold. "Happy Valentine's Day."

Mike's gaze swung toward his wife. His lip curled into a sneer. "What the hell is this, Angel."

"Is that a question, or a demand?" She strode into the room and stood behind her client, Frank Sand, placing a hand on his shoulder.

"Seriously? You have five minutes to—"

"There's the problem," Angel said, cutting Mike off. "You've always thought you were the one calling the shots. You never were. You never will be."

"I—" Mike started to stand.

"I wouldn't do that if I were you," Frank growled. "I'd love to pull this trigger. Using my gym to get cozy with my wife, then fucking her behind my back. Give me one good reason and I'll gladly blow your goddamn brains out."

Mike froze.

"I'd listen," Angel said, the corner of her mouth twitching into a momentary smile. "Frank is a client. I asked him not to shoot you," she glanced at her nails. "At least not yet." She paused, meeting Mike's gaze, holding it as she continued. "He usually takes my advice, but he doesn't *have* to."

Mike settled back into his seat. "What do you want?" His gaze shifted from Angel to Frank.

"Well, now, that's an interesting question. I want what all women want. Safety. Security. The ability to live my life in peace. And you, my dear, dear, husband, are getting in the way of that."

"What do you plan to do?" This was the first time Angel had ever seen fear and perhaps remorse in her husband's eyes. It was a nice change. Not enough to divert her plans. *Too little too late.* But, still, it was nice to see.

50

TYRONE

Present
June 19

Tyrone and Jackie approached the county attorney's office, armed with all the information obtained through their investigation. It was barely eight o'clock in the morning. The search of Frank's restaurant and subsequent interviews had taken all night. Tyrone was running on fumes, but he wasn't going to waste time sleeping. Not when they were so close to the answer.

"Are you here to see Miss Harper?" The overly cheery woman at the front desk said.

"Yes."

"Come on in," she motioned to a door next to her. "I've unlocked it. Miss Harper is waiting."

Tyrone and Jackie stepped through the door to the county attorney's office. It was far busier than anyone would expect while standing out front, because the building sat tucked away on a side street, serene in its silence. Paralegals typed at their computers, their nails *clack, clack, clacking* against their keyboards. The witness coordinator's voice wafted from her small office in the corner as she spoke into the phone. Bells chimed, phones rang.

Tyrone wondered how anyone could get legal work done in such a hectic environment.

"The two people I wanted to see." Harper appeared outside her office, motioning for Tyrone and Jackie to follow her back in.

They did. Harper's office was spacious and sparsely decorated. The style was relaxed with earthy tones and a row of potted plants lining the windowsill.

"Have a seat." Harper indicated two vintage-looking wooden chairs across from her desk. She lowered herself into her office chair and waited for them to get situated. Then she steepled her fingers and said, "What do you have for me today? I hope it's good."

"It is," Tyrone said.

"You sound confident." She did not.

Tyrone slid his notes across the desk. He'd made Jackie drive to the county attorney's office while he scrawled the highlights of the case onto a legal pad. It was nowhere near an official report, but there was no time. They were closing in on a murderer.

"We've got him," Tyrone said.

Harper's eyes widened. She grabbed the notepad and started reading. He could see her eyes tracking from left to right along the page, starting at the top, then working their way to the bottom. When she finished, she set it down.

"There's no reason for Mike Malone's wallet to be in that freezer, is there?"

"No," Tyrone said. "Mike and Frank did not get along by any accounts. Nobody has drawn any ties between Vivian and Mike. They worked out at the same gym, but they didn't seem to interact."

"Vivian must be too old for that philanderer's attentions," Harper said, raising one eyebrow.

"Yes, well, I don't know about all that."

"So, we have a frozen body and a freezer with a wallet, right?" Harper said.

"Yes."

"We don't have a definite cause of death yet, but the medical examiner is working on that. Asphyxiation is the likely, but she wasn't positive. She said she'd need to 'open the body' for that," Harper said, scrunching up her nose at the last bit.

"Hypothermia?" Tyrone said. He hoped not.

"It could be. Nothing is set in stone, but I've been told he had petechiae in his eyes."

Petechiae was when blood vessels burst in the whites of a person's eyes. It almost always meant strangulation.

"But why put him in the freezer?" Tyrone asked.

"To throw us off on time and date of death."

Tyrone thought for a long moment. "Do you think Frank was trying to make it seem like Mike kidnapped Molly and killed her?"

Harper shrugged. "Maybe. But we are missing a lot of facts here. All we know is that Frank went to great lengths to keep others out of the restaurant freezer and Mike's body was in there at some point."

"Molly's too," Tyrone said.

"You're stretching with Molly," Harper said.

"Her hair was in there. Several pieces of it. Forensics will have to examine them, but I'm sure they belong to Molly. Vivian has blond hair and Molly's is browner. The hairs in the freezer are the exact same shade as the hairs found in that pig pen. Those belonged to Molly. I'm sure these ones will, too."

"Yeah, but she was married to the owner. She could have gone in there for a legitimate reason. And why didn't you find blood? Molly's murder was different than Mike's. We didn't find a body, but there was so much blood at that scene. She bled out."

"You can't say that," Tyrone said with irritation. He could feel the imminent arrest and glory slipping through his fingers. Jake was going to take the credit for his work. He knew it. "She could have been strangled and frozen just like Mike. The blood could have come from the pigs. They *ate* her. They literally tore her apart and devoured her."

"You're saying the blood could be postmortem, not the cause of death," Harper said, tapping a pen against her chin.

"Yes."

"That's a theory, but it seems like a lot of blood for a heart that isn't beating."

"But—"

"Regardless, it still doesn't get us to a next step."

"We need to know who was at Legends Park shortly before that hiker found Mike's body," Tyrone said.

"Bingo."

"How do we do that?"

"Simple." Harper tapped her fingernail against the desk. "A Geofence warrant."

A geofencing warrant was a warrant asking for all the user data of individuals using any Google application within a specific area during a certain timeframe. In this case, it would be Legends State Park within an hour or two before Mike Malone's body had been discovered. This kind of warrant was effective because almost everyone had some Google owned application running in the back of their phones without even knowing it. They didn't have to be actively using the application for the data to pop up.

"What if Frank didn't have his phone on him at the time?"

Harper shrugged. "Then we tried." She turned toward her computer and started typing a search warrant. She asked Tyrone and Jackie a slew of questions about the execution of the search warrant at Frank's restaurant, evidence discovered, witnesses interviewed, and plugged all that information into the Geofencing search warrant.

Tyrone watched her in awe. She made it look so easy, like throwing together a grocery list. When she finished typing, she sat in silence for a long moment, reading through the document, then pressed print and snatched it off the printer.

"Read through it," she said, handing it to Tyrone. "If it looks good, sign on the line for Affiant and I'll sign as the assistant county attorney. I can take it over to one of the district court judges now."

Tyrone scanned the document, reading through each numbered bullet point. Then he signed and handed it back to Harper.

She was up and dashing to the door within seconds. "Back in a flash."

She left Tyrone and Jackie alone in her office. It was awkward sitting there without Harper present, but Tyrone busied himself reading news on his phone. True to her word, Harper was back in what seemed like a flash with the signed warrant in hand. He was shocked by how much easier search warrants were when everyone was awake and right there. That wasn't reality, most crimes occurred at night, but it was interesting to see how quickly things could get done when given direct access to the right people.

"Now, we need to get this puppy to Google and then we're off to the races," Harper said. She placed the signed search warrant in a scanner and scanned it into her computer, ready to shoot it off to whoever could provide her the information.

"What now?" Tyrone asked.

"Now we wait."

Tyrone hated waiting, but it was part of his job in law enforcement. TV made his job seem exciting, but the reality was *hurry up and wait*. He had to hurry up to gather the information, then wait to find out what it all meant. Had to hurry up and get to court but wait in the hallway until it was his turn to testify. Hurry up and arrest the perpetrator but wait while the jailer booked and processed the person. It was infuriating, but there was nothing he could do about it. So, he went back to reading news on his phone.

Ten minutes passed, then there was a pinging sound on Harper's computer.

Harper looked up at the sound, clicked a couple buttons, then said, "Bingo."

Tyrone lowered his phone. He and Jackie exchanged a look. The excitement was palpable. *Bingo* was something a person exclaimed when they had won.

"What?" Tyrone asked.

"The nice thing about a hiking area like Legends is that few people go there."

This was not the answer he was looking to receive, but she was building up to it. His entire body was on edge. He needed to know what she knew. He wanted to grab her shoulders shake her, and say, *out with it, woman*. But he didn't. He played along. Placated her.

"I suppose," Tyrone said.

"There were only two phones active in that area at the time the body was dumped."

"Two? That's all?"

"One belongs to a user called *FrankSandRules*. Who do you think that might be?"

"Frank Sand."

The only other person it could be was Frankie Sand, Jr., but he always called himself *Frankie* and his social media was the same. The kid didn't like his father and he didn't want people to confuse them.

"I'm sure a cell phone tower ping will place Frank's number there as well. I'll get that warrant, just to tie things up with a bow, but we've got our man."

"Who was the other user?" Tyrone asked, mostly out of curiosity.

"HikerMan5000."

"That must be the hiker that found the body."

"I'm not a betting person, but that's a horse I would back."

"Should I issue the arrest warrant?"

"Yes. For Mike Malone's murder only."

"Not Molly?" Tyrone's heart sank. He wasn't surprised, but it stung all the same. He wasn't investigating Mike Malone's case. That was a whole separate team that included Jake. He didn't know Jake well, but Jake did not seem like someone who was willing to give credit where it was due.

"Not yet. Let's see what happens when you arrest Frank. He might say something dumb. Otherwise, we need to wait for forensics."

Tyrone groaned. That could take weeks or months. This was the problem with attorneys, they were so cautious.

"Don't look so glum," Harper said. "Go get your man. He'll probably crack under the pressure. Men like Frank always do."

51

ANGEL

Past
February 14

Angel grabbed two objects off the counter. A phone cord and an empty plastic bag.

"Remember what you said to me that night that you attacked me?" Angel said. She was orbiting the table, walking around to where the island met the counter, then turning around and retracing her steps.

Frank's eyebrows shot up, but he kept his gun and his gaze trained on Mike. Angel's husband was not a small man. One wrong move and Mike could gain control of the situation.

"My temper got the best of me. I'm sorry," Mike said.

Angel scoffed. "Oh, you're sorry now. Of course, you're sorry. You're staring down the barrel of a gun. But you know what?" She stopped next to Mike and slammed a fist on the table in front of him. She paused, then leaned forward and lowered her voice. "I don't accept your apology." She turned her head and spoke directly into Mike's ear. "It means nothing when it's forced. Besides," she straightened and continued orbiting the table, "it's too late for that."

"Too late?" Mike said.

"You threatened my children."

"*Your* children. I thought they were *ours*."

"Oh, now they're *ours*. Just days ago they were 'bitches like me,' remember?"

Again, Frank's eyebrows shot up, but he said nothing.

"I didn't mean that."

"Shut up!" Angel shouted. "I already told you that your apologies mean nothing. You had more than a week to make even a half-assed apology, and what did you do?" She let the question hang in the air, "You screwed another woman. That's what you did."

"I—"

"My wife," Frank said. His hand started to shake.

There was so much anger, so much venom in Frank's voice. It was ironic, considering Frank had been running around with Rebecca for months. He was furious with Mike, but the two weren't all that different. A hypocrite. Angel would deal with him later.

"You came to my gym on a free membership because of Angel here," Frank nodded to Angel.

She said nothing. She continued orbiting and fiddling with the phone cord in her hands.

"You cornered my wife. *My wife*. And then you started messing around with her. What is this? Who owns this place?" Frank gestured around him.

Angel had only told her client the bare bones of the situation. *I know where they are, they are probably screwing now.* As she had expected, that was plenty of information to get Frank rushing to unlock his gun safe.

But Frank knew little of the master plan. He had no idea Vivian and Nolan were next door with Molly. He had no idea that they were even involved. He thought this was a plan he and Angel had hatched on the fly. Men like Frank always thought they ran the show. Angel encouraged that false mindset. For now.

"How did it start?" Frank said.

"I don't know."

Frank leaned forward, holding his arm outstretched so the gun was pressed up against Mike's head. "I said, How. Did. It. Start?" Frank spoke through clenched teeth. His agitation had tripled in the matter of minutes. This kind of anger would lead to sloppiness. Frank might pull that trigger and then they'd have quite the mess to clean up.

"I told you—"

"*Enough!*" Angel shouted.

Frank looked up at her and slowly leaned back in his chair, keeping the gun pointed at Mike. The two men glared at one another, both ignoring the one truly deadly person in the room. That was just fine for Angel. She took the bag and the phone cord. She shoved the bag over Mike's head then twisted the phone cord around his neck. He bucked, and she thought for a moment that she wouldn't be able to hold it, but he quickly ran out of steam. The bag was tight to his face. It took seconds for him to weaken and moments for his breathing to stop.

When it was over, Frank's face had taken on a greenish hue.

"Don't throw up," Angel said.

"Um," Frank swallowed hard, "okay."

"Now, get this body out of here," Angel said.

"Where? Where do I take it?"

Angel's gaze lifted to the ceiling, and she reminded herself to keep her cool. "Take it to Old Main. Put it in the freezer. Remember? That was the plan. That was the whole reason we paid Vivian off."

"Oh, yeah. Right."

What Frank didn't know was that whole "paying Vivian off" thing was a ruse. A way to shift blame to Frank when it came time for his turn for punishment.

"Keep the body frozen until the summer when the weather gets warmer. The body will thaw quickly. By the time investigators find him, he'll be a regular body and they will think Mike's death was recent."

"Okay." Frank looked around, a bewildered expression on his face. "But where's Molly? I thought she would be here, too?"

"I don't know," Angel said. "She was supposed to come here. Maybe something spooked her."

"Maybe."

"She's probably at home. You should go check there," Angel said.

Frank nodded.

"But first, take care of this body."

Angel watched Frank grunt and strain under Mike's dead weight, wrapping it in a tarp and carrying it to his truck. When it was fully wrapped, it looked like a bundle of construction supplies. She watched him drive off. When he was gone, she returned to the neighboring duplex.

52

TYRONE

Present
June 19

Frank's arrogance was Tyrone's only hope. There was plenty for an arrest in Mike's murder, but Tyrone wasn't assigned to the case. But if Frank confessed to Molly's murder, he would be able to arrest him for that, too.

With that tiny thread of hope, Tyrone applied for the arrest warrant. Once it was issued, Tyrone and Jackie drove over to Frank's gym and marched inside.

"Hello, again," Riley said. His voice had a slight shake to it.

"Is your boss in?" Tyrone asked.

Riley pointed toward a long hallway to their right. Tyrone marched down the hallway, passing several small offices, all with gold placards listing a name and the person's job title. The very last office had a far larger placard reading *Frank Sand, the man*. Normally, Tyrone would consider a title like this distasteful, but it fit their situation just right. Frank Sand was *their man*. Tyrone was there for that very reason. To arrest him.

Tyrone didn't knock. He twisted the doorknob and pushed the door open.

Frank was at his desk, his back turned to Jackie and Tyrone. He was looking through a large window at the back of his office, watching the back-side of a woman running on a treadmill. Tyrone had only been at the gym for a matter of minutes, but even he was tired of the rampant misogyny. He couldn't imagine how Jackie felt.

"Frank Sand," Tyrone said, his tone grave.

Frank swiveled around in his chair. Sweat sprang to his brow the moment his gaze fell on the two officers. "What, what, can I, uh, do for you officers?" His voice shook. Gone was the arrogant man Tyrone had known so well.

"You're under arrest for the murder of Mike Malone."

"M-murder." He repeated.

"Yes. Now stand up and turn your back to me."

Frank complied and Tyrone removed his handcuffs, sliding them around the businessman's wrists, clicking them into place and double locking them so they wouldn't tighten during the trip to the jail. While he was busy doing that, Jackie read Frank his *Miranda* rights. She read from a card that Tyrone had instructed her to always carry.

Miranda was a series of words that had to be said in a very specific way. It was easy to screw up in a high stress or high excitement situations like this one. They couldn't afford to screw this up. Reading Miranda word for word was the only way to ensure accuracy.

"Having these rights in mind," Jackie said after reading the full card, "do you wish to speak to us?"

"I want my lawyer."

Tyrone's gaze shifted to the ceiling, and he fought a groan. That was not the series of words he was hoping to hear. "I'm not sure you have a lawyer anymore. You killed her husband," Tyrone said.

Frank's eyes flashed. "She's still my lawyer."

Tyrone nodded and led Frank out of the office and down the hall toward the front door, trying not to lose faith. He and Jackie kept silent, hoping the pressure of it would break Frank's resolve. If Frank wanted to volunteer information, he could. But Tyrone could not ask anything until Frank's lawyer was present, and Angel Malone was not going to let Frank talk.

53

MOLLY

Past
February 14

"Nolan," Molly squeaked, when her closest friend and confidant entered the duplex and stood leaning against the counter. Even he had betrayed her. Brought her to this place to die. Had it all been a trick? Had he offered his grandmother's duplex from the start to lead her to this very place at this time? She didn't know what to believe anymore.

"Sorry, girlie," he said, his gaze shifting to the ground.

"How could you?" Molly was heartbroken. "I invited you into my home. Introduced you to my kids. We loved you."

Nolan's gaze shifted back up and met hers. Tears sparkled in his eyes. "I..." He trailed off and they fell into an intense silence.

Then Molly heard the unmistakable sound of the front door opening *again*. Who was it this time? Angel reentered the kitchen. Angel nodded to Nolan, but said nothing, and went to stand at the other side of the kitchen.

"You're all in this together," Molly said, her gaze shifting from one stony face to the next.

"It isn't what you think," Nolan said. "You needed help and Angel needed help."

"This is real helpful, Nolan. Thanks so much," Molly spat.

Nolan flinched but continued speaking. "Mike needed to go. He was spiraling. It was only a matter of time before he killed either you or Angel or both of you."

"This is about Mike?" Molly was more confused now than ever.

"It was time for him to go," Angel said. "He had threatened to kill me, threatened my children. He was blackmailing you and raping you."

Tears sprang to Molly's eyes, and she looked to Angel for the first time since she reentered the duplex. Angel looked exhausted, wrung out.

"How did you get rid of Mike?"

"It's better that you don't know," Vivian said.

Vivian had a point.

"Now, we are both free," Angel said.

"You may be free," Molly said, "but I've escaped one cage for another."

"Well, now, that's why you are going to have to die," Vivian said.

Molly's throat dried. She knew it. This wasn't about Mike. It was about Mike *and* Molly. Angel didn't believe Mike raped her. She thought that was an excuse. And now Molly was going to die for it. Death was a form of freedom, but not an avenue Molly wanted to explore.

54

ANGEL

Now
June 19

If anyone was going down for the murders, it was going to be Frank. Vivian and Angel had made sure of that. But Angel had tried to avoid it. She'd told him to dispose of Mike's body at Legends State Park, a park that was beautiful for all the overlooks, but dangerous with its steep hiking trails and sharp drop-offs.

She'd instructed Frank to wait until the temperature got hot so that Mike's body would thaw quickly, then shove it off one of the higher drop-offs. It would look like Mike had killed himself. So consumed by his guilt from kidnapping and killing Molly that he jumped to his death. Frank couldn't even do that right. She hadn't specifically told him to choose a less traveled hiking trail to delay discovery time or to remove the bag from Mike's head and the phone cord securing it into place from around his neck. She thought that was a given. Apparently not. And now, once again, she was cleaning up another one of Frank's avoidable messes.

It was early morning. The call came in from a restricted number. As always, Angel had answered.

"Angel Malone, here."

"My Angel. I need you."

"Don't call me that." She was officially done with this *my Angel* business. If she was ever an angel, she was a fallen one.

"But—"

"I don't belong to you."

"Okay." No apology. Frank would never apologize.

Angel sighed. "Where are you?"

"I'm at the jail. They arrested me and I—"

"That's enough. This line is recorded."

"But I—"

"What's your bond?"

"A million," Frank said. "Cash."

"How much of that do you have?"

"In cash? Maybe two-hundred thousand. Two-hundred and fifty max."

"I'm on my way there. Do not say a thing until I get there."

She was already walking through the door of her office and toward the staircase by the time she hung up. She passed George's office too fast for him to call out to her, and she did not stop at the front desk. In the hallway, she paused to wait for the elevator. It was coming too slow. She took off her heels and raced down the stairs, dialing her phone as she ran.

Vivian answered after one ring. "What's he done now?"

"They arrested him."

"How much does he need?" She didn't sound disappointed or mad. She sounded gleeful.

"His bond is one million. He has two-hundred thousand. Can you come up with the rest?"

"I hate that man," Vivian said, but there was excitement in her voice.

"You'll get it back when trial's over."

"I'll get it back sooner than that," Vivian said. She was right, of course. They would never get to trial.

"So, you'll post the bond?"

"Reluctantly, yes. I'll use my house as collateral. This better not go sideways."

"He won't run," Angel said.

Vivian would get every dime of her bond money back so long as Frank didn't run.

"He'd better not."

"There won't be time," Angel said. Then she hung up, certain Vivian would follow through. She continued down the stairs, taking two at a time, then slipped her feet back into her shoes and rushed out the door and down the street.

She was at the jail in less than five minutes. She hoped she'd made it in time.

Angel smoothed her hair and straightened her jacket, then approached the jailer at the front desk. The man looked up as she approached, watching her through wary, knowing eyes.

"I'm here to see a client."

"Frank Sand?" the jailer asked.

"Yes."

"You do realize he's here for murdering your husband."

"Yes. I still need to see him."

"He's dangerous."

"I'll be fine."

"You're not going to hurt him, are you?"

Angel's heart fluttered, but she forced her features to remain even. "Look at me," she gestured to herself. "I'm barely five-foot and I have no muscle. I couldn't hurt anyone to save my life."

"Those shoes could be a weapon." He nodded down at her stilettos.

She lifted an eyebrow. "Do you make male attorneys remove their shoes to speak to their clients?"

"No."

"I want to speak to my client. *Now*."

The jailer was stalling, and she was beginning to wonder why. Was Tyrone up there interrogating her client without her knowledge? If he was, she was going to be furious. The story Frank might be telling is one that could bring this whole house of cards crashing down.

"Which attorney-client meeting room?" he asked.

There were two types of rooms, one with a partition, and one without it.

They all had cameras, but they were incapable of recording sound. It was the only way to preserve attorney-client privilege.

"The one without the partition."

"Are you sure? The man is a killer."

"I've represented Frank for a lot of years. He isn't violent."

"Yet he's in here for murder."

"Just do it," Angel hissed. She was tired of his retorts and the deadpan delivery.

The jailer had her sign in before he unlocked the front door, allowing her to step back into the secured portion of the building. He led her down a long hallway and into the attorney-client room. It was sparsely furnished with two blue plastic chairs sitting on either side of an old desk.

"Have a seat. I'll go get Frank."

The jailer left and Angel sank into one of the chairs. This was where her grand plan could go off the rails. Everything had run so smoothly. Something like this was bound to happen. But she was a planner, a lawyer, someone who knew how to pivot. Today, the plan was pivoting.

A few moments passed and then the jailer returned with Frank. The hours seemed like they had leeched years from Frank's features, and the bright orange jumpsuit highlighted his pasty white skin. She'd never fully appreciated Frank Sand's ugliness. He was so unattractive, but his money helped to mask it.

The jailer led Frank into the room. His arms and legs were chained together, so he could only move by shuffling his feet. The jailer followed him, allowing Frank to use him for balance until Frank was safely seated in one of the chairs.

"I'll step out," the jailer said. "Press that button when you are done." He nodded to a small intercom with a silver button. "I'll come get Frank, then I'll let you out next. These doors will be locked."

Angel nodded. There was a warning to the jailer's tone, but Angel was not bothered. Frank was not going to hurt her. He needed her.

55

MOLLY

Then
February 14

"I don't want to die," Molly cried. Tears leaked from her eyes, smearing her makeup, leaving trails of dark mascara cutting ravines in her foundation.

"Stop that sniveling and pull yourself together," Vivian snapped. "You aren't going to die."

"But you just said..."

Another person entered the house, causing Molly to trail off.

An old girlfriend of Nolan's stepped into the kitchen and made her way to Nolan's side. A woman called Naomi. Molly had never met her in person —Frank didn't allow her to have a social life—but she'd seen plenty of pictures. Molly wouldn't describe Naomi as pretty in a traditional way. There was a masculinity to her features that veered toward handsome, but she was striking all the same. A confidence radiated from her that kept Molly's gaze glued to her.

Naomi had a large bag strapped across her chest. It was black with a red cross. She stopped next to Nolan and slowly, gingerly brought the strap over her head and lowered it to the floor. Then she looked up, met Molly's gaze, and said, "I'm going to take some blood."

Molly opened her mouth to answer, but she didn't know what to say. She had no clue what was going on.

Nolan turned around and plucked two items off the counter. He turned and displayed them. A bag of Oreos and a box of black hair dye.

Molly shook her head. Just when she thought the day couldn't get weirder or more confusing, it did.

"You're not going to die," Angel said, her tone softer than Molly had ever heard it. "You're going to pretend to die."

"That's why I will be taking your blood. I'm going to come by every eight weeks to take blood," Naomi said, her voice as kind and open as her face.

"We will gather blood and use it to fake your death," Angel said. "It will take several months, so you are going to have to be patient."

"We can only take a liter at a time," Naomi said. "And we have to wait eight weeks between withdrawal."

"Eight weeks between withdrawals," Molly said. "How long total?"

"We are thinking four months," Angel said.

"No. I can't," Molly stood, and she was surprised that they'd allowed it. She must not be a prisoner anymore.

"You have to, honey," Nolan said, coming to her side. "This is the only way you will ever get away from Frank."

"What about the kids?"

"We'll all look out for them," Vivian said. "Frankie Junior can get into the house, so he'll check up on them all the time."

"Frankie hates the kids."

"But he loves you and he hates Frank more," Vivian said. "Besides, they are his brother and sister. He'll do it. Trust me."

"Okay." Molly lowered herself back into her chair. "What will I do all that time?"

"You'll stay at Nana's duplex," Nolan said. "I'll stay there with you. We'll spend the next four months eating Oreos, watching trashy TV, and changing your appearance." He nodded toward the box of hair dye.

"But how are we going to fake my death? You won't have a body."

"I have a solution for that," Angel said. Then she launched into a story about a man called Old Pete and his pigs.

Molly's gaze darted from one face to the next—Naomi, Vivian, Angel—and settled on Nolan. "Will it work?"

"We think it will," Nolan said.

"What about Mike?" Molly's gaze shifted to Angel. "He's at the duplex. We can't go there."

"Oh, don't you worry about Mike," Angel said, her tone turning dark. "He won't be bothering you anymore."

56

VIVIAN

Present
June 19

It was physically painful to shell out seven-hundred-thousand dollars for her ex-husband. Sure, it was temporary, but not temporary enough. She drove with a vice grip on the steering wheel of her white Maserati Levante.

"Slow down," Nolan whined from the backseat, "You're going to get us killed."

Vivian glanced at the speedometer. She was going sixty-five in a fifty-five. She was speeding, but they weren't exactly breaking the sound barrier. "It's been too long since you've been in a car," Vivian said.

"Yeah," Nolan said. "No kidding."

Nolan had been hiding out with Molly at that crappy little duplex for four months. He hadn't left once. Angel and Vivian had taken care of all their needs. Why? She sometimes asked herself that very same question. She didn't like Molly, she'd never cared much for Nolan, but she hated her ex-husband.

She'd spent years waiting for the moment she could finally get even with him. Nobody cast her aside like that. *Nobody*. She didn't know when or how she'd do it. All she knew was that she was going to make it happen.

Then she learned about Molly and Mike Malone's affair. That had her casting her attorney aside so she could speak directly to Angel Malone. And then voila. Magic. Vivian had always been intelligent, but when combined with Angel's wit, they were genius.

"What if he sees me?" Nolan said.

"He won't." They were on their way to pick up her despicable ex-husband from jail. He'd been released, thanks to Vivian, or rather, Vivian's cash, and Angel couldn't do this next part herself. It would be too suspicious. "You're in the back and those windows are tinted as dark as the law allows. Nobody can see you."

"Okay," Nolan said, but he didn't sound any less anxious.

Vivian pulled into a parking spot next to the jail and glanced in the rear-view mirror, looking for any sign of Nolan. He wasn't in a seat; he was crouched down behind the passenger seat. She couldn't see him. Frank wouldn't either.

She turned her attention to the door just as Frank stepped out. Angel was behind him. She pointed to Vivian's Maserati. Frank met her gaze with bloodshot, tired eyes. He looked *terrible*. A sight that brought a burst of pure joy through Vivian. He trudged toward the vehicle.

"Stay down," Vivian said, holding a smile and talking through her teeth. She kept her gaze straight ahead, but she was talking to Nolan.

"Okay," Nolan said. There was a crinkling sound, like the sound of an empty Sun Chips bag.

"And stay quiet."

"Sorry."

Angel gestured to the front passenger door and walked around to the driver's side. Vivian rolled her window down. The passenger door opened, and Angel passed an object to Vivian. Vivian passed it back to Nolan. It happened within seconds, while Frank was distracted getting into the car.

"What took you so long?" Frank said, closing the door with a loud *slam*. "I had to sit there twiddling my thumbs with my babysitter," Frank's gaze shot to Angel, "for forever."

"You wouldn't need a babysitter if you had half a brain," Angel said, crossing her arms.

"How was I supposed to know?" Frank said.

"Common sense," Angel said.

It had taken hours for Vivian to arrange everything. She didn't have that kind of cash in any one account. She had to move money around, and that took time. "Maybe," Vivian turned and faced her ex-husband, "you should try thanking the people who have *helped* you rather than criticizing us. How about that?"

"Whatever. You wanted to help."

This was how he'd always been. A favor for him was not a favor at all because, in his mind, people *wanted* to do it. That meant he was doing them a favor by allowing them to help him. It was a self-centered warped reality, but it was Frank's world, they were just living in it.

"I'll take it from here, Angel. Thanks for babysitting," Vivian said, turning back to the window. She winked; Angel nodded. Then Vivian rolled up the window and put the SUV into reverse and backed out of the parking lot.

"Put your seatbelt on," Vivian said.

"Put your seatbelt on," Frank mocked, but she could hear the click of it going into place. "You're a nag, you know that. It was annoying when you were young, but now, it's *really* annoying."

Vivian started driving toward the duplex. As the car moved, Frank kept talking, likely issuing backhanded insults, but she wasn't paying attention. She was willing Nolan to do his job. She waited, and waited, and waited, for what seemed like forever, then finally, she saw his pale arm emerge from the backseat. He was holding a syringe. The object Angel had handed to Vivian through the window. It was full of insulin. A life-saving substance for Angel's daughter, but a killer to the non-diabetic. Nolan plunged the needle into Frank's arm and pumped the substance into his body, then his arm disappeared back into the backseat. It was over in a second.

"What the fuck was that?" Frank said, turning in his seat to look behind him. "*Nolan*. What the hell is going on?" Frank's gaze swung to Vivian. "What is this fairy doing in your car? And what the fuck did he just do to me?"

"Well, Frank. Nolan and I have a bit of an alliance."

"An alliance," Frank wiped sweat from his forehead. "I, uh, what's happening to me?"

"You're overdosing," Vivian said.

"My heart. It's uh, racing," his words slurred at the end, like he was falling asleep just sitting there.

Vivian pulled up outside the townhome and Nolan hopped out. Vivian backed out of the driveway and continued driving.

"I'm so thirsty," Frank said, then he started having a seizure.

She'd drive him around until he stopped moving, then she'd take him to a hospital and say he'd complained of symptoms consistent with a heart attack.

A gurgling noise came from Frank.

Vivian glanced at him. It was an odd sight to see, and she almost felt sorry for him, with his face contorted like that. *Almost.* This man had tortured and tormented women for decades. He kept his wives in a gilded cage until he was ready to kick them out and replace them with some new young, easily manipulated, woman, each a bit more beautiful than the last. Vivian was first, but Molly would be his last.

The women in Frank's life were tired of it. Just like the women in Mike Malone's life were tired of his bullshit. They couldn't change these men. They couldn't escape them either, not without serious repercussions. So, they'd done what women do best, they manipulated both men. And soon, they would both be dead.

This plan, the one where Vivian got to watch her ex-husband die, it was not the original idea. It was a contingency that came into play when Frank was dumb enough to get arrested for Mike Malone's murder. It was only a matter of time before Frank would rat Angel out, and they couldn't have that.

57

ANGEL

Present
June 20

Angel stepped through the front door of the duplex for what would be the last time. Nolan was waiting in the living room. Two women were with him. Naomi, the home-health nurse who had been instrumental to their plan, and another woman. Naomi nodded in greeting, but the dark-haired woman didn't look up. She sat twisting her fingers together, nervously.

The dark-haired woman did not look like anyone Angel knew, but Angel did know her. The last time she'd seen this woman in person was on February fourteenth, when she'd been brought in on the plan. Since then, she'd used cheap hair dye to color her hair black. She'd cut her hair into a jagged bob, a decent home cut, and gained twenty or thirty pounds. Molly Sand was unrecognizable.

Angel joined the group in the living room where they waited in silence. Angel's gaze flitted from object to object, settling on the home-health bag that Naomi used. Naomi had been coming to the house for months now, drawing Molly's blood. Molly pulled strands of her hair out during that time, too, ripping them out at the root one by one and gathering them in a plastic bag.

That's what Angel had used on June fifteenth when she'd gone to stage the murder scene. She'd driven out to Old Pete's farm with memories of an earlier *pigs eat everything* conversation swirling in her mind. She'd then taken large hunks of meat and wrapped them in Molly's clothing, tossing them to the pigs. When they were busy eating, she'd cut open the bags of Molly's blood and poured them everywhere. Pools and pools of it. There had to be enough blood that Molly's death would not be questioned. Then she tossed the handbag, using gloves so she never touched it, and did the same with Molly's high heels. The hair was tossed inside the pen as well, and that was it.

Angel left and Molly was declared dead.

The sound of tires on the drive pulled Angel out of her thoughts. The tension in the room doubled. The time had come. Three doors slammed and small voices trickled in from outside.

"Where are we?" a little boy said.

Molly stiffened, freezing mid-fidget.

"Just go inside," Vivian said.

The door opened and two small children stepped inside, moving slowly, tentatively. The boy was older, and he was first, standing in front of his little sister like a protective barrier. Then his gaze fell on Nolan, and he gasped. The little girl pushed past her brother and ran at Nolan, throwing her little body into his arms.

Nolan laughed, tears springing to his eyes. "I missed you, too."

Molly stood. The little boy, Matthew, looked at her. He studied her for a long moment, taking in her features, trying to reconcile why she looked so familiar. Then it clicked and his expression changed. "Mommy?" he said, his voice small.

Genevieve froze, turning her head so she could look at Molly.

Molly nodded, and both children ran at her, throwing themselves into her arms. Tears streamed down their faces, and they clutched at each other like their lives depended on it. Angel turned away, heading for the door. Eager to get home to her two little angels.

When she was almost to the door, Molly called after her. Angel froze.

"Thank you," Molly said to Angel's back.

"No, thank you," Angel said without turning around.

She left the duplex with no intention of ever returning.

Everything was already settled. Nolan and Molly would move away, taking the children with them to raise in Arizona with Nolan's mother. Vivian had guardianship of the kids, that was part of Frank's "succession plan." Angel would file the documents that would transfer guardianship from Vivian to Nolan in the morning. Vivian gained control of all Frank's businesses, and Frank's money was split evenly—in trust—to his three children. Molly would assume a new identity and they'd live modestly off the children's trust until she'd finished school and could support them on her own.

In the end, everyone won, except the two men who had spent their lives destroying women and ignoring their children.

EPILOGUE
TYRONE

Present
July 15

Frank's death simplified everything. It meant that there would be no trial, no defense attorney picking apart the evidence, so they could officially name him as the killer of both Mike Malone and Molly Sand. Case closed. Tyrone had solved his first two major murders.

Within a week of the resolution, he received a call from the sergeant of his old police department in Chicago. He picked up right away.

"Ty, how's it going?" Everyone in Chicago called him Ty. It had been that way since his first week on the job and the Chief had said *Tyrone. We already have a Tyrone. You'll be Ty.* He'd never earned a nickname in Fort Calhoun. Not even one out of convenience. He wasn't a good ol' boy. He never would be.

"It's fine," Tyrone said.

"Losing your mind in that podunk town yet?"

"Something like that."

"I saw you solved those murders."

"Sure did."

"Do you have any interest in returning?"

Tyrone's heart skipped a beat. "To Chicago?"

"No. Cincinnati. Of course, Chicago, you idiot."

Tyrone chuckled. He'd forgotten what banter with another officer felt like. Everyone kept such a wide berth from him in Fort Calhoun. "I'm sure you've filled my old position."

"We have. But there is a detective spot open."

Tyrone had jumped at the idea. He was online and applying for that position before they even hung up the phone. A couple weeks and a few interviews later and he was packing his things to head back to his hometown. Back to Chicago, back where he belonged. He was more than excited to hand in his two weeks' notice and get out of dodge. His only hesitation was Frank Sand's death. It was too convenient. Too simple.

In Tyrone's experience, things were never that simple. A death by cardiac event right after a murder arrest seemed suspect to him. Yet, the medical examiner had determined it was death by natural causes and the body was cremated in accordance with Frank's Last Will and Testament. It just didn't feel right to Tyrone, but that wasn't enough reason to open an investigation into it. The case had garnered national news and it was solved, tied up with a perfect little bow, that didn't even require a jury or a trial. Nobody, not even the prosecutors, wanted to revisit it.

He'd packed up his office and was on his way out the door when his phone rang. The number belonged to the criminalistics laboratory in Ankeny. He'd take one last call.

"Gully here," Tyrone said.

"Hi, Detective, do you have a minute?"

"Sure," Tyrone said, more curious than anything.

"I've got some weird test results for Molly Sand," the criminalist said.

"Okay."

"The blood had an anti-coagulant in it."

"A what?"

"It's the stuff that they put into donated blood. It's so the blood doesn't coagulate before its needed for a transfusion."

"What does that mean?" Tyrone asked.

"I don't know."

Tyrone didn't either, but he had a suspicion. Could Molly Sand be alive?

Not my problem anymore, Tyrone thought as he ended the call and left the law enforcement center for the last time. He was going back to Chicago. He had a cold case to solve.

UNSYMPATHETIC VICTIMS
ASHLEY MONTGOMERY LEGAL THRILLERS #1

When a defense attorney becomes the defendant, one small town is forced to reconsider their ideas of good and evil.

When successful public defender Ashley Montgomery helps acquit yet another client, people in small-town Brine, Iowa are enraged. Following the verdict, a protest breaks out — and the hated defense attorney quickly finds her life in danger.

But little does Ashley know, things are about to get worse — much worse. One of her clients turns up dead, and Ashley is arrested for his murder. As local investigators Katie Mickey and George Thomanson dive into the case, they start to suspect that Ashely is being framed — but by whom?

With Ashley's freedom at stake, Katie and George are desperate to find out the truth. And soon, they uncover a sinister plot born of corruption, greed, and misplaced loyalty that will leave the whole town reeling — and questioning their faith in the people they trusted most.

Get your copy today at
severnriverbooks.com

ACKNOWLEDGMENTS

Writing a first draft is solitary work. But bringing a book to publication takes a team. It requires the hearts and minds of many. I have numerous people to thank for assisting me in my journey to publication of this book.

First, I must thank my family. My husband, Chris, and children, H.S, M.S, W.S, for their ever-present love and support. You make every day an adventure. I am fortunate to have all of you in my life. I want to thank my parents and my extended family who have provided me with a foundation that has led to my success.

A special thanks to my agent, Stephanie Hansen, of Metamorphosis Literary Agency. Her constant determination and encouragement created the gateway for my books to see publication. She believed in my writing from the moment we met at a writers conference and I pitched the idea for my very first book. Without her, none of my books would not exist. She has quite literally made my dreams come true.

Thank you to all members of the Severn River Publishing Team. You saw potential in my books and in me. Especially Cate Streissguth who is my go-to person for all book-related questions. Your professionalism, organization, and attention to detail has transformed my life as a writer.

Finally, I want to thank all the women out there who choose to support other women. Especially the three that I have grown up alongside, Ashley, Amanda, and Kristen. You are my ride or die, my "bury the body" friends. I hope every woman has at least one person like you in their life. True friends don't come easy, but they are forever.

ABOUT THE AUTHOR

Laura Snider is a practicing lawyer in Iowa. She graduated from Drake Law School in 2009 and spent most of her career as a Public Defender. Throughout her legal career she has been involved in all levels of crimes from petty thefts to murders. These days she is working part-time as a prosecutor and spends the remainder of her time writing stories and creating characters.

Laura lives in Iowa with her husband, three children, two dogs, and two very mischievous cats.

Sign up for Laura Snider's newsletter at
severnriverbooks.com